Deadly Little Games

The Daring Brotherhood
Book 1

Jenna Daring

THE DARING
BROTHERHOOD

DEADLY LITTLE GAMES

JENNA DARING

Formatting by Smoking Hot Covers

Cover Design by Artista Grafico

Editing by Messenger's Memos and More Than Words

When the journey takes a dark turn, I take my brothers' hands and we walk into the gates of hell together.

Contents

Prologue
Freya

There's one rule in Daring: don't cross over the train tracks unless you're looking for trouble. I've never been one to play by the rules, and that's probably why my best friend lives on the other side of the tracks, in Daringville, and why I'm sneaking into one of their parties yet again. I love gate-crashing them and the thrill that comes from the possibility of getting caught at any moment.

When you live on my side of the tracks—Daringhood—you are just a peasant. You do all the dirty work that those elite from Daringville don't want to do. It fucking sucks. I once vowed never to come here again after what they did to my mother, but now, twelve years on, the pain doesn't sting as much as it once did. I've grown to accept it—because we finally have an escape plan. I may as well have some fun before we leave.

My brother, Alec, eases his car out of the trailer park, hitting the gas. The farther away we get from the place I call home, the more I can breathe. If I had to spend another second inside that shit hole, I would have gone crazy or had

1

to deal with my high mother, and I have better shit to do with my time. I spend enough of it looking after her ass.

I just want a night out. To be somebody else for a little while.

I pick up my blonde wig from the passenger-side floor and place it over my brown hair. Pulling down the shade visor, I use the mirror on it to pin my fake locks in place. It's like putting on a mask, a new identity, and I fucking love it.

"I'm still not happy about you going to this party in Daringville. Why can't you just go to one of the joint parties?" Alec sighs, shifting gears.

I hold back the urge to roll my eyes. We've already had this conversation tonight and I'm over it. "I'll be fine. How many times have I been to them? And I always come back. Why are you so worried all of a sudden?"

He lets out a heavy breath. "I'm always fucking worried about you, Frey—you know this. I'd lock you up in your room if I knew you'd actually stay there and not pick the locks in twenty seconds."

I laugh. "I'll be fine. I'll be with Amirah, and I can take care of myself." Lifting my phone out of my pocket, I find a text from her telling me to hurry my ass up.

"Just promise me you'll be careful?" Alec asks, and I nod.

"You know I will," I say.

"I've got something to tell you, and don't freak out, but—"

"What?!" I cut him off. "You got in, didn't you?!" I scream, and Alec laughs.

"You know me too well, Frey. Yes, the scholarship for Bexley College got accepted."

I squeal, leaning over the console and wrapping my

arms around Alec. The car swerves before he rights it again and pushes me away, laughing.

"Oh my God, this is so exciting. You have to come with me to celebrate tonight. Please," I beg, settling back into my seat. I can't believe it—this is our ticket out of here. We can start fresh and get Mom on the straight and narrow.

"I can't, I'm meeting someone," he says, and I frown, turning to face him again.

"Who?"

"Someone from Daringville," he admits.

I take in a sharp breath. "What the fuck?"

"Don't fuck this up for me. She's cool, and you'll approve once you meet her, but not tonight," he says, and I scoff.

"We'll see."

Every girl my brother has ever dated I've had a problem with. They are either too bitchy, rude, or just don't even acknowledge me. They are never good enough for my brother; he deserves the world.

"What's her name?" I ask, hoping he'll tell me so I can find out everything about her from Amirah.

"Uh, Mia," he says, and I nod.

"So when can we leave?" I ask, staring out the window, watching the dark streets zoom past.

"We've gotta save up a fair bit of money. It's not a full scholarship, and I got early acceptance so I can choose when to start. It might take a bit, but we've got a one-way ticket out of here and a chance to give Mom a fresh start."

I can't wipe the smile off my face. This is something worth celebrating.

We spend the rest of the drive in comfortable silence. I love my brother. He's one of my best friends and the closest thing I have to a real father. We've always had each other's backs. As we are only a year apart, I've followed him around since we were young. It's always been us against the world, but the older we get, the more time we spend apart. He's got his shit and I've got mine.

Alec pulls his car off the main road, hitting the dirt track. The trees tower over his car on either side the farther we drive. He stops at the end of the road just before the massive silos. I lean over the console, pressing a kiss against his cheek and rustling up his mousey-brown hair. He swats me away, laughing.

"Text me if you need me and I'll be there," he says, and I nod.

"Love you. Bye," I reply, opening my door, sliding out, and slamming it shut before he can say anything back.

The beams of his lights illuminate the path, leading me through the trees until I finally reach the fence. I quickly crouch down and slip under it, entering a spacious paddock. I love this part—when his headlights disappear down the road and I'm left alone in the pitch-black night, my heart racing as I anticipate a boogeyman lurking nearby. I can feel the weight of the knife in my boot as my hand glides over it, ready for any situation. *Bring it on, anyone who dares to come out of the shadows.*

I grab my phone and there's a text from Mom. My stomach sinks. The words are a jumbled mess, a reflection of her chaotic state of mind. I send Alec a text to check on her when he's done with the new girl. I need a night off from all the drama at home.

The cool night air whips my hair back from my face, and I pull my sweater tighter around my body. I lift my phone up, pressing *call* on Amirah's number. She answers within two rings.

"Where the hell are you, babe?" she says, and I grin.

"Just coming through the paddock, about to hit the train tracks. Are you on the other side?"

The darkness gradually gives way to a lighter hue, revealing massive spotlights shining down from above the tracks.

"Yep, hurry. The coast is clear, but we don't have long," she says, then hangs up.

I swiftly slide my phone into the back pocket of my denim shorts and increase my pace. The closer I get, my heart races and the excitement grows, just as it always does. This is what I live for—the thrill, that feeling that builds from the pit of my stomach. With a burst of energy, I sprint the last few feet, coming to a halt just as the paddock comes to an end. The grass brushes against my calves, sending a tickling sensation up my legs. I turn my head to the left and then to the right, taking in the sight of the train tracks that stretch endlessly in both directions.

It's dead silent. All I can hear is the rustling of grass, and I can just make out the shadow of a body pressed against the wall of the train station building where guards usually patrol. I scan the tall fence, my eyes searching for any signs of bodies hanging from the wire, but thankfully, there are none tonight. Thank fuck.

Amirah kicks off the wall, waving me over. She probably distracted the guards by sending them to get something for her. She's got that kind of pull in Daringville. Her family is high up in the ranks. The Ledgers were some of the first people to settle in Daring before the founding families divided everything.

With one final breath, I take off running, the gravel crunching beneath my boots, and I don't stop until I crash into Amirah on the other side. I hug her so tight I feel like I might snap her in half.

"I'll never get tired of watching you run for your life," she says. Pulling back, she takes my hand and we are off once again. I sneak a glance back at the train tracks and then at the paddock beyond, a smile spreading across my face.

"You know how much I live for that shit," I say, then giggle.

"Yep, come on. You need to get out of those shoes and into something a little more Daringville." She lets go of my hand and presses a button on her keys, and her expensive-as-all-get-out car lights up the quiet car park. Once we're inside, I can finally breathe again.

"Your dress and shoes are in the back," Amirah says, her dead-straight, long black hair falling gracefully behind her ear.

I grab the bag of clothes from the back seat, feeling the weight of it in my hands, and eagerly unzip it to discover a stunning black sequin dress. I squeal, yanking it out. "This is perfect. Thank you, thank you, thank you," I say, reaching in to find a matching pair of sparkling pumps.

"That's what best friends are for, and as always, you'll fit right in. You know I'd be lost without you, and I'm always grateful we secretly rekindled our friendship because no one gets me like you do," Amirah says.

"Aww, are we having a moment?" I playfully tease, and Amirah's laughter echoes through the air.

"But in all seriousness," Amirah says, her grip tightening around my hand, "if anyone catches me sneaking you in here, it won't be pretty for me." She doesn't have to spell it out for me; I know what's at stake here. If The Brotherhood found out, she would pay. I've seen the bruises that line her stomach, and it kills me that she's risking that for me.

"I don't want you to get into trouble with them. I can go back," I say, and Amirah laughs it off.

"No, fuck that. You're already here and they don't know. Let's just let our hair down and have a good night." She revs the engine before we fly down the road, heading toward the private estates.

A few cars drive past, but I'm safe now with Amirah. Well, not completely, but the hard part of sneaking over the tracks is done. I'm ready to unwind and let loose, leaving all my worries behind for the night.

While I struggle to put on my clothes, my heart races as Amirah takes a sharp turn, the sound of tires squealing filling the air. My groan is met with her infectious giggle, and she immediately reaches over to turn up the stereo. "Escape" by Kx5 plays, and I bob my head along to the beat.

After kicking off my shorts, I shimmy down the dress until it covers my ass. I shove my clothes back into the bag, throwing it on the back seat. Slipping my feet into the heels feels like slipping into a second skin—a perfect fit.

When I flip down the mirror, I see my blonde wig in disarray, strands sticking out in every direction, so I quickly readjust it, carefully arranging my bangs. The wig sits right above my shoulders in a cute bob. It's totally different from my long brown hair, and that's the whole idea. I'm unrecognizable here. No one questions Amirah—especially not me, her best friend from upstate.

After driving for a few more minutes, we finally come to a halt just outside the exclusive private estate. Amirah winds down her window, letting in a rush of fresh air as she presses in the code and watches as the black wrought-iron gates slowly open. There are a couple of security guards lined up, and some patrolling the area, and they wave us through.

Even though I was born and bred in Daringville, Amirah's house still stuns me. Instead of the familiarity of home, it's like entering a lavish five-star hotel. A tingle runs down my spine as the three-story mansion comes into view. These mansions may have beautiful exteriors, but behind closed doors lurk the deadliest of individuals, using their wealth to manipulate and acquire whatever they desire as members of The Brotherhood. They run the whole town of Daring, no matter where you're from.

Amirah isn't like them. She's different. She thinks it's bullshit, the divide our ancestors created after the gang war between the rich and poor. They thought this was the solution—a peace treaty. The Brotherhood was formed, and they made a pact to divide Daring into two parts, resulting in where we are today. There are still riots from my side when gangs try to take more than what their birthright affords them, but nothing ever gets out of hand. The Brotherhood won't let it.

The closer we get to the house, the more fancy cars are parked off the main driveway—cars that cost more than the whole trailer park.

Amirah pulls into the garage and parks next to a familiar deep-red Range Rover. My stomach flips. Is *he* going to be here? It is his house, too, but I've never seen him at these parties.

"It's time to fuck shit up. Are you ready?" Before I can even answer, Amirah jumps out of the car with a huge smile on her face. Determinedly, I trail behind her, closing the distance as she rips open the garage door, granting us access to the house.

The booming thump of bass pounds in my ears, drowning out all other sounds as I firmly shut the door. The house is totally crowded. The massive foyer is cast in darkness, illuminated only by the flickering strobe lights. Everyone's dancing around me as I move through the crowd. A few even rub their bodies against mine, and I itch to dance— after I've had a little drink.

I push past this chick with two guys hanging all over her and follow Amirah into the kitchen by the entrance. It's brighter in here, and I can see properly now. The kitchen is so spacious that it could easily fit my entire trailer. The shiny marble wrap-around countertop is cluttered with bottles and bags of coke. I wrinkle my nose—feels a little too much like home.

I eagerly accept the sealed bottle of vodka from Amirah, and with a grin, I twist off the lid, releasing the familiar scent of alcohol. With each sip, the liquid ignites a trail of heat down my throat until Amirah abruptly grabs it from me and takes an enormous gulp.

A shiver works its way up my neck as I feel someone staring at me. I look out into the crowd and come face to face with a familiar set of mossy-green eyes. His black wavy hair peeks out of his back-to-front baseball cap. It's been twelve years, but I'd know his dark hair anywhere—it's exactly the same as Amirah's. I lick my dry lips, casting my eyes down his body. With his loose-fitting gray T-shirt and black jeans, his tattooed sleeves are on full display. Gage Ledger is a full-grown man; he'd be about twenty-two now a year older than me. I shouldn't let him have this kind of power over me or my body.

When I look up at him again, he scowls and grabs a blonde chick who's walking by. She fights to get away from him, but when she recognizes him, she stops and wraps her arms around his neck. As he leans in close, his eyes remain fixed on mine, his tongue tracing a path along her collarbone. My thighs clench and my cheeks warm. Without looking, I snatch the bottle from Amirah, but I can't hear what she yells. I bring the bottle to my lips, swallowing until it's taken away again.

As I'm locked in a staring contest with Gage, the sharp snap of fingers grabs my attention, breaking our eye contact. I give Amirah a look, and she shakes her head.

"Excuse me, were you checking out my brother?"

"What? No!" I scoff.

"Good. He's bad news, Freya. Surely you'd remember that, after everything that happened."

"I know," I say, taking a drink from the bottle. "I'd never touch him."

"Good, 'cause no one can know who you are—remember what's at stake," Amirah says, taking the bottle from my hands, and I nod.

"And who's this? You didn't tell me you've got a new friend, Amirah." His deep, gravelly voice goes straight to my core. *Down, girl.*

He steps right in front of me, and his earthy aftershave makes me forget for a second that he's a complete asshole. He'll remind me any second now. His intense gaze follows my every move, causing my heart to pound against my ribcage. Does he recognize me? He was only thirteen and I was twelve when I last saw him. It's been too long since I've been this close to him. He had grown up so much that I almost didn't recognize him, making me doubt if he would remember me.

Amirah rolls her eyes. "Piss off, Gage. Leave us alone."

She takes my hand and drags me into the crowd. The weight of his gaze lingers on me for the next couple of hours as we dance, laugh, and continue to drink. My head and body feel light, and I forget everything that's going on in my life. It's perfect.

Amirah disappears in the crowd, and I realize I've got to go to the bathroom. Badly. Pushing my way through the throng of people, I finally reach the stairs that lead up to the bedrooms. I waste no time and bound up the stairs, taking them two steps at a time. Moans and the sound of a headboard smacking against the wall come from Amirah's bedroom, and I smile. *That's my girl.*

I make it down the dark hallway, reaching the bathroom between her room and the guest bedroom, but there's a line. *Great.* I cast a glance down the other end of the hallway, toward *his* room. There's no one down there because they know the rule—don't go near Gage's space—but I do like to play with fire, and besides—I'm about to pee myself. It's an emergency.

I sneak past the staircase and walk up to his door, pressing my ear against it until I'm certain no sound is coming from inside. That's the last thing I want—to walk in on him balls deep in someone else's pussy.

I check one more time to make sure no one's watching, then I open the door and disappear inside.

Someone neatly made Gage's bed with luxurious, silky black sheets that would cost more than my entire closet. The walk-in wardrobe door is ajar, giving a glimpse of the meticulously organized clothes inside. Nothing is out of place. It's very clinical.

Shaking my head, I move toward the other door into the bathroom where I take care of business in record time. I lock eyes with my reflection in the mirror, taking a moment to fix my blonde wig.

The bedroom door creaks open, and I freeze. Oh, shit. It slams shut, and my heart races against my chest. I frantically scan the bathroom, searching for any possible escape route or hiding spot. There's no window—just a god damn skylight. Rich assholes. I could lie down in the bathtub, but he'd see me straight away if he walked closer. The door handle turns, and I move like a light is up my ass, diving behind the door.

He goes to the bathroom and heads straight for the toilet. He zips down his jeans, freeing his cock, and I can't keep my eyes away as he wraps his hand around his length. I'm meant to be getting away. *Remember, move your ass.* I sneak by the door, about to bolt.

"I wouldn't run if I were you. I do love a good chase."

I jump and spin around as he quickly puts his cock back in his jeans and washes his hands at the sink.

"Well, I'm a fast runner, so good luck with that," I say, then I do exactly that and run.

I barely make it out of the bathroom before he's breathing down my neck and grabbing me by the waist. I squirm under his grip, trying to pull free, but it's useless. He's too fucking strong. I give up, and his breath tickles my collarbone.

"Keep fighting me, baby. Keep rubbing that tight body on me. Gets my cock so hard," he says, running his tongue along my nape, and my body reacts, wanting more.

No, you hate him, remember? He's one of them. Remember?

"That's the only way you get women, isn't it?" I ask, finally finding my voice, but it comes out all hoarse. Damn it.

He flips me around, shoving against my chest until I'm falling. I hit his bed with a huff, then he's towering over me. His hand grips my throat, and I'm done for. Heat pulls between my thighs, and he smirks, causing his sexy-as-fuck dimple to appear.

"Let's see how much you don't want this. Shall we?" he

says like he's asking for my permission—but he's not. He never would. He's that kind of guy.

His fingers glide up my inner thigh, going higher and higher until he reaches my lacy underwear. He pushes my thong to the side and runs his finger along my slit. I close my eyes and he growls. I shouldn't—damn it, I so shouldn't. But it's not as if he knows who I really am. He'd never guess it was me. The thrill of it all—what if we get caught? What if I bring the Prince In Training of Daringville to his knees? —is too much to refuse.

"Eyes open and on me. I wanna watch when you come apart," he commands, and my eyes peel back open.

I want to tell him to fuck off, to get off me, but the words are stuck in my throat and my pussy wants this. *Just take what you need from him, then leave.* When two fingers push inside me, his thumb rubbing against my clit at a rapid pace, there's no turning back.

My eyes stay on his as he makes me climb higher and higher. My legs shake and I'm about to come. I squeeze my eyes shut, ready for the release, but he pulls out and I glare up at him.

"What did I tell you?" He smirks, placing his fingers in his mouth and sucking them clean. Fuck, that's hot.

"Just shut up and fuck me so I can go," I snap, pushing up to my elbows, ready to leave. This was a mistake. I can't do this. What was I thinking? "Actually, you know what? I'm leaving. This never happened," I say, glancing toward the door.

"You're not going anywhere." He pauses, smirking. "Freya, from the hood."

My whole body locks up. He knows. Who the hell told him? I'm fucked. Shit. I need to leave. Now.

I roll off the bed and run toward the door, but he's on

me, grabbing my shoulder and shoving me until my back hits the wall. Pain slams into me and I groan. He looks down at me, the corner of his mouth lifting, causing his stupid dimple to appear. Why does he have to be so hot? It's always the assholes that get the good looks.

"Nothing happens in our town without me knowing about it. How did you think you'd been getting past the railway tracks every time, hmm?" He laughs. "You didn't think you were just that good, did you?"

I swallow hard, wanting to punch that smug look off his face. Of course, he fucking knows. How foolish of me to think Amirah could pull one over her brother. That I could get over the tracks without *them* knowing about it. He's the heir of Daringville with the other two guys he's always with —they're next in line to rule over the entire Brotherhood.

Before I can open my mouth, he yanks up my skirt, pulling down my thong until it sits at my feet. His jeans drop to the floor and his hard cock springs free. I lick my dry lips.

"There's no way I'm having sex with you after that. I'm leaving," I say, pushing off the wall, but he pins me back, his hand wrapping around my neck, and he brings his other one up to rest over my racing heart.

"You want this—the way you look at me with those hood-rat eyes. I see right through you," he says, biting into his deep-red lips that I want.

"Pfft, if you really knew me, you'd know I'd rather fuck a hood rat over you any day of the week," I say, pursing my dry lips together.

"Liar."

He grabs my pussy, running his fingers over my soaking-wet lips. *Damn it. We don't want this.*

"Your body never lies," he says, and I hate to admit it, but the asshole is right—that traitorous bitch.

He leans forward, pulling a condom from his pocket. Ripping the packet open with his teeth, he grabs it and rolls it down his cock in a one-handed move he's clearly perfected. Then, in one swift thrust, he sheathes himself inside me, balls deep. I gasp, dropping my head back against the wall. *Okay, maybe I do want this. Fuck.*

He keeps his grip on my throat, leaving just enough room for me to breathe before thrusting in and out. My body comes alive, and I can't stop the moan spilling from my lips.

He pins me with a heavy stare, watching as he builds me up and up. A deep animal-like groan falls from his lips, and my legs become weak, stars clouding my vision.

The door swings open and the light flicks on.

I take a second to adjust to the brightness and I scream, shoving against Gage's chest until he pulls his cock from inside of me. Amirah's face turns eerily white.

"You didn't?" Tears pool in her eyes as she looks between the both of us. My heart breaks in two. *What the fuck have I done?*

"Amirah, I'm so sorry. I didn't . . ."

"After all I did—sneaking you in here? If Dominic found out, he would have made me pay in the worst possible way . . ." Amirah's voice wobbles.

"Is that your concern?" Gage jeers, pulling up his pants. "Or are you worried that your little hood rat prefers my cock to your friendship?"

Amirah bolts and I freeze, the wall holding me up, but my knees tremble. What have I done?

Gage zips the fly of his pants, the movement snapping

me out of my shock. I forgo my underwear, tugging down my dress so I can run straight after Amirah.

I sprint down the stairs, watching as Amirah rips open the front door and rushes into the night. Footsteps pound in my wake, but I don't dare look behind me. All I care about is my best friend. I can't lose her. I can't.

The cool night air kisses my cheeks, and I look left and right, trying to find Amirah. There are cars everywhere still, and a few people from inside have spilled out onto the lawn.

Finally, I spot Amirah in the trees next to their house, pacing back and forth. I walk toward her, but a hand lands on my shoulder. Whirling around, I come face to face with Gage.

"Let me go. I need to fix this," I say, taking a step back.

Hurt passes between his eyes before he shakes his head. "Go back to where you came from, Freya, and never return. You aren't welcome here in Daringville anymore—you never were, you hood rat. Go back to your junkie mother and be gone."

His words hit me like a nail in my heart, and I don't know why I thought anything else would come out of his mouth. Hazen and Lucas, the other members of The Brotherhood, stride over from the steps of the house to flank either side of him, scowling at me with so much hate.

With one last breath, I storm off into the trees, ready to save the one thing I hold dear. I can't lose her. Even though I fucked everything up, I will do whatever it takes to fix this.

Chapter One

Freya

One year later

Alec pulls his car into the dirt parking lot. It's full of a mixture of cars from both sides of the tracks. Some belong to those who are rich as shit, and some are absolute bombs that look like they're about to fall apart.

Before Alec can give me another lecture about being safe, I've unbuckled my seatbelt and am out, slamming the door shut. He curses, following me. We usually go to these parties together, and I always feel his eyes watching me. It is a little annoying. I can't really let my hair down when my brother is here.

I follow the concrete steps down into the forest, and the music echoes louder around the trees. People come into view as the forest clears. A massive bonfire sits in the middle of the area, and tonight there are people every-where. They're talking in groups, with the elite sticking to their circles and a lot of hood people mingling in between, passing around the elite's drugs and God knows what else. Even if it's neutral ground, we're still running after them.

That familiar curtain of black hair moves in my direction through the crowd, meeting me as I jump off the last step. The person it belongs to crashes into me, wrapping her arms around my neck.

"About fucking time. You know how much I hate being here without you," Amirah huffs out. Then she pulls back, and I smile at my best friend.

She waves over my head at Alec, and we head into the sea of people together. I look back over my shoulder and catch Mia, his girlfriend, running into his arms. He smiles down at her like she's the only woman in the world. I'm happy for him, but I don't trust her. Every time we chat, she manages to rub me the wrong way.

Amirah shoves a red cup already full of something into my hands, and I chug most of it in one go. These parties on the tracks, a mix of the elite and the everyday people, are the best I'm going to get for a while. After everything that happened last year, I don't want to go back to her house again, afraid Gage will be there, and Amirah thinks that's for the best. It's part of our treaty, the reason she forgave me —I'm never to be alone with her brother again. That hasn't been a problem for me, given the hateful words that spilled from his lips, anyway. I'm better off staying on my side of the tracks. Fuck him and The Brotherhood.

"Ahh, what are they doing here?" Amirah blurts out, pointing across the fire. "They never come here."

His eyes clash with mine. He licks his lips, and I fight the urge to flip him off. A redhead runs her fingers down his chest and jealousy flares deep within me, but I shake it off. Next to him are Hazen Hendrix and Lucas Fox. They both watch me intently.

Hazen runs his tattooed hand over his chiseled jawline.

Lucas grips his bottle, bringing it to his lips. His blond hair is brushed back out of his face, and his throat bobs up and down as he swigs his drink. For a moment, I'm caught like a deer in headlights. It's unfair that three friends should be so incredibly good-looking.

My eyes move of their own accord back to Gage, and he pulls the redhead forward, his lips touching hers. I look away before I do something stupid. There's no way I'm going to be pulled back into that drama.

I won't be losing my best friend again. He wasn't worth it; he still isn't. Nothing good ever comes from The Brotherhood.

"I wish he'd just fuck off and let me have one night." Amirah huffs, glaring at her brother.

"Just pretend he's not here. Don't let him ruin our night," I say, finishing off the contents of my red cup while trying to take on my own advice. The strong booze in my last mouthful burns a trail down my throat. It's a welcome distraction.

"You know what it's like having an overprotective brother. But at least Alec doesn't watch your every move—he lets you have your own life." Amirah sighs, and she's right. Alec's here somewhere, probably keeping an eye on me, but he's not overpowering like Gage is. He actually lets me live my life without interfering too much.

More people come down the dirt track and into the pit. Music pumps through the massive speakers and the DJ from Daringville mixes up some dance beats. Before I can reply, Amirah moves toward the sea of people dancing in front of the DJ. She dances up against a cute guy, and he grabs her hips, moving to the beat of the music.

I grab another drink from one of the open coolers, twist

off the cap, and sit on a log next to a couple of guys from Daringhood. They nod and I smile back. One of the guys pulls out a glass pipe and a lighter. He takes a hit then passes it my way, but I shake my head. No fucking way I'm touching that shit, not after what it's done to my family.

I sit back and watch Amirah, not having any desire to dance. I'd much rather people watch—at least until I have more alcohol in my system.

The guy dancing with Amirah freezes, looking past me. He steps back, throwing up his hands, then moves my way. I look over my shoulder and roll my eyes. Gage beckons the guy over with a lazy smirk. Hazen's arms are hooked around a preppy girl's shoulders, and Lucas looks bored as he flicks his lighter.

A hand lands on my shoulder, and I jump, whirling back around and coming face to face with a pissed-off Amirah. Oh shit. She stands in front of me, staying quiet, watching her brother and his two friends talk to the guy she was dancing with. Then she crunches up her cup, throwing it into the fire.

"I'm so over this. He needs to learn a lesson," she snaps, grabbing my hand and pulling me closer to her brother. I try to pull back, but it's useless—Amirah's grip is too tight.

The air around us changes the further we get from the fire. Goosebumps scatter over my arms, and I have no idea if it's from the chill in the air or because we are getting closer to Gage.

Amirah lets go of my hand and pushes against her brother's chest before she grabs his drink from his hand and throws it at his top. I snort-laugh, covering it with my bottle of alcohol. The guy she was dancing with runs off without a backward glance.

"What the fuck, Amirah?" Gage growls and looks wild. He snatches a bottle from Lucas, who's laughing at him. He downs the rest and throws the bottle to the forest floor. He catches my gaze before lifting his soaking top over his head in one swift movement and chucking it into the flames of the fire. It's gone, evaporated in the blink of an eye.

My gaze runs over his tattooed, muscular chest, and my core clenches. I want to run my fingers over each and every muscle. Fuck, I need to get laid—but not by my best friend's brother. He's off-limits, and I won't put Amirah in danger with her family again.

"You deserved that." Amirah smirks, and Gage steps closer toward us, giving me a better view of his chest. Fuck. I need more alcohol to deal with this.

"Why? Cause I fucked your best friend?" Gage asks so casually I choke on my drink.

Amirah scoffs. "No, you idiot, because you won't let me have one night out without scaring away anyone who dares to get too close to me. I'm so over it. Just leave me alone."

"Never," Gage growls. "They just want to use you. Then they'll throw you away like you're nothing, and you're better than that—and them."

My eyes widen, and I look at Gage in a different light. I never thought I'd see the day something that nice would come out of his mouth.

"Unless you like being the town whore, then I could arrange a job for you with the Daringhood hookers." He smirks, running his thumb over his bottom lip.

All thoughts of him being nice vanish. Amirah shoves his chest again, and I've just about had enough. I drop my drink and step between them, placing my hand on Amirah's and then Gage's chest. Ignoring Gage, I look at Amirah.

"Can we please just drop this and keep the peace for one night?" I plead, and Amirah huffs but nods.

She takes one last look at her brother and then walks away toward the drinks in the coolers. I go to follow her, but someone grabs me around the waist, pulling me into a hard body. Goosebumps scatter over my arms and the hairs on the back of my neck raise. His breath tickles my nape, and it takes everything in me not to lean into his touch.

With a deep inhale, I elbow Gage in the ribs and step out of his embrace. He holds his side, the corner of his mouth lifting, and his stupid fucking dimple sits there on his perfect face.

Gage, Hazen, and Lucas surround me, blocking off my view of the fire and my escape.

"I thought I told you to stay on your side of the tracks?" Gage says, resting his finger on his jaw.

Hazen studies me with interest, his gaze heavy on my body as he slowly eye-fucks me. I frown, unsure how I feel about his attention.

I should be afraid of them. They rule Daringville, which in turn means they own my side of the tracks, Daringhood. But I've always liked playing with trouble.

"This is neutral ground, Gage. You, of all people, should know the rules. After all, wasn't it your family who created them? Hmm?" I raise my eyebrow with a smirk.

Lucas laughs, not bothering to hide it from his friend, who smacks him over the head. He curses, rubbing the back of his neck.

Gage steps forward, right into my personal space once again, and I don't dare move an inch. The air around us changes like I've been shoved into the fire. My skin burns when his chest meets mine. I feel like the whole party is staring at us, judging our every move. What will Amirah think? I block out everyone around us, focusing on Gage. He looks down at me with a heavy glare.

"Stay the fuck in line, or you'll be sorry, little Freya from Daringhood trailer park, lot number 138." He pauses, and I try not to show any emotion, but inside, my heart's beating rapidly. He knows where I live. Fuck. I should be afraid, but I live for the fear; it keeps me breathing. "It would be too easy to burn you and your trailer to the ground. I'm sure you'd love to see your junkie mother burn down with it, wouldn't you?" he asks, and I hold back from revealing any emotion. He doesn't know shit.

I go to open my mouth, but my brother sweeps in next to me.

"Back off, Gage," Alec says, and Gage steps back slightly before chuckling under his breath.

Hazen studies my brother with a heavy stare, running a hand through his short-clipped hair. "You've got some nerve, kid, I'll give you that. Come see me later. I've got a job for you." Hazen nods at my brother, who swallows hard. This isn't good—this isn't good at all. My brother working for them would be trouble. Fuck.

Hazen's eyes come back to me. He slowly looks me up and down. My traitorous body burns with need or hate—I have no idea. But I won't be going there.

"Bye, Freya. Be a good little hood rat, won't you?" Gage grins, and I glare daggers right through him.

They all leave, moving into the crowded dance floor, and I finally release the breath I was holding in.

"What the hell have I told you, Frey?" Alec snaps. "Stay away from them."

"Did you not notice? They stopped me from leaving," I snap, crossing my arms over my chest.

Alec rolls his eyes. "You know everyone from

Daringville only uses us for their benefit. It's how our town works."

"What about you? Hazen just asked you to come see him about a job," I say, raising an eyebrow.

His fingers wrap around the necklace I got him that mirrors my own. It's one you give to your best friend. I gave it to him when I was ten, and he's never taken off his half of the small heart pendant with our initials on it. Neither have I.

"Don't worry about that—I'll handle it. We need to lie low. It's only six months until we are out of here and can start fresh. It's not ideal, but you know how much we need the money. I've lined up a place to stay with Levi and it's more than I thought," Alec says, and I nod.

He's right. Doing a job for them shits all over a shift at the diner. I just hate the thought of him getting caught up in Daringville politics.

Amirah bumps into my hip. "What did my brother want?" she asks with a hint of suspicion. She's got nothing to worry about with him and me. One and done. Never again.

"Just to remind me of the rules and to threaten me. You know, the usual." I shrug, watching the guys leave. Everyone in their path moves aside. I shake my head. Pathetic.

Mia, my brother's girlfriend, pushes through the crowd, grabbing Alec's hand. "Come on, baby, let's go."

He shifts uncomfortably, taking a step backward. I have no idea why he doesn't just break up with her already. She's way too needy, and besides, she's from Daringville.

We are allowed to fuck each other, but only if they initiate it first. The whole system is fucked, and I'm not the only one who thinks so. That's why there are riots happening almost every night, mostly initiated by fans of 18 Hood music. Those guys sure know how to rile up the masses.

Alec presses a kiss against my forehead.

"I'll see you later," he says, and I nod.

There's a ball in the pit of my stomach as I watch him go up to Hazen, Gage, and Lucas. As they walk up the hill, Lucas looks over his shoulder. The corner of his mouth lifts and he winks. Then they are gone, and it takes everything in me not to race after them to see what they are going to do.

* * *

A loud bang followed by rattling wakes me from a deep sleep. Opening my eyes, it takes me a moment to remember where I am. Bottles and butted-out smokes line the surface of the coffee table in front of me, and the TV plays in the background. I grab the remote, turn off the TV, and flick on the living room light.

There's more banging, and then the door of the trailer swings open. My mother falls onto the dirty carpet floor face first. She laughs with her face on the ground and ass in the air.

I groan, rubbing the sleep from my eyes. Fucking hell, not again. Every night is the exact same. When I turned eighteen, I swore I'd get my own place, but three years later, I'm still here under the same roof, putting up with the same shit. If only money did grow on trees.

I push myself off the couch and head to the door, then lean down and try to lift her up. She pushes me away, digging her nails into my flesh and mumbling something under her breath. I should leave the bitch on the ground. If the roles were reversed, she'd do that to me, but unfortunately, I have a heart.

Loud, heavy footsteps sound behind me. "Aren't I glad to see you?"

Every part of me freezes, turning to ice at the sound of his voice.

Oh, fuck.

Chapter Two
Freya

Glancing up, I find her pimp daddy, Gavin, standing just outside our trailer, a smoke to his lips. He sucks in a drag, the red bud casting shadows around his face. The streetlights aren't working as usual, so it's pitch black. Not ideal when you live here.

I've seen some fucked-up shit happen in this trailer park, and it never changes. The cops won't even come here anymore, deeming it too dangerous for them to enter.

"What are you doing here, Gavin?" I spit, lifting my mother off the ground.

She tumbles, mumbling, but it's all just gibberish. I manage to put her on the couch, and she falls straight to sleep, snoring her ass off. One of her arms flops to the ground, and the track marks dotting her inner elbow make me so angry. He did this, turning her into an addict. A crack whore. Gone is the mother I once had. Now she's a shell of nothing, always begging for her next hit and selling anything and everything we have.

Turning around, I bump straight into Gavin's chest. He runs his hands over my ass, and I shove him backward. My

27

heart races, pounding in my chest. He grins with his smoke between his teeth.

"I do love it when they fight. Makes my dick so much harder," he says, taking a step forward, and I don't move a muscle.

"Piss off," I growl, praying he just leaves, but that's wishful thinking. When Gavin wants something, he won't stop until he's had it. Then he fucks off.

"Nah-uh, your mother owes me, and I've come to collect five hundred. Cash." He licks his cracked lips, casting his beady eyes down my body. "One fuck, and this week's debt is cleared."

Sweat rolls down the back of my neck. The nerve of this guy. I swallow past the lump in my throat, ready to smash his face in.

The flywire door squeaks. Gavin's head snaps toward it, and he takes a couple of steps back. Alec fills the door, glancing between us both with a feral look in his eyes. He raises an eyebrow at me, silently asking me if I'm okay, and I nod.

"Well, I better be off, and remember what will happen if your mother doesn't pay up, Freya," Gavin sneers, brushing past Alec.

Alec grabs his arm, pressing five hundred dollars into his chest. *Where the hell did he get that?*

"This should cover it," he says. With a grin on his face, Gavin saunters out into the night, but not before he takes a final glance over his shoulder, giving me a flirtatious wink. My stomach rolls, and I can't resist flipping him off.

Once he's finally gone, the tension in my shoulders melts away, and I release a long, overdue breath. I could've dealt with Gavin myself, but having my older brother show up was a relief.

"You good?" he asks, shutting the door and flicking the flimsy lock in place. It wouldn't do much if someone actually wanted to break into our trailer, but at least it's some kind of protection.

"Yeah, it wasn't the best way to wake up, but you know Mom," I say with a shrug, and Alec takes one look at her on the couch before shaking his head.

"I'm going to get enough money for us to get our place. Fuck her." He unzips his little man bag that's strapped to his chest and pulls out a wad of cash. My eyes widen before I snatch it from his hands.

"Where the hell did you get this?"

He shrugs. "Been saving up from our shifts at the diner."

He'd have to save for a year to get this kind of dough. Memories from the party flicker through my mind. Oh, God —Hazen asked to see him.

"Alec?" I press. "Where the hell did you get this? And please don't tell me it has anything to do with a job for *them?*" I snap, running my fingers through the fifty-dollar notes.

We've never had money like this before. Well, maybe once when Mom won at the slots, but the next day it was gone and that kicked off her habit again.

"Don't worry about it. Just go get some food tomorrow. This should bolster our savings," he says, grabbing a cup from the cupboard and filling it with water from the tap.

"You know I'll keep worrying about it until you tell me, right?" I say, placing the money on the kitchen table.

He retrieves his antidepressant medication from the cabinet and removes a tablet.

"Yes, but just let me be the big brother and look after us. You've got enough shit to deal with already." Alec

29

approaches me, plants a gentle kiss on my forehead, and then takes the wad of money. He quickly swallows his pill, puts the pack back on the shelf, and disappears into his bedroom, closing the door.

If the source of his money has anything to do with Hazen, Gage, or Lucas, then nothing good will come out of it. Once you work for them, The Daring Brotherhood, there's no going back. I just hope he knows what he's getting into, and it doesn't come back to bite him or me in the ass.

We have to get out of here so he can use his scholarship to college and make something of himself. He was able to defer for up to two years. We just need enough money to get us there, and a safe place to stay. Alec already has everything lined up for us—we just need a bit more in our savings.

Taking one final glance at my mom slumped on the couch, I pick up my water bottle from the table and make my way into the room next to Alec's. I secure the small lock and finally unwind for the first time today.

My room's a mess. There are clothes strewn across the floor and bed from earlier this evening. I'm too lazy to tidy up, so I just kick my clothes off the bed and let them fall to the floor. I collapse onto my narrow bed, tucking my phone into my tracksuit pocket before shutting my eyes.

The memories from earlier tonight keep replaying in my mind. The way Gage watched me intensely when he took off his wet shirt. Then when he mentioned where I live and to stay in line. Fuck. I blink my eyes open and shut a few times to erase the image, praying my thoughts will stop so I can sleep, but it's useless.

Gavin's beady, dark eyes lingering over my body. The threats. The worry when Alec pulled out all that money.

Fuck this shit. I quickly sit up, grab my phone out of my pocket, and pull up a text to Kai.

You busy? Can't sleep.

Within five minutes, there's a light knock on my window. I smile, pulling open my curtain, then window, to find my partner in crime Kai. He's dressed in a black hoodie, jeans, and beanie, blending into the dark streets.

"Good timing. I was just walking home. Are we hitting up another party or did you have something else in mind?" Kai asks, taking my hand and hoisting me out into the crisp night air. My feet hit the ground and Kai pulls my window shut before wrapping an arm over my shoulder. I lean into him, absorbing his warmth.

"No more parties. I have to blow off some steam or my head's gonna explode," I say, lifting my hood up.

"You good?" he asks.

"No, but I will be," I reply, and Kai doesn't answer, just squeezes my shoulder. He gets it, he gets me, and that's why he's one of my best friends.

We've known each other since we were kids—met at the basketball courts, and never left each other's side. Everyone always presumed we were together, but it's not like that with us. He's like a brother to me. We kissed once when we were teenagers, but soon realized that it just wasn't right.

Moving silently, we make our way through the dark lanes of the trailer park, passing a couple of locals who perk up and mouth off. Once they realize who Kai is, they quickly shut down, offering him their respect. They know better than to start something with him. He doesn't just look scary with his big build, but he's part of the 18 Hood gang.

We hit the courts. As we approach the abandoned high-rise community center, the sound of kids laughing and the thud of a ball hitting the pavement grows louder. When I reach for the ladder to the fire escape on the left-hand side of the building, Kai grips my waist and lifts me effortlessly. I quickly grasp the railing, the metal cold beneath my fingers as I start climbing. Release—I am free at last. The higher we get, the more I can breathe properly. With each step toward the top of the ladder, my heart beats faster, creating a rhythmic thumping in my ears.

Kai follows closely behind me. I peer down, grinning, and he laughs. The ladder abruptly stops, and a surge of anticipation tightens my chest, preparing me for the climb ahead. The part I love the most.

Grabbing hold of the jagged bricks, their sharp edges dig into my palms as I begin to climb. I've done this countless times, my feet and hands effortlessly navigating the holes until I reach the top. Hanging onto the ledge, I can't help but notice the rush of wind against my face as I contemplate the consequences of letting go. How my body would feel floating, then *bam*. Splat. I never would jump, but it's the thought that keeps me alive. The ringing in my ears, the light-headedness. Fuck yes, I need this.

Sweat drips down my palms. My hand slips.

Chapter Three
Freya

From somewhere below me, Kai's curses echo, but I block them out, concentrating on my tight grip on the edge of the building and avoiding glancing down at the daunting ten-story plunge. My gaze snaps to the hard cement basketball courts and a whole heap of pain. I try to focus on pulling myself back up, but it's useless—I don't have enough strength with one arm. A strong hand force-fully pushes against my ass, propelling me forward with enough force to grasp onto the ledge and pull myself up with a desperate scramble.

I roll onto my back on the rooftop, the sound of my laughter filling the air.

"What the fuck, Frey? That was way too close of a call. Even for you," Kai growls, standing over me. I take his outstretched hand, rubbing off the dirt on my ass as I'm lifted to my feet.

"It's been a night," I say, following him to the edge and taking a seat. Looking out into our neighborhood, my legs dangle and I lean back on my hands. There are a few small fires scattered throughout the trailer park, with people talking amongst themselves and drinking. Typical Friday night.

"You're telling me. Shit's been popping off on the streets tonight. There was a huge brawl between Daringhood and the cops. We weren't even there, but you know as well as I do, we will get the blame." Kai sighs, pulling out a joint from behind his ear.

He's not wrong. Being part of 18 Hood, the rap group, doesn't do him any favors with the force. Half the time they aren't involved; they just rap about what's happening on the streets.

"That's bullshit. You know how to get your revenge— through your words," I say.

"How was the party down at the pit?" Kai asks, changing the subject.

For the next few hours, I fill him in on what happened tonight while he smokes his joint and we watch Tony stumble around, picking fights with anyone he can find. By the time Kai drops me back at my trailer, the sun is rising, casting a warm golden glow across the park, and I curse. I've got work in a couple of hours and it's going to be hell. But at least I've had my adrenaline high, and this time, when my head hits the pillow, I fall into a deep and restful sleep.

* * *

The air is filled with the scent of cleaning chemicals, while sweat drips down my forehead and my arms ache with each movement of the mop. Each hour has felt like an eternity as I anxiously await the moment when I can finally say I'm finished. Reluctantly, I accepted a double shift from seven in the morning until ten at night, and now I'm starting to regret it as exhaustion seeps into my bones.

The only thing pushing me forward is the realization of how crucial this money is for us—especially for Alec. He deserves to collect his scholarship at college and get the fuck out of this place, and I know he won't leave unless I can come with him. No one but us knows about our plan, not even my two best friends, Kai and Amirah. It's easier that way because whenever you have something good going for you in Daringhood, there's always someone lurking in the shadows, ready to snatch it away.

Eager to check my messages, I reach into my apron pocket and retrieve my phone, feeling its familiar weight in my hand. None of the messages I've sent to Alec have been read, which is quite disappointing. Where the hell is he? He's meant to be working in the kitchen with the other cook, but he didn't show up, which is totally out of character. He knows how much we need this.

The echoing sound of the doorbell fills the empty diner. I leave the restroom and enter the diner, ready to announce that we're closing, but I quickly close my mouth instead. Lucas Fox confidently strolls in, giving off the impression that he is the rightful owner of the place, and chances are, he is. He's wearing casual, loose-fitting cargo pants and a black polo shirt that strains against his muscles. Underneath his flipped-back black hat, his light-blond hair is neatly slicked back. Swallowing hard, I find my voice as I grip the mop tightly.

"We're closing," I say, dunking the mop in the water.

Lucas pays no attention to me as he keeps moving, finally settling into the booth that's snugly nestled against the smudged windows, providing a view of the parking lot. With a roll of my eyes, I continue to clean the floor while deliberately avoiding eye contact with him.

I get halfway down and find myself right next to his table, within arm's reach.

"Didn't you get the message? We're closing in five minutes," I snap, completely ignoring the fact that he could get me fired with just a snap of his fingers. It's been a long-ass day, and I don't want to be dealing with this. All I want is for this shift to be done so I can find Alec.

His dimple becomes visible as the corner of his mouth lifts, and his eyes lock onto mine as if he can decipher every thought in my mind. Curiosity shines in his light-brown eyes, along with a mysterious glimmer I can't decipher.

"Looks like you'll be staying open for a little while longer for me." He pauses, eyes fixated on my shoulder, no doubt where he can see the rose tattoo. The one Kai did for me. "Something tells me you need the money, so I wouldn't go complaining, thorn."

"Thorn?" I ask, frowning.

"Yeah. Rose doesn't seem very fitting for you. You're more of a thorn, with all the prickly edges." He grins.

Pinching my lips together, I hold back the "fuck off" I want to scream in his face.

"Did you want something to eat or drink, or are you just here to piss me off?" I ask, leaning the mop against the end of the booth.

"Nah, nothing for me. I'm meeting a business associate who's late as per usual," he says, checking his phone.

"Business on this side of the tracks?" I raise an eyebrow, then laugh. "Wow, must be desperate."

Lucas opens his mouth just as the front door chimes and my stomach drops.

Gavin enters, shoving a small, transparent bag into the pocket of his torn jeans. I grab the mop and bucket, ignoring Lucas, and continue cleaning with my back turned to

Gavin. I'm really hoping he doesn't notice me. I don't want to handle him tonight, or ever again, for that matter. The encounter from last night was enough to last the entire week.

A hand lands on my lower back, and my knees lock. Gavin bends over, his lips close to my ear as he whispers, "Little Freya, aren't I happy to see you here." His bad breath lingers all around me, and I fight back the urge to knee him in the balls. If we were any place else I would, but I need this job.

I take a step forward and swiftly turn around, lowering my voice to ensure my boss doesn't hear me from the kitchen.

"Piss off, Gavin, we're closed," I say between gritted teeth.

"It won't be long until your mother is coming back to me again. And you know what that means . . . I'll need to collect." He looks salaciously at my chest, and my fists clench onto the mop so hard that it might snap. I'd rather shove this right up his ass, but he isn't worth losing my job over.

"Gavin," Lucas snaps, and the sleaze scurries away, meeting him at his booth.

"Two coffees, thorn."

"Please," I mutter, but I go fill their order and dump the pot and two mugs on the table.

"No milk? No sugar?" Lucas seems far too amused.

"No. Figured you'd want it black, like your heart," I reply, then head back to the kitchen to rinse the mop head.

The diner is empty after I finish, and while I'm happy Gavin is gone, I can't help but wish Lucas was still there. I have no idea why, and I don't want to give it much thought. He's one of them. End of story.

Oscar, my boss, shuts the cash register, leans across the counter, and hands me an envelope containing my wages for the week.

"Lucas left a nice tip for you. I put it in there. See you next week," he says, switching off the lights.

I quickly open the envelope and find an extra fifty-dollar bill. What the fuck? I don't need his charity. I work for my money; this is too much of a tip for just serving two coffees. Rich dick.

"Oh, did you get ahold of your brother?" he asks, and I shake my head.

"I'll make sure he gives you a call when I run into him," I say, and he agrees. I slide the envelope into my back pocket, remove my apron, and make my way out the front door.

Stepping out into the cool night, a light breeze brushes against my face, so I pull my hoodie over my head and tuck my hands into the front pocket. I lean back against the wall, taking in the stillness of the mostly quiet parking lot. There is no mistaking the owner of the magnificent black Bugatti La Voiture Noire that's right in front of me. Within a matter of moments, I recognize the person leaning against the car. With a smooth motion, Lucas brings the sleek, black e-cigarette to his lips and inhales a long drag. The light above me flickers, creating creepy shadows all around.

Ignoring him, I bring my phone back to my ear, desperately trying to reach Alec again, only to be met with silence.

"I don't know where you are, Alec, but you were supposed to drive me home. If I get rolled by a bastard in a Bugatti, it's on you."

After leaving the message, I feel a throbbing headache coming on and pinch the bridge of my nose. This isn't like him. He'd never normally leave me to walk home like this.

What if he's been hurt? What if something bad has happened?

"Damn it," I mutter, angrily typing out another text message to him. I can always count on him to be my designated driver, ensuring I get home safely. Now I'm going to have to walk.

"Who are you waiting for?" Lucas approaches and stands by my side, the scent of blueberry lingering in the air as he exhales.

"Don't you have somewhere else better to be?" I ask instead.

"Yeah, I do, actually," he says, a smile spreading across his face as he pushes off the wall and strides confidently toward his car. "It's where your brother is waiting."

He . . . what? Running to catch up, I stumble after him.

"What do you mean?" I ask.

He opens the passenger-side door for me. "Hop in and I'll show you," he says, but I shake my head, crossing my arms tightly over my chest.

"Hell no. Tell me where he is. Now," I say, my voice growing louder with each word.

Lucas's playful smile fades away as he shakes his head, his expression turning serious. Taking a firm hold of my arm, he squeezes, inflicting a sharp wave of pain that forces me to clench my teeth.

"Get in the fucking car. I won't ask again," he warns, his words tinged with a touch of menace, sending a chill down my back. Under different circumstances, I would delight in the excitement that comes with defying him, but my brother's safety is at stake, and I can't afford to take that risk.

I manage to break free from his firm grip, my heart racing, and quickly slide into his car. With a forceful slam, he shuts the door, and I immediately sink into the plush upholstery, the leather soft against my skin. Beads of sweat form on my palms and I anxiously rub them on my shorts.

Lucas jumps in, the engine roars to life, and we speed out of the parking lot.

"Where are we going? Just tell me." The intense speed and sharp turn force me to hold onto the seatbelt tightly, basking in a mix of excitement and fear.

"To the masque ball in Daringville, little thorn," he says, and the sound of my racing heartbeat drowns out everything else.

My brother is at a masquerade ball with some of the wealthiest, most dangerous people on the wrong side of the tracks?

Damn it, Alec, what the hell are you doing?

Chapter Four
Freya

Lucas races through town at a breakneck speed, his fingers tapping away on his phone. I'm on edge the entire time, gripping onto my seatbelt.

Alec is a big boy and can look after himself—but what if he's in trouble? He always has my back, and it's unlike him to leave me to get home from work by myself, which makes me worry that something is seriously wrong. Has he been seeing his therapist? He's been a little on edge lately, but I have, too, with the stress of getting enough money to get out of here. He isn't like he was before—he has something to look forward to. A way to get out of here for good. It doesn't stop me from worrying, though.

Unfortunately, the only person who can give me a ride to him is this jerk, who happens to be one of the heirs of The Brotherhood.

Something jumps out in front of the car. My scream fills the interior of the vehicle as I instinctively latch onto his thigh, my nails digging deep into his flesh.

Lucas narrowly avoids hitting whatever the hell that thing was. My heart pounds in my chest, a restless rhythm begging for action, demanding a release of this built-up adrenaline. Shifting in my seat, I subtly cross one leg over the other, my hand still tightly gripping his thigh. It's as though it's keeping me from falling off the edge and doing something reckless.

"Deathwise" by Stand Atlantic rumbles through the car and my eyes lock with Lucas's. His mouth quirks up at one side, his eyes leisurely taking in every inch of me, leaving me paralyzed. I don't dare move. I can't. He continues driving, constantly shifting his gaze between me and the road.

"Don't tell me you're one of those girls who can't handle a little reckless fun?" he asks, switching gears and turning back to watch the road.

A scoff escapes my lips as I exhale the breath I've been holding. "You'll have to figure that out for yourself," I say. I refuse to give him any details that he could twist and use against me. He's the enemy, and the only reason I'm here in his car is because I'm worried about my brother.

I remove my hand from his thigh and instinctively pull away, but he reaches out and grabs it, guiding it to his crotch, where I feel his hard erection. Holy crap.

"That's what the thrill does to me." He smirks, his voice filled with an intoxicating combination of excitement and danger, and I quickly withdraw my hand.

"Touch me without my permission again, and I'll bite off your dick. I don't give a fuck who you are," I snap. His frown deepens, and his eyes shimmer with an indiscernible glimmer.

"Damn, thorn, I think I just fell in love. Keep talking to me like that and I'll get down on one knee for you." He laughs, and I turn in my seat to look out the window, praying we get there soon.

I'm done with this car and him. The entitled asshole. I

can't get to my brother soon enough. He expertly maneuvers around the main streets of Daringhood, and I can't blame him for wanting to steer clear of the chaos. The car would be completely totaled by the time the thugs figured out its owner.

The train tracks come into view as we swiftly fly over them, completely bypassing the security point. They must be familiar with his car, otherwise they would be chasing us at full speed.

His phone suddenly vibrates, grabbing his attention, and Gage's name lights up the screen. A lump forms in my throat, but Lucas ignores it, quickly silencing his phone.

The further we venture into Daringville, the more extravagant and ridiculous the houses become. Despite the darkness, their lights cast a glow that pierces through the night.

We come to a halt in front of a gated community, and the hairs on the back of my neck stand as memories threaten to overcome me. No, I can't think of that now. I just need to get through this, find Alec, and leave. Fuck them and this place. I can't let my mind go back there. The grand gate looms before us, no doubt adorned with rigorous security features. Daringhood and this place are like two different worlds. The poor versus the rich. No middle class here. The whole system is fucked.

The gates swing open, and we drive down a winding driveway that seems to stretch on forever. Streetlights illuminate the road, large well-manicured hedges scream I'm rich, and it takes everything in me not to jump out of the moving car and run back over the train tracks. It's maddening how we have almost nothing and they have all of this, even though we work so hard. Half our earnings go to them just because they put it in the treaty all those years ago. The Brotherhood rules, and we have no say in it.

And to think I used to be one of them.

A house comes into view that can only be described as a gothic mansion, sitting on the edge of a cliff. He parks right in front, and a staff member hurries over to open his door for him, but before he gets out I ask, "Is this where the ball is?"

"This is my place and I'm hosting." He grins, then slips from his car and shuts the door.

I've never been to his place, only Amirah's. I stay in the car, doubting my decision once again. No turning back now. I'll go to this stupid masquerade, find Alec, and go home. Simple as that. But the longer I stay in the car, the longer it will take.

I find the door handle and step outside into the cool night air. The crashing waves against the cliff top surrounding Lucas's home send shivers down my spine as I imagine the treacherous drop below. I resist the urge to approach the edge, where I can almost taste the salty spray of the wind and feel the exhilarating whip of the waves on my cheeks.

The rev of engines comes down the driveway and more people start arriving dressed in beautiful gowns and suits. They eye me with suspicion, and I shift uncomfortably.

"Come on, little thorn," Lucas says from the front door with a smirk. "We've got to transform you into a princess for the masquerade ball."

I scoff. "I don't need anything, just need to find my brother and go back home. I don't belong here."

"You used to," Lucas whispers so low I almost don't hear him. I can't think of that time. Not now, not ever.

I join Lucas, and he swings the front door open with a

forceful push, barely giving me time to enter before it slams shut.

The foyer is a whirlwind of activity, with staff darting around frantically, balancing trays of food and drinks, while masked figures navigate through the house.

I need to find Alec—he's got to be here somewhere. I can't help but notice people stopping and staring, their heads turning to catch a glimpse of my diner uniform and the sound of their whispers filling the air. I keep my head held high. I don't give a fuck what they think. Navigating through the crowded living area, I search desperately for my brother, scanning the faces of countless people, but I can't see him. Music echoes through the house, coming from outside.

A hand grabs onto mine and I spin around, finding myself face to face with Lucas. His grip on me tightens as he pulls me away, and I desperately try to escape, but it's futile. I try to keep up with Lucas, but he's like a ninja, dodging everyone until we arrive at a black staircase. He bounds up the steps, two at a time, with me chasing closely behind, eager to escape the bustling foyer.

"You're right, you don't belong here, but that's the best part. Besides, you won't be able to go undetected wearing that uniform. You need to blend in with the ladies of Daringville. Or would you prefer being the center of attention?" Lucas's voice echoes through the long hallway as he moves, disappearing through a door and into a bedroom.

I follow in after him, and in the center of the room, a grand king-sized bed dominates the space. Its black four-poster frame exudes an air of elegance, adorned with deep-red covers and soft, plush cushions. Lucas opens up a set of double doors, revealing what appears to be another bedroom. Scratching the back of my neck, I fight the urge to turn around and head back out the front door.

Lucas reappears, his arms full of long dresses and high-heeled shoes, which he haphazardly throws onto his bed.

"Why on earth do you have women's clothes? Are you a cross-dresser?" I ask with a frown. "Totally cool if you are. That's your business."

With a laugh, he pulls his T-shirt over his head and lets it fall to the ground. My eyes trace down the lines of his defined chest to the trail of hair that disappears beneath his pants.

"Nah," he says, licking his lips, "these clothes are souvenirs from the women who leave them at my door."

I scoff. "I'd rather not know what poor women they belong to."

He unzips his cargo pants, and they effortlessly slide down his legs, revealing his black briefs. Swallowing hard, I quickly move past him and begin browsing the gowns, feeling the soft fabrics between my fingers. I can't believe how far I'm willing to go for my brother's sake.

From the corner of my eye, I catch a glimpse of his muscled bare ass fading into the bathroom. He leaves the door slightly open, but I resist the urge to glance back and give him the satisfaction. The dresses are absolutely stunning, and as I run my fingers along the smooth silk and delicate lace, I discover a beautiful black gown with a gracefully low neckline.

The shower starts running in the background, and I peer over my shoulder, locking eyes with Lucas through the misty shower window. His hands firmly grip his cock, and I can't help but roll my eyes.

Turning my back on Lucas, I lift my top over my head and drop my shorts. I lift the silk dress, exposing the elegant black lace bra and thong with tags hanging off them that perfectly complement it. Who on earth has these kinds of things hanging around?

Shaking my head, I remove my old, worn cotton bra and underwear that I've had for way too long and replace them with the lacy set. There's no way I'm wearing my old pair in this dress. I pull the dress over my head and shimmy into it. The garment fits snugly, accentuating my curves, but I'm cautious as I take a seat, hoping it won't rip.

I pick out a set of silver heels, holding them up to admire them for a moment before I place them on the floor and slide my feet into them. The shoes are a perfect fit, although I'm unsure if I can walk in them, but I'll give it a try.

The water turns off and a few moments later, Lucas walks out with a towel around his waist, water dripping from his blond hair down his neck and chest. Gripping the bed linen, my fingers ache with the desire to trace their way down his sculpted torso. I can't even remember the last time I got laid. I'm flooded with memories of that unforgettable night with Gage one year ago. The hate fuck that almost ruined my relationship with my best friend for fucking her brother. Ever since that night, Amirah has been throwing countless guys my way, but none of them interest me. I don't want them. It's annoying as fuck. I don't want Gage to have any control over me, but my body still reacts to him.

With a purposeful stride, Lucas makes his way across the room until he towers over me, his erect cock at eye level. My gaze instantly locks with his, and I'm met with that familiar playful smirk. From somewhere in the house, pulsating beats of loud bass start up, and the bed beneath me practically trembles.

"I've always thought hood pussy tastes sweeter than the

elite. Why don't you lie back and let me have at it?" he suggests, gently running his fingers along my jaw.

I take a deep, shaky breath, feeling a rush of excitement that dampens my panties at the idea of him eating me out. Fuck.

"You think you can have anything you want," I say, and I hate the tremor in my voice.

"I don't think." He laughs, low and sinister. "I know."

"You can't have me." Danger sends a pulse to my pussy.

"I know, little thorn." His fingers move from my jaw, down the column of my throat, and linger on the swell of my breasts. "There's something . . . special about you."

"I bet you say that to all the girls." I try to laugh it off.

Fire flashes in his eyes. "Trust me." He runs his fingers over my breast and my nipple pebbles. "I don't."

I should fight this—I should. But he's so damn fine, and something about how wrong this is makes it feel so right.

He kneels, positioning himself between my legs, they naturally spread apart slightly until I feel the tight pull of the dress, and I instinctively lean back onto my elbows. As he bends forward, I can feel the gentle pressure of his chest against mine. His stiff cock brushes against the soft silk.

There's a loud knock on his bedroom door, then it opens not a moment later, Lucas curses.

"What the fuck is going on here?"

His voice turns my damp panties dry. The moment our eyes connect, a chill runs down my spine as if Gage's glare has the power to extinguish my existence.

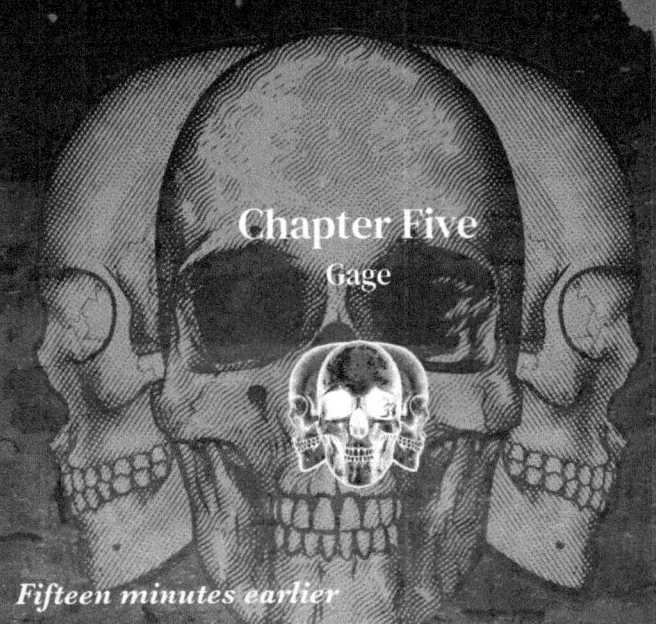

Chapter Five
Gage

Fifteen minutes earlier

Fuck Lucas. He was supposed to meet me down at the docks to deal with a shipment and some useless workers, but he ghosted me and didn't even bother picking up his damn phone. I had to deal with those useless members myself.

I reach into my glove box and grab another wipe, using it to carefully clean the blood off my knuckles. I hate getting my hands dirty; that's why I'm so mad. As I discover more on my steering wheel, my chest tightens, and a heavy weight bears down on me. Fucking gross.

As long as I remain untouched by blood, I have no qualms about eliminating my enemies with my firearm. However, tonight presented a challenge as I found myself facing a group of five on my own. You have no choice but to get your hands dirty to get out of a situation like that.

I pick up my phone and quickly send a text to Phillip, my personal assistant. He responds right away, promising to pick up and clean my car from Lucas's. At least I can rely on him, not my so-called best friend.

Lucas's house comes into view, along with his car in the driveway. So he is here, along with a swarm of other people pulling up in gowns and suits. Fuck, I forgot about the stupid ball. Why does my best friend love to party so damn much? Could this day get any worse? All I want to do is bury myself in a bottle.

I drive my car straight into the underground garage and park it there, so no one messes with my Bentley Mulliner Batur. Only Phillip is allowed, and even the thought of him in it makes my skin crawl.

I brush off the staff and take the elevator up to Lucas's floor. When I open his bedroom door, I freeze. The moment our eyes lock, a wave of blood floods my head, intensifying the connection. What the fuck is *she* doing here in Lucas's bedroom? And why is he naked in between her legs?

The girl who won't leave my every fucking thought. The girl who blew my fucking mind. The girl who I vowed to never see again after I tried to protect her, put her before The Brotherhood, and paid the ultimate price for it. Yeah, I fucking hate her, and now here she is again—underneath my best friend.

Lucas remains perfectly still, his lips curling into a subtle smirk. He's dead.

I slam the bedroom door shut, the sound reverberating through the room, and stride confidently toward the bed, my footsteps echoing on the hardwood floor. My fists clench against my sides.

She places her hands on Lucas's chest, attempting to push him away, but he stays firmly in place.

"Care to explain?" I growl, folding my arms over my chest.

Lucas's gaze playfully shifts between Freya and me, his lips curling into a mischievous smile. "Just about to eat her out. Here to watch?"

My nostrils flare, and he opens his mouth, but Freya momentarily distracts him by throwing her body sideways to evade him, and then she scrambles to her feet.

"That would never happen. In your fucking dreams," she snaps, looking back at Lucas. Something crosses over her features, and I clench my teeth. *She's a liar.* "I'm just here to find my brother, then I'm gone."

Her brother? Interesting. He's becoming a great asset to The Daring Brotherhood, according to Hazen. The kid has skills, ones that we have been taking advantage of.

I frown. "I'll deal with you later," I say, giving Lucas a side-eye. Lucas just shrugs and saunters into his walk-in closet like it's no big deal. "And you." I look back at Freya, trying to ignore the way her black silk dress clings to her body, accentuating every curve. With her straight brown hair flowing down her back, she nervously bites her plump bottom lip, a habit she can't seem to break. God damn.

Memories of that night come rushing back, threatening to consume me with their power. The way her eyes lit up when my hand was around her throat. She loved it. And when my cock was buried deep inside her—fuck. Her pussy clenched around my dick like a damn vice.

I clear my throat, trying to ignore everything that happened that night. "You just don't fall in line, do you? You just love playing with trouble."

With a roll of her crystal-blue eyes, she delicately runs her fingers down the smooth fabric of her gown. "You've got me all figured out, don't you?"

"You wear your heart on your sleeve, Freya. You're too

easy to play with." The corner of my mouth lifts and her fists tighten at her sides.

"I'm done playing games. I've got more important shit to do."

Lucas reappears, dressed in a stylish black suit with a white shirt unbuttoned at the collar. He holds a black lace mask and passes it to Freya. She takes it and walks toward the door, brushing past me on her way. It takes everything in me not to grab her by her throat and fuck her against the wall for the second time. Nope, never happening again. She's one of them. I only fuck women of the elite. She was the one exception because she once was one of us, and it clearly worked out terribly.

She reaches the door and rips it open.

"The games haven't even started yet, little Freya." My voice lingers in the air as she storms out of the bedroom. I whirl around, glaring at Lucas. "What the fuck was that?" I breathe out. "You know she's off-limits."

With a casual shrug, Lucas's lips curl into a faint smile before he strolls into his bathroom, paying no attention to me. I storm in after him and dart my hand out to grab the collar of his shirt tightly. His smirk remains plastered on his face, and I have to restrain myself from forcefully knocking it off. I shudder at the thought of more blood touching my skin.

"She's off-limits to you, but not me," he says, licking his lips. "You never mentioned how sweet her pussy—"

I smash his head into the tiles, and he moans in pain.

"If you don't stop talking," I snap, my voice dripping with irritation, "you'll regret it."

Lucas finally gets the hint and nods. I let go and put some distance between us, leaning back against the vanity.

"Is this where you've been all night? I needed you at the docks," I say, releasing a long breath.

"Oh fuck. Sorry, brother. I had to meet up with that scumbag Gavin to collect, then I ran into her, and she was looking for her brother. She's sure something," Lucas says, kicking off the wall like what he just said isn't a big deal.

He never thinks any girls are special. He fucks nearly every night of the week, but then they are gone, thrown out like the trash. He grabs some gel from the cupboard, running it through his hair.

"Don't let it happen again. I'm using your shower." I don't bother waiting for him to leave—it's not like he hasn't seen everything before. We grew up together, our lives intertwined so tightly it's impossible to imagine a world without him and Hazen.

I toss my dirty clothes on the black tiles and hop into his shower, the water turning on automatically. It takes me twenty minutes to scrub away every trace of blood and grime.

Lucas is chilling on his bed, scrolling through his phone when I walk into the bedroom and head straight for his closet. He'll have something in here for me to wear to this ball. Thank fuck we're the same size.

As I rummage through his vast array of clothing, my gaze lands on a pair of black slacks that closely resemble his. Beside them, I spot a button-up shirt in a rich, deep shade of red. I can almost feel the smoothness of the slacks and the silky texture of the shirt. These will do nicely.

* * *

Hazen leisurely leans back against one of the bars, a joint dangling from his lips, and a glass of amber liquid in his hand. I slide in next to him and snatch the joint from his lips, and he rolls his eyes. I blow out a smoke ring and the wind catches it, wafting it away, fuck I hope this weed will help calm my anger. There's been a constant stream of drama tonight, and all I want is to relax and unwind, but it seems like that won't be possible. When you are The Brotherhood heirs and practically rule over Daringville, you never stop. There's always something to take care of. It's fucking exhausting.

"How'd the docks go?" Hazen asks, bringing his glass to his mouth. He scans the crowd, his eyes darting from face to face, no doubt searching for his next target. Lucky for him. Ever since that night, I haven't been able to properly scratch that itch. Since *her*.

She's fucked with my head, and I hate her for it. She's the forbidden fruit, tempting me with memories of its sweet taste that I long to savor once more. I won't. She's a distraction, one I can't afford.

"Fucking nightmare. You need to recruit more workers for the docks, but make sure they're trustworthy. You'll find the shit in the garage, start . . ." I spot her in the midst of the bustling crowd who are milling around the pool. She's still here. Her eyes meet mine as the black lace mask hides her identity and her long brown hair cascades down her back. I want nothing more than to wrap that hair firmly around my fist and watch her swallow my cock.

"Start what?" Hazen asks, but I pretend like I didn't hear him.

She's scanning the area, checking out every guy to find her brother, no doubt. It's why she's here. Lucas steps in front of me, obstructing my view of her, and then turns his head to look in the same direction I am. He turns back around with a playful smirk on his lips. He whips out a bag from his pocket and does a line of coke on the bar behind us before turning back around.

"Oh, looks like the little thorn is lost and needs a helping hand. See ya," he says, and with a determined stride, he sets off toward her. Fucking hell.

Lucas catches up to her and leans down, whispering something in her ear. I'm dying to know what he's saying. I need to know. She says something back to him, then they stare at one another, exchanging words for far too long before she shoves her empty glass into his chest and walks off.

"Dude, focus. That's the second time you've ditched this conversation and not even to get laid—for an eye fuck. Don't tell me you're still obsessed with her?" Hazen says, sparking up another joint.

"Shit, yeah, sorry. Can you get the shit from the garage, baggie it up, and start circulating?" I snatch a glass of champagne from a waiter and down it. It tastes like shit, but it'll do.

Hazen pushes off the bar and disappears.

I spend the better half of the night watching her every move. No matter how hard I try to avoid her, her presence lingers like a shadow. It's driving me fucking crazy. She shouldn't be here, for starters. I should get her kicked out and drive her back over to her side of the tracks, but part of me wants her here . . . and it's fucking with my head. Any other fucker from Daringhood would be dead already, but not Freya LeClair. With an air of self-assurance, she waltzed into the place, leaving everyone unaware of who she is. They think she's one of us. How wrong they are.

Her attention is abruptly captured by something, causing her to gulp down the rest of her drink and swiftly retreat indoors. I follow after her, my footsteps barely audible like a predator stalking its prey. Everyone gets out of my way and it's not long until I've caught up to her.

With each step, her high heels create a distinct clicking sound on the tiled floor, effortlessly drawing attention to her confident walk and the gentle sway of her hips. My dick hardens, and not for the first time tonight. She's really starting to get on my nerves. She's too much of a distraction for me to handle.

With a lunge forward, I extend my hand, firmly gripping her arm, and she reacts with a surprised gasp, swinging her fist in defense. Just in time, I manage to duck and narrowly avoid her hand, then I spring back up and pin her against a nearby wall. Her body tenses as she tries to break free, her piercing gaze locking onto mine.

"Let go of me now, or I swear to God I'll . . ." Her nostrils flare and I smirk. She's too easy to play with.

"You'll what? I don't think you've got it in you."

She takes a deep breath, a gentle smile gracing her lips. She pushes her hips forward, getting so close that her berry scent overwhelms me. Fuck.

When her lips meet mine, I forget who she is and why I hate her.

Gage - Age Seven

The piercing screams carry through the walls of Hazen's house, fueling the fire of anger within me. I storm toward Dominic's office door, my clenched fists trembling with rage. Peering through the crack, my heart races in my chest. Dominic is leaning over Freya, her body trembling under his, and her eyes widen with terror as he abruptly withdraws his hand. A loud slap fills the air. I flinch as though he's hit me. He pulls down her pants and the anger I felt before is nothing compared to now. This isn't right.

She's so small compared to him. She's only six. I have to

help her. Without thinking about the consequences, I push open the door and run straight up to Dominic. He has one hand down his pants and the other moving over her stomach. With a trembling fist, I lash out, connecting with his side, my voice escaping my throat in a shaky scream. "Don't hurt her!"

He whirls around so fast I lose my balance and fall straight onto the hard floor. Her bright blue eyes bore into me as she lets out a chilling scream that sends shivers down my spine. Dominic's fist hits the side of my face, my vision blurs and her screams are the final thing I hear before the ringing in my ears takes over, and everything goes black.

A loud bang of metal against metal clangs in my ears, bringing me back to consciousness in a dark room. No, please don't let me be here. Anywhere but here. The walls gradually narrow, suffocating me as Dominic secures the bars with a resounding click, trapping me in this claustrophobic prison. Clutching onto the cold, unforgiving metal, I look up into his dark-brown eyes, pleading for forgiveness and praying he'll let me out.

"I'm sorry, please don't leave me here!"

I know it's weak to beg for mercy, but I hate this place. The memory of my previous visit lingers in my mind, a consequence of my defiance toward Dominic that I have no desire to relive. I was locked in here for two days that time, without any food or water, only me and my thoughts. I don't want to experience that again.

"This is what happens when you put a girl before The Brotherhood. You will be punished. No one comes before us. Your brothers are kings, and anyone who breaks our code isn't one of us. Understood?" His menacing growl sends chills down my spine, and I struggle to suppress the knot of terror constricting my throat.

"Yes, I understand."

I have to forget about Freya—she's a distraction, and she's the reason I'm now getting punished. Because I tried to protect her, to save her from him. I'll never make that mistake again or I'll pay the ultimate price.

Chapter Six
Freya

Thirty minutes earlier

G age and Lucas can play whatever games they want, but I just want to find my brother and get back over to our side of the tracks. The streets may not seem safe, but they're still safer than being here. Money equals power, and being around The Brotherhood means he's not far away. I never want to see Gage again.

I slam Lucas's door shut with Gage inside, leaving them to sort out whatever they need to. In the quiet hallway, I secure the mask over my face, concealing my identity, and cautiously descend the stairs toward the music that will lead me to the ball and my brother.

I squeal when someone grabs my shoulder and I spin around, grabbing a slender throat. Amirah's eyes widen, and I quickly let go, stepping off the last stair.

"What the hell?" I snap, and Amirah takes in a few deep breaths.

"I was just about to ask you the same thing. What are you doing here?"

"Sorry, you know better than to sneak up on me. I'm here to find my brother. Apparently, he's here. Have you seen him?"

Amirah hooks her arm with mine, and we make our way through the foyer, heading to the open-plan kitchen that has an incredible view of the massive garden. In every direction I turn, my eyes are met with a sea of people adorned in glamorous outfits and mysterious masks, gracefully sipping from their champagne-filled glasses. I don't recognize anyone.

"I saw him earlier with Hazen and was going to message you, but didn't want you freaking out," Amirah says, grabbing two glasses from a waiter. She passes one to me. I finish the drink in one gulp. He's with Hazen? That's more important than work and walking me home? That's so not like him. I have to find him.

"Where is he now?" I ask, glancing around the room, but I can't see him.

"No idea. Let's go look." Amirah takes my hand, the sounds of chatter and footsteps surrounding us as she leads us deeper into the sea of people. They watch our every move, probably because they know who Amirah is. A shiver runs up my spine as I feel the weight of their gazes on me. A wave of anxiety washes over me, making me want to bolt out the front door. But I won't.

The parties at Daringhood are so different from the ones they hold here. We hang around a fire pit with deafening hip-hop and techno music. Wearing short skirts and crop tops and drinking wine straight out of a cask. Here they show up in expensive dresses, snort cocaine, and drink from crystal glasses. And to think I came from here. Nope, not going there tonight.

Overlooking the expansive lap pool is a DJ setup, with a

few people dancing while the rest form circles, engaging in conversations. A few girls approach Amirah, but I completely ignore them as I search everywhere for a glimpse of my brother or Hazen. I pick up my phone and dial his number once more, but it goes directly to voicemail, just like the countless times earlier tonight. Fuck.

Regret fills my stomach, churning like a storm as I realize I should have asked if he was okay last night. I'm probably overreacting and everything will be fine, but I won't stop until I find him. Then he's going to hear about it for the rest of the week—or year.

I feel a sudden weight on my shoulder as a hand touches me, and I freeze. Cautiously, I lift my gaze and meet a pair of light-brown eyes staring directly into mine. Lucas's touch sends a shiver down my spine, causing goose-bumps to ripple across my arm, tempting me to continue what we began in his bedroom. The other part of me wants to push him away.

His lips softly brush against the sensitive spot below my ear, creating an electrifying sensation.

"Tell me why I shouldn't bend you over one of the tables and finish what we started, little thorn?"

I take a deep breath, refusing to let his mind games affect me. He's a distraction, and no matter how much my body wants the release, I won't give in.

I purse my lips and confidently place my hand on his chest, exerting a slight force that moves him back a step, and his eyes lock on mine. A smile touches my lips. "Because you and I both know you won't be able to handle me."

His eyes sparkle. "Want to test that theory?"

"Elite cock doesn't do it for me. I'd rather be with a hood rat. They know how to fuck harder," I say with a grin. His silent stance is accompanied by a glimmer in his eyes, and he opens his mouth, but I abruptly thrust my empty glass into his chest and slip into the surrounding crowd.

For the next hour, I search high and low, desperately scanning every corner for any sign of my brother or Hazen. I even talk to a few of the elite, ones with their lipstick not quite perfect, their dresses designer but not couture, and ask them if they've seen my brother—but no luck.

Gripping my glass, I take another sip of wine. Hazen's short, neatly styled hair catches my eye as he swiftly grabs a bite to eat from a passing waiter and seamlessly fades into the bustling crowd inside the house. Finishing off my drink, I hand it to the waiter before following him.

People close in around me and my heart rate rises with every step. I can't breathe, but I won't stop. I've spent the entire night tirelessly searching for my brother. I'm done with this place, and I just want to go home.

Moving with a purpose, Hazen bounds up the stairs, confidently taking them two at a time. He's the last person who saw Alec—maybe he'll tell me where he is. Intent on keeping up, I begin to follow, only for a large hand to grip my arm tightly, preventing me from proceeding. I pivot around, launching a punch, but he deftly ducks, narrowly avoiding my strike. In the next heartbeat, Gage swiftly pins me to the hallway wall, our bodies hidden from potential onlookers.

I try to resist his hold, but his mossy-green eyes, reminiscent of a lush forest, hold me hostage.

"Let go of me now or I swear to God I'll . . ." I say, my voice rising with each word, and he just smirks. God, I hate him. Every second I waste here, Hazen is moving further away.

"You'll what? I don't think you've got it in you," he says, leaning further into me. His body presses firmly against mine, and the hard plains of his chest tempt me to run my fingers over them.

I take a deep breath. If he wants to play, then I'll play. With a subtle tilt of my mouth, I surge my hips forward, savoring the exhilarating feeling of his cock pressing against my belly.

Our lips touch, starting off slow, then he intensifies the kiss. I tangle my fingers in his curly black hair, pulling his head back a little, and he lets out a deep growl that goes straight to my core. It takes me a second to remember why I kissed him in the first place.

I draw back, biting down hard into his lip until I taste the metallic tang of blood on my tongue. He takes a step back, creating just enough distance for me to place my hands on his chest and give him a firm push. With a stumble, he swipes his finger across his bottom lip, collecting the blood. The look in his eyes instantly changes, turning dark.

I spin around and sprint up the stairs. Gage curses, then his shoes pound against the stairs after me. The music starts to fade, and I reach the final step, glancing left and right. Light spills into the hallway from the slightly open door across from Lucas's room. Voices rise the closer I get, and when I push the door open, I freeze.

My brother's sitting there with a block of off-white powder, little baggies, and a small knife in his hand. My heart stops beating.

What the fuck have you done?

Chapter Seven
Freya

My brother jumps up, kicking back his chair, and it falls to the ground with a thud.

He takes a step toward me, and I take one back, hitting a wall of muscle. I look over my shoulder, meeting Gage's green eyes once again. He shuts the door behind him, and I create some distance between us, stepping further into the room.

There are two rows of tables set up, one with bricks and bricks of white powder, tubs of various chemicals, and other tools. Seems like this is a little drug operation. Shaking my head, I can't believe this. My brother is working for them and dealing with drugs that have torn our family apart. Doesn't he remember why we were forced out of here in the first place? I can't go back there.

It's no surprise that The Daring Brotherhood imports and deals drugs across the two towns—everyone knows that. They are in charge of everything. The only question is why the fuck is my brother involved? He hates drugs and how much they've fucked our family up. It's one of the main reasons we are moving away from here. So we can get Mom clean and give her a fresh start.

"I can explain," he says, and that's exactly what Mom used to say. Before I can even think twice about the consequences, I grab a bunch of already made-up baggies from the table in front of my brother and storm into the tiled en suite straight ahead.

"I wouldn't do that if I were you." Hazen's deep voice follows me into the bathroom. Despite the shiver working its way up my spine, I choose to ignore him.

Alec races behind me. "Freya, no! I can explain, don't —" He reaches for me but he's too late. I throw the baggies into the toilet bowl and flush. The plastic swirls and disappears down the toilet. Shit. Did I just get Alec in more trouble?

"Now would be the perfect time to explain, Alec," I say, turning around. He's standing in the middle of the bathroom doorway, his face pale. Lucas is standing behind him, gazing at me with such intensity, as if he's attempting to understand me. The playful signature smirk has vanished, and in its place is a furious scowl.

Alec turns around, facing him. "Give us a minute?"

Lucas scoffs. "Seriously? It's my house, but whatever. Have your little family chat. Just don't go flushing anything else down that toilet or there will be more than hell to pay, Freya."

Alec closes the door, leaving them outside, and I release a long, audible breath.

"I'm doing what I have to do to get out of here. We need this money, Freya." He steps forward, reaching for me, but I stumble backward, hitting the vanity. "Please understand."

"How can you do this? What if it ends up with Mom?

What if the next time she collapses through the trailer door, it's all your fault?"

He looks as though I've slapped him, his face pale. He takes a step back, hitting the door. His fingers wrap around his necklace and mine itch to do the same to mine.

"Look, we can go tell them you're not doing this anymore. We don't need the money that badly—"

"We do! I want to get you out of this place now. I want to help Mom now—not after I've been at college for a few months and saved some extra dollars." He pauses, takes a step closer, then tucks a lock of hair over my ear. "I'm doing this for you, sis."

My stomach churns. "Fuck, I know we want out, but anything but this, Alec. Anything."

A knock sounds at the door and Alec's body stiffens. He steps forward, his hands reaching out to grab onto mine. I look down at his big hands wrapped around mine.

"Let's not do this here. Just let me be your big brother and look after you."

I look up into his crystal-blue eyes, which are identical to mine. "Like how you forgot to pick me up after work tonight?" It's a low blow, but fuck him, I can't lose him to this shit. He's better than that, and we have a plan.

Alec drops my hands, running one through his dark-brown hair. "Fuck. I'm so sorry, Freya. I-I just had a lot on my mind with all this stuff. It won't happen again. Promise. Let's just—"

The door opens and Hazen's presence fills the space as he looks back and forth at us.

"Finished your little mothers' meeting?" he says, and I brush past Alec, stopping in front of Hazen.

"Move," I snap through gritted teeth. I need to get out of

here. Everything's fucked, and I need to do something. Anything to release this built-up anger.

The corner of Hazen's mouth lifts before he crosses his arms over his chest, showing off his bulging muscles and colorful tattoos that look way too good on his tanned skin.

"I'm sorry, Freya," Alec says from behind me, and I shake my head. No amount of apologizing is going to fix this.

"We'll talk tomorrow afternoon," I say, pushing Hazen aside, and I stride back into the drug den.

Gage is blocking the exit, and Lucas looks bored with his phone in his hand where he sits on one of the tables.

I need to get out of here. As I approach the door, Gage stands in my way, running his fingers along his jaw as he watches me. With a deep exhale, I forcefully barge into him, causing him to move aside as I stumble into the hallway. Without warning, Gage, Hazen, and Lucas close in on me, trapping me in the hallway.

"You're not going anywhere, Freya," Gage growls in a gravelly voice, and my knees become weak.

"Yeah. Seems you owe us about a hundred grams of coke. How are you gonna pay for that?" Hazen asks, raising an eyebrow.

"I've got an idea," Lucas counters with a wicked glint in his eye. Midnight deeds flash in my mind before I can stop them, and I blink them back because it doesn't matter how attractive these three are—they're trouble, and that's the last thing I want.

Shit. Maybe I shouldn't have flushed their product down the toilet.

No, fuck them and fuck the consequences.

"If your idea has anything to do with you shoving your

dick down my throat, forget it. I'd rather choke on a cactus than have your cock."

Lucas laughs, running a finger down my cheek, then my neck. Goosebumps scatter over my arms and my belly tightens. "It didn't seem that way earlier when I had you on my bed, ready to drop my head between your knees and—"

"Enough," Gage snaps, moving closer until his knees hit my thighs, and he wraps his hand around my throat.

My eyes widen and I stumble backward until my back slams into a wall. They all surround me. My underwear soaks and I hate myself for it. Why do I get so turned on when a guy wraps his hand around my throat? I have no fucking idea, but there's just something between pain and lust that gets me off.

"You know we've gutted guys for less than this, right?" Gage says, tightening his grip and cutting off more of my air supply.

"Do it," I say, my voice coming out all husky.

Gage's eyes darken and Lucas kneels at my feet. He runs his hand up my leg, getting higher and higher. My breath hitches and Gage moves my head back to him. Hazen has a pocketknife in his hand, flicking it open and closed. Shit.

Lucas's hand disappears up my dress until his fingers run over my soaking underwear. My eyes close for a second before I snap them back open.

"What the fuck is going on here?" someone yells, and Gage curses but doesn't move. Not until my best friend Amirah pushes us apart. I gasp in several deep breaths, rubbing my sore throat. Fucking Gage.

"Thank God you're here. Let's go," I say, moving toward her and grabbing her hand.

"What have I told you? Stay away from my friends," Amirah says, glaring at her brother.

Gage laughs. "Hey, she came to me and caused problems. Like usual. Keep your girl on a leash from now on or you won't see her again."

A sudden chill sends a shiver cascading down my spine. There's not a doubt in my mind that he can and will get rid of me if he wants to. They rule everything and everyone. You are stupid if you go up against them. Guess I'm the stupid bitch here.

Gage disappears back into the room, with Hazen and Lucas following closely behind him. Lucas throws me a wink and I shake my head.

"Don't tell me you're fucking my brother again?" Amirah asks, tugging me through the hall.

"Fuck no, you know that won't happen again," I say, shaking my head.

"Okay, then what the hell was that?" she asks with a sigh.

"I'll fill you in later. I've gotta get out of here," I say, pulling my hand out of hers and running down the remainder of the stairs.

Amirah yells something, but I don't hear her over the ringing in my ears. I kick off my heels when I reach the front door and stumble out into the cool, crisp night.

I need to release this built-up tension and there's only one way. Goosebumps scatter over my bare arms and I don't think twice as I run to the edge of the cliff face that surrounds Lucas's mansion. When I was a kid, I'd come here with Amirah, and the landscape feels familiar to me. Like coming home in some crazy fucked-up way, even though this place hasn't felt like home for years.

Angry waves crash against the rocks and it's like music

to my ears. Thunder booms from somewhere in the distance. The night sky lights up with a crack in the air. My heart pounds faster and faster. Don't do it. Part of me screams, but the other part eggs me on.

I need this.

My toes curl over the edge of the rock. Closing my eyes, I jump.

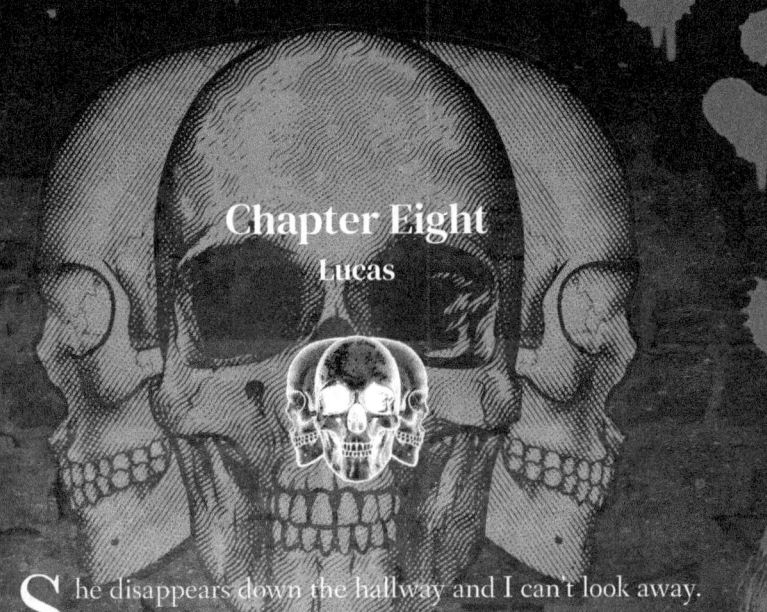

Chapter Eight
Lucas

She disappears down the hallway and I can't look away. Her dress clings to her body in a way that drives me wild, and I can't help but fantasize about discovering every detail underneath it. My cock twitches against my pants, begging to be touched. Fuck.

No one's ever made me feel like this. Why her? So many women throw themselves at me, but it has to be Freya LeClair who ignites something deep within me. Women have always served one purpose to me. To stick my dick in for release. No feelings attached.

That's all I've ever wanted, but since the café earlier today, I can't get her out of my mind. She's always been hot —but I didn't know how fiery she was. How protective of her family she is. And it's a fucking turn-on. I'd do anything to protect my sister, too, and that's exactly why she isn't here tonight—she's at a friend's place.

I want to know everything about Freya. What she likes to eat. Who she really is beneath the mask. What she likes to do. Everything. I want to strip away all the layers until only her innermost, most sinister thoughts are exposed. My

parents have been pressuring me to settle down, to repro-
duce to keep our bloodline going strong for future heirs, and
she's exactly the trouble that will piss them off. When it
comes to finding a worthy queen for my empire, she's definitely sparked my interest.

When I walk back into the room, Alec is carefully
portioning the cocaine into baggies while Hazen stands
nearby, giving him instructions.

"Micromanage much?" I ask with a smirk.

With an eye roll, Hazen swiftly takes one of the bags
from Alec's hand and forcefully dumps its contents back
into the large pile of white snow.

"That one was over, do it again," Hazen snaps, his jaw
ticking. He moves one of the scales so it forms a straight line
with the others.

His fucking OCD drives me insane sometimes. Hazen
is on the verge of breaking, and I can't say I blame him. It's
been a hell of a night, and all I want to do is forget that little
thorn whose pussy I'd love to be balls deep in.

"When are the others getting here?" Gage asks. "We've
got a lot of work to get through tonight." He leans back
against the wall, head in his phone, typing away.

"Soon. Just wanted to get Alec here caught up on the
operation before leaving. He's the new guy and we need
this extra work done," Hazen replies, and I yawn, ready to
head back out to the party. Give me drama and partying any
day of the week, not this business shit.

"Lucas, darling." My mother's voice floats through the
door, and I frown, turning her way. She glides into the room
in a tight-fitting pink dress, her blonde hair neatly arranged
in a bun on top of her head. I reach out to her, pulling her
into a tight embrace. Her strong floral perfume clings to me,

and it's like coming home. I pull back, pressing a kiss against her cheek.

"What are you doing up here?" I take a step back, creating a small distance between us.

We've always been close. She's always put me first, protecting me no matter the cost, but my mother will always be my father's prized possession. No matter how hard he pushes her, she never breaks. She's always by his side, putting on the perfect mask and acting like everything is perfectly fine.

That's the problem with the elite—they're all living a lie. Putting on a show for one another, always fighting to be the best, but really, they are the most unhappy fuckers on the planet. At least the gutter rats on the hood side of the tracks don't need to pretend. They are real. You know what you're going to get, unlike here. I have to watch my back because there's always a snake in the corner ready to pounce, and with my father getting sicker by the day, it's not long until I'll lead alongside my brothers.

"I just wanted to see my precious boy. You haven't been home much lately. I've missed you," she says with a pout, pulling me in for another hug.

"Missed you, too, Mom," I reply.

Looking past me at Alec, she pulls back and raises her eyebrows while I shake my head. Here we go.

"And who do we have here?" she practically purrs, moving over to the table and leaning over, her fake tits on full display.

"It's Alec LeClair," I say, and my mother narrows her eyes, studying him intently.

"From the hood," I explain, and her eyes widen slightly.

"Well, I won't hold that against you," she replies with a

laugh, and I groan. I wish that was all she wanted to hold against him.

"My son is going to lead The Brotherhood one day, and everything will be how it should be," she says, staring at Alec intently, waiting for him to reply.

I love my mother, but I can't deal with this side of her— the overprotectiveness. She needs to get her own life. Fuck this, I'm out.

I storm out of the room, leaving my mother behind without speaking another word. It's time for another drink, or maybe I should opt for something stronger. Moving down the stairs two at a time, I head straight for the bar.

I reach out to take the bottle of whiskey from the waiter, my fingers eagerly ripping off the lid with a satisfying pop. The warm liquid slides down my throat, leaving a fiery sensation in its wake, and I don't pause until half of the bottle is empty. A few girls surround me, but I don't give them an ounce of attention like I usually do. They are nothing compared to her, and that makes my blood boil. Why is she on my mind so much?

Moving through the sea of people, I reach one of the windows that overlooks the cliff and sea. The constant sound of crashing waves has become a comforting backdrop to my life, living here on the edge of the ocean. Knowing there's a whole other world out there gives me a sense of peace. It's humbling to realize I'm only a small blip in the grand scheme of things. That at any moment, it could swallow me whole. And I'd let it.

A hand touches my shoulder, and someone forces a blunt into my mouth. I bite into the paper and Hazen flicks a lighter, setting the end ablaze. Inhaling, it hits the back of my throat, and I hold my breath as my body relaxes. I blow out a ring of smoke, watching it float lazily before disappearing.

Gage takes the bottle from my hand and pours some into his glass.

As I'm raising the blunt to my lips again, a sudden movement on the cliff catches my attention.

Her dark-brown hair whips through the air, and she looks so wild and free. Her dress clings to her body like a second skin, making my cock strain against my pants. Just before I can make a move, she jumps. The smoke falls from between my lips and my heart stops.

Chapter Nine
Freya

The sea air whips through my hair. For seconds, I am weightless. My heart stutters. My pulse races like a bullet train, thundering through my veins. Finally, the constant chatter in my mind has ceased, bringing me a sense of peace.

With each passing second, I draw nearer to the icy depths of the ocean, the wind rushing through my dress as my body hurtles through the air.

I open my eyes and am met with an endless void of darkness stretching out before me. I unleash a scream that fills the void until my throat feels parched, yet a subtle smile graces my lips. I'm okay.

The water engulfs me, its coldness seeping into my bones as I am swallowed whole by its powerful embrace. Giving in to the ocean's whims, the weight of my worries dissolves as if carried away by the waves.

I remain submerged in the water until my lungs are emptied of air and I am on the brink of taking my last breath. Breaking through the surface, I breathe in deeply. As the cool night wind touches my face, I shiver in response.

Fuck, it's cold. Laughter bubbles up my throat. It's the middle of winter and I'm in the freezing-cold ocean.

I really need to figure out another way to release these built-up emotions. Something other than putting myself in danger. But as the thought hits my mind, I shake it off. There's no way I'm doing drugs or using any kind of substance to numb the pain. I've seen firsthand how much it can change and destroy everything.

Putting myself in danger has helped me get through life without ending it all. Everything becomes too much sometimes, and I need a release. This is it for me. Putting myself in a dangerous position and then *bam*. Everything fades away. The adrenaline that pumps through my veins is like no other high I've ever experienced. No drug could replace that.

My dress clings to my body, making it harder to swim, but I keep moving my arms to pull myself forward until my feet hit the sandy ocean floor. A dark figure appears on the beach, running straight toward the water and me. Who the fuck is that? My body tenses and I freeze, unable to move— not even when they run straight into me, taking us both flying back into the water.

Strong arms wrap around me and pull us both to the surface. I cough up water as I gain my footing, then push away from the hard chest pressed against me.

"What the fuck are you doing?" Lucas yells, stumbling backward, the water churning around him.

A wave knocks us both over, and I laugh as Lucas tries to regain his stance. He looks at me with so many questions, yet he doesn't ask any more. My heart pounds harder and harder. His white shirt clings to his body, showcasing his defined chest in the light of the full moon. He runs a hand through his hair, pushing it back off his face. Water drips down his cheeks, running over his plump, kissable lips. Fuck. I want him just as much as I want to run away from him. I need to keep my distance. I can't afford any attachments.

"I just needed to get away from all of that in there." As I start explaining, Lucas locks eyes with me for several heartbeats as if he's searching for hidden meaning in my words.

"I get it," he says before a sly smirk reaches his lips. "But there are safer ways to quiet the noise."

Before I can think about changing my mind, I move toward the shore, unzipping my dress and letting it fall into the water, leaving me in my underwear. I turn back, watching my dress get taken away by the crashing waves.

Lucas advances toward me, and I don't dare move an inch—I can't. My feet sink into the sand like glue, the water threatening to push me over with every wave hitting the shore. Warmth fills my back, his breath tickles my neck, and his lips brush against my ear. Goosebumps spread over my arms and my belly churns.

"You always did love that cliff. One thing I can't understand is why you, of all people, can do this to me," he whispers into my ear, pushing his hard cock against my back.

I swallow hard, trying to remember why this is a bad idea. Crazy. We've just come out of the ocean, freezing cold and . . . and . . . All thoughts vanish when his hand runs down my belly, disappearing into my underwear. His fingers cup my pussy, one of them circling my clit, and warmth fills my belly with a deep need to release. *Let him give you that, then you can leave,* reasons my sex-deprived mind. I give in, resting my head back against his chest. He runs his fingers through my slit, keeping his thumb on my clit and slowly circling. Teasing me.

"I'm about a second away from leaving if you don't pick

up the pace," I snap, and Lucas's chest rumbles with amusement, his breath warming my neck.

"As you wish, little thorn."

He pushes one finger inside of me, then two, hitting the right spot. His thumb continues to circle my clit, building me up and up until my knees grow weak. He runs his tongue along my neck, then kisses the same path. Waves crash against our feet, threatening to push us over. My eyes shut, and a moan falls from my lips, drifting out into the quiet night.

"I want to record that sound coming from your lips so I can hear it all day long," Lucas whispers into my ear, picking up the pace. My back arches further into his body, my stomach clenches, and his name leaves my mouth as I fall apart.

He slowly removes his hand, sliding it up my chest, carrying my release on his fingers. Another wave crashes against the back of our thighs, I tumble forward a couple of steps before righting my balance.

"Hey, little thorn," Lucas calls from behind me. I look back over my shoulder, and his white shirt is now open. I can't help but admire his chest.

"Yeah?" I reply. Another whip of wind hits me, and my arms begin to shake. I clutch my hands around my shoulders.

"You owe me for that," he says, then laughs.

I flip him off over my shoulder and can't help the smile that forms on my lips. There's no way this will ever happen again, so he'll be waiting for the rest of his life. I won't get caught up with a guy from Daringville, let alone one of them. This was just a bit of fun, nothing more. Alec and I are leaving soon, and nothing will hold me back from giving our family the life they deserve. A fresh start.

The sand bites between my toes as I make my way along the beach, and my body begins to shake. A shiver dances up my spine and not from the cold. A twig snaps from the trees that lie ahead in front of the cliff, and I swear I see a figure there. Oh shit. Lucas is too far away to save me this time.

What have I done?

Chapter Ten
Freya

A s I look around into the dark night, the trees sway back and forth, creating an eerie atmosphere that fills me with unease.

I haven't been down here in years. I fight back all the memories that threaten to play in my mind. Memories I've locked up deep within me, then thrown away the key. Nothing good ever came from living here. Only bad.

I move toward the wooden stairs that lead back up the cliff to Lucas's place, watching every shadow that dances around me. A towel, and a black hoodie sit on the bottom step, and I freeze. I look around frantically, but no one's there. Lucas is slowly making his way along the shore, watching my every move.

I quickly grab the towel, dry myself off, and throw the sweatshirt over my head. It falls above my knees, and Gage's signature sandalwood and spicy scent overwhelms me. He left this here for me. Why? He hates me and I hate him. This makes no sense.

Lucas comes up behind me, taking the towel from around my neck, and he starts drying himself off, removing his wet shirt in the process. I try to avert my eyes from his naked chest, but it's near impossible. I need to get out of here before my body decides to take over again.

I bound up the stairs, taking them two at a time, eager to reach the top of the cliff.

"See you around, little thorn," Lucas yells, and I flip him off again over my shoulder.

Gripping the handrail tightly, I struggle to regain my breath at the top, feeling lightheaded and dizzy. The house seems alive with the constant ebb and flow of people, accompanied by the echoing melodies of music.

With the hood pulled over my head, I keep my gaze lowered as I make my way to the cliff edge, searching for where I dropped my phone. I pick it up and find my brother's number. My fingers tremble as I press dial and silently pray that he's still around to give me a ride home. With each ring, hope rises, only to be dashed as the call is sent to voicemail. Fuck. I've got a couple of missed calls from Amirah, along with texts asking if I'm okay. I quickly type back telling her I just jumped off the cliff and ask if I can borrow her car or get a lift from one of their drivers.

My phone vibrates in my hand.

Thank fuck you are okay. You scare the shit out of me when you get all weird and do reckless shit. Richard is waiting—the black Rolls Royce. Text me when you get home x

I reply, thanking her, and make my way over to the front of the mansion, keeping my head down to avoid making eye contact with anyone. Spotting the car waiting for me, I hurry to it and eagerly climb in, settling back into the plush passenger seat.

Resting my head against the door, I struggle to keep my eyes open, fighting off sleep. Even though I trust Richard and have known him pretty much my whole life, I need to stay awake. Be alert. I'll never drop my guard again because when you do, people take advantage of it.

"Just drop me at the tracks please, Richard," I say with a yawn, and he nods.

Richard pulls up shortly after, and I take a moment to thank him before getting out. The asphalt bites into my feet and I grit my teeth. While I walk away from the car and into the cool night, the outpost house is engulfed in headlights, almost blinding me, but providing light for the path over the tracks. Four guards stand directly in front of me. I flip back my hoodie and one of them steps forward, eyeing me up and down.

"What are you doing on this side of the tracks?" one of the guards says, moving closer, and I fight the urge to punch that smug look off his face. I'm tired and I just want to sleep.

I sidestep him, ready to sprint over the tracks, but he blocks my path again. "I'll make this easy for you, since you clearly need help. You move, and I go back over there to my side of the tracks. Simple, right?" I smirk, placing a hand on my hip.

He laughs, a wicked gleam in his eyes. "If you want to go over there so badly, get on your knees, baby, and show me how much you worship elite cock." He grins, cupping his dick through his pants, and I roll my eyes. I'm so done with this fucking asshole. It's been a hell of a night, and all I want to do is roll into bed and sleep for days.

I start walking, barging past the guard whose mouth needs washing out with gasoline. I get a couple of steps over the tracks before a hand grips my arm, pulling me to a stop.

"Get the fuck down on your knees. Now," he growls.

All the humor from before is gone, and I swallow hard.

Sweat drips down my back. He could kill me, but not without their approval. I fall to my knees.

Tires screech to a stop from somewhere behind us, a car door slams, then a gunshot rings through the night. The guard drops his hand as he stumbles backward, checking himself for injuries. I look around, my knees digging into the road.

The headlights from the car blind me. Lucas storms over, gun in hand, aiming it at the guard. His lips curl back and he looks me over, his eyes softening for a second before hardening again. The guard's arms are shaking, and I feel sorry for him for a split second before I remember what he did to me.

Another loud gunshot splinters my ears, and the guard falls to the ground. He killed him. Oh God. But why? Was it for me? My heart pounds harder and harder as Lucas turns his gaze on me, and he looks scary. His chest rises and falls, and I can't move. I can't breathe.

There's a loud whistle over the tracks and I break eye contact to find Kai and a couple of members from 18 Hood surrounded by a bunch of people who have stepped out from the shadows and into the light. Bear and Zion flank Kai and look like they are ready for war.

Kai's wearing a black oversized hoodie with their written logo on the front. He eyes me up and down before meeting my gaze. I press my lips together, and he nods.

"Let her the fuck go, or I won't hesitate to put a bullet between your eyes. I don't give a fuck about the conse-quences," Kai growls, taking a step forward so his foot lands over the first track. He looks lethal, glaring at Lucas with his rifle in his hand, ready to fire if they make one wrong move.

Lucas laughs, shoving his gun into the front of his slacks. "Watch your fucking mouth. We're the ones in charge here—not you. One wrong move, brother, and I'll kill you all."

Lucas reaches down, offering me his hand. Kai raises his weapon, finger on the trigger, and I'm ready to bolt, not wanting to be stuck in the middle of a shootout. Part of me wants to protect Lucas from them, and that confuses the fuck out of me. I should hate them. My family is on the other side of the tracks, not here. Not in Daringville—they abandoned us.

"I'm fine, Kai," I say, and he nods but doesn't lower his gun.

I take Lucas's hand and let him pull me to my feet. He heads over to his car opening the back door and pulls out a black bag before passing it to me. I look inside finding my uniform and shoes.

"I'll be seeing you real soon," he says before grabbing the back of my neck and pulling me in for a heated kiss. Butterflies scatter through me and then it's over. He pulls back and walks over to his car.

Pulling my black sneakers out of the bag, I step into them before walking across the tracks straight to Kai, who messes up my hair, his fingers getting caught in the wet tangles.

"You fucking scared us, Frey," he says, hitting me in the arm. I shove him away playfully. "And tell me my eyesight is fucked because I swear I saw you kissing the enemy."

"Yeah, you're seeing shit," I reply, having no idea what to say about that. He's right, I did, and I have no idea how I feel about that.

"Hey, kid," Zion says, scuffing up my hood, and I swat him away, laughing.

We don't move until the guards disappear into their security box, carrying the corpse with them. Kai keeps his arm over my shoulders as we walk through the streets. My wet hair clings to the back of my neck and the hood keeps me warm, but only just.

Music echoes through the streets, and they are full of life. A few people walk around with bottles in their hands, muttering to themselves, and others are huddled together talking smack.

"You weren't really going to shoot them, were you?" I ask.

Bear scoffs, but doesn't say a word. He hardly ever talks, and most people don't understand his silence. They are afraid of it because they feel they have to fill in every moment of silence. But I find it refreshing, and if they'd been through what he has, then they'd understand.

"You know I'd start and finish a war for you," Kai says, squeezing my shoulder, and I smile, believing every single word. He's my ride-or-die, and I'd do the same for him.

"Now are we going to get fucked up or what?" Zion asks, picking up a rock from the ground and throwing it at a traffic sign.

"Yes, I need to forget tonight ever happened," I reply, and Zion hollas into the sky.

It's about to get messy.

* * *

If I hear one more tick from the clock in the diner, I'll murder somebody.

My head's throbbing, threatening to crack under the pressure, and I wouldn't blame it if it did. One last area to clean before my shift's over, and it couldn't come quickly enough. The day has gone by painfully slowly, and I blame Zion for making me chug that wine from the cask. That pushed me over the edge. Bile threatens to come back up my throat at the thought of it. The taste of burned fruit lingers in my mouth.

The diner's empty by the time I finish cleaning. I lock the door, leaving the key in the lockbox, and pull out my phone. My messages to Alec have gone unanswered, and I try not to worry. He's a grown-ass guy, and he can take care of himself, but it doesn't stop the churning in the pit of my stomach.

He missed another shift at the diner, and they are threatening to fire him. He needs this job, but apparently, he doesn't seem to think so. He's so caught up with this little drug operation that he's throwing away everything else. I just hope he doesn't get into trouble. Nothing good comes from getting involved with guys like that.

After pulling Gage's hoodie out of my shoulder bag, I throw it over my head, lifting the hood up. I should have torched it the moment I got home, but I haven't. It's warm, and it's the only jumper I have without holes in it. That's the only reason why. Not because it belongs to him, and I can still smell his signature aftershave. No fucking way. I don't do things like that when it comes to guys like him. Only desperate groupie bitches do. Fuck that.

I look around the empty parking lot, hoping to find my brother's car, but he's nowhere to be seen, yet again, and there's a small part of me that hoped Lucas would be here. A really stupid, pathetic part of me. I don't need anyone to come to my rescue—especially them.

I sigh, starting the walk home, the streetlights illuminating the empty parking lot.

My phone vibrates in my hand, and for a split second I pray it's Alec, but Mia's name appears over the screen. I frown, sliding it unlocked. Before I can even say hello, she rushes out, "Have you seen Alec?"

"No, why?" I don't bother telling her he didn't show up for work or that I'm worried about him. She's one of them, and I don't trust her. Never have.

"He's gone missing." Mia starts crying through the phone and I pull back, squeezing the bridge of my nose.

"Mia, listen, he's going to be fine. He's just caught up in some stuff. He'll be back soon."

She continues to cry, then eventually hangs up without saying goodbye. I shove my phone into my back pocket and squeeze my eyes closed. Fuck, now Mia is worried and I'm no closer to finding him. My head pounds behind my eyes, and I just want everything to go back to normal, with Alec home safe.

After opening the door to our trailer, I shut it behind me and flick the lock automatically. It's pitch black inside, and a shadow moves from somewhere to my right. I jump, flicking on the lights, fists up and ready to attack. My mother stares back at me, eyes as wide as saucers, and she cocks her head to the side. My shoulders relax slightly with the realization it's just her and not someone else. She's clearly off her face, and I can't deal with this. I raise my eyes to the ceiling, shaking my head slightly.

"What the fuck do you want, cunt?" she growls out, her jaw moving from side to side.

"It's me, Freya. It's okay, Mom," I say, taking slow steps toward the kitchen. She watches me intently before throwing her head back and laughing like a loon. She falls onto the couch and stares out the window into the darkness.

She starts mumbling to herself, and I leave her, heading to my bedroom and locking the door behind me. It's a necessary precaution in case Mom tries to get in later to steal some more things to sell to support her habit.

My phone vibrates against the pocket of my pants and there's a message from Mia telling me to call her if I hear anything about Alec.

I'd know if anything bad happened to him. Amirah would have told me if things with the boys had taken a turn for the worse, and I'd feel it in my bones. Everything is going to be fine. We are so close to getting out of this town—it has to be. Right?

Chapter Eleven

Freya

Another day of the same old shit—working until my body aches.

I just need some time to chill. By the time I start heading back home, my legs protest with a dull ache. I shake my head when I arrive at my trailer to find it unlocked. No wonder I never feel safe here. Mom always leaves the screen door open so anybody can just walk on in. I shut the door behind me, flicking the lock in place.

The trailer is dark and empty as usual. I check Alec's room, but he's not there, and his bed's a mess with clothes scattered around the room. Since the party three nights ago, I haven't heard a single word from him, even though he made a promise to talk about it the following day. He hasn't read my texts, and when I messaged Amirah yesterday, she said she hadn't seen him. I don't usually trust Mia's judgment, but maybe she's actually right this time. The urge to take matters into my own hands is growing, and I'm almost ready to storm over the tracks and start searching for myself.

I shut the bathroom door behind me, strip down, and step into the shower. The cold water blasts me, and I'm out after a minute. It seems that we forgot to pay the bill for the hot water. Damn it.

The front door swings open and forcefully shuts. Peering through the bathroom door, I catch a glimpse of Mom stumbling in, donning a short denim skirt and a crop top. She throws her bag on the ground, its contents spilling out onto the floor, and promptly collapses onto the couch, succumbing to exhaustion. Shortly after, the sound of her soft snores fills the air. I sigh in relief—at least she's home and safe. No matter what she puts us through, I'll always love her and have hope for her.

I spend the next couple of hours lying on the couch beside her, reading one of the romance books Alec gave me from the thrift shop and trying to get tired enough to fall asleep. With my eyes growing heavy, a loud knock on the door breaks the silence. I turn to see my mother snoozing on the couch, mouth wide open. If this is one of her dealers, I'm going to scream. She's finally sleeping after her bender, and she doesn't need any more temptations banging on the door.

As quietly as I can, I make my way over to the door, slowly opening it to find a large figure towering over me. Hazen's wearing loose-fitting black cargo pants with a plain white top. The colorful tattoos on his tanned skin add a striking contrast to his clothes.

"What the hell are you doing here?" I ask quietly, swallowing hard.

Is Alec okay? Did something happen to him? Is that why he's here?

Hazen runs his thumb over his plump lips. His ocean-blue eyes run over my body, and I instantly regret not putting on any pants. My old, ripped 18 Hood T-shirt hangs just above my knees.

"Where's—?"

"Shut up! Don't wake my mom." I point out the door. "Wait there a second."

He walks into the dark night. I'm torn between telling him to fuck off and slamming the door, and wanting to know why he's here and to find out if he's heard from Alec.

Still, I haven't heard from or seen Alec in the last two days, and now Hazen's shown up at my door. It can't be a coincidence. I need answers, and hopefully, he can give them to me. A chill slides down my spine. What if Mia was right?

Shit. I can't let anything happen to my brother.

I put on some high-waisted black skinny jeans, squeeze into them, and tie my T-shirt in a knot above my belly button. I slip on my favorite pair of Nike kicks I got at a garage sale and head out, making sure Mom's still out cold.

When she finally sleeps after a bender, she doesn't come out of her coma for days, and when she wakes, they are the best days. When she finally regains consciousness, we get our mom back. She makes us dinner, talks about getting out of here, and sings, laughs, and smiles. But that only lasts a day before she gets that hungry look in her eyes, then she's out finding her hit. That special gold liquid she calls the magic serum, making all her thoughts vanish. It's a vicious cycle that I've learned to deal with over the years. One that I'll be glad to set aflame when we get out of here. If we take away the temptation, she'll be able to get help and we can move on. Be a happy family again. Like we once were.

Shutting the door softly behind me, I find Hazen leaning back against my trailer with a joint between his lips. With a flick of his lighter, his face is bathed in a warm, flickering glow.

"What do you want?" I ask, folding my arms over my chest.

Hazen's mouth twitches at the corner, revealing a fleeting hint of emotion before transforming into a stern, firm line. He falls into silence, taking several seconds to inhale from the joint before extinguishing it against the sole of his shoe.

"I want to know where your brother is. Is he in there?" he asks, pointing to the trailer, and I frown. Hasn't Alec been with them? A sickening sensation spreads through my stomach, and I can almost taste the remnants of the dinner I had threatening to resurface.

"What the fuck are you talking about?" I ask, raising my voice and moving closer to Hazen until he's only a step away. "I was about to knock down your door and start asking questions since the last time I saw him, he was with you."

Tilting his head to the side, Hazen's dark-blue eyes bore into mine, filled with intensity. Something passes between us—my body responds, wanting to be closer to him, and I don't understand. "Are you sure?" he asks, and I nod, licking my dry lips. "Well, your brother owes us a fucking lot of money. So you better find him."

Where the fuck are you, Alec? I knew working for them was a bad idea. Fucking hell. I need to see him. If he isn't with them, then he has to be somewhere here.

I turn around, the gravel crunching beneath my feet as I start walking through the trailer park. The dirt path leading to the quiet main road is illuminated by the lights from the trailers.

"Hey, wait!" Hazen calls from behind me, but I ignore him and keep going.

Old man Ronald from down the street storms out of his

home, beer in one hand and a knife in the other. He raises his head toward me, and I nod in response. I quickly look back and see him watching Hazen with a mix of fear and anger. He doesn't budge until we're out of sight.

Hazen reaches me, the sound of his shoes scuffing the dirt.

"What are you doing?" I scowl.

"Stalking you. Trying to take you on a date," he replies dryly, and I roll my eyes.

"Hilarious. Look, you can either help me find him or you can fuck off. Your call," I say, darting my eyes around the park and taking in every detail. Hoping Alec just pops out of one of the trailers or out of the bushes.

Hazen laughs but doesn't leave. He's my shadow, following my every move. "I'm not going anywhere. I've got a lot riding on your brother, so lead the way."

The unsettling sensation in my stomach intensifies, threatening to overpower my every thought. Alec is fine. He is okay. He'll be back soon. I repeat those words over and over until I start to believe them.

I'll find him at one of the guys' places or at a party. Then Alec and I can leave this fucking town with our mom, but without a "see you later."

"When did you see Alec last?" I ask, climbing through the fence and out onto the road.

"That night at the masquerade party," Hazen replies, falling into step beside me once again.

The wind whips my hair behind my back, and I try not to freak out. That was three nights ago, and I haven't seen him since then either. Even though my brother prefers to be away from home when Mom is there, he never forgets to send me messages to let me know he's doing okay. I'm sure he's fine. He has to be. We are so close to getting out. He could have already skipped town and gone to college to settle in, but again, why wouldn't he tell me?

I swallow hard, running my fingers through my hair. "He's probably at one of the gatherings at Junction Street," I say confidently. "You sure you want to come? I mean, it's not really your scene. So you can run back over the tracks to your little safety net, and I'll let you know when I find him," I say with a smug look, and Hazen scoffs.

"Those little hood rats don't scare me. They know their place. I've got a job to do, and I won't be going home until it's done." He punctuates his statement with a grunt, pulling out another joint from his pants pocket. He offers it to me, but I shake my head.

We walk through the streets, the only sound being the soft shuffle of our footsteps. It's quiet except for a few people walking by, giving Hazen suspicious looks like they always do when the elite are on our turf. It's a sure sign of trouble. Guys like Hazen only come over here for business, to clean up, or to sort shit out. Never socially. They prefer to stick to their own, just like we do. It's easier that way. Less complicated. We have the divide for a reason: to keep everyone in line, which keeps the peace.

I used to feel at home over in Daringville with them, but now I know this is where I belong. This is home. They abandoned us. Threw us over the tracks and never looked back. I'll never forget what they did to us.

Turning down the familiar suburban street, the sight of abandoned houses, their windows covered in boards and graffiti, paints a picture of neglect and decay. There are still people squatting here because they had nowhere else to go when the rent got raised and they got evicted. The Brotherhood holds all the power. The divide was initially intended to grant us autonomy and our own set of rules, but as the years passed, the lines began to fade, resulting in their complete domination. We have the freedom to do whatever we want, but there is always a cost attached.

"Your precious Brotherhood did this," I say, pointing at the empty buildings, and Hazen freezes in front of a red-brick home.

Before I can intervene, he defiantly pushes through the broken wire fence and ascends the steps.

"I did this," he whispers, his voice barely reaching my ears.

I follow him through the fence, the rough metal scraping against my fingertips. He halts suddenly, and his eyes remain fixed on the house, a mix of guilt and shame etched across his features. His face turns pale as all color drains from it, and he shoves his hands into his pockets.

What did he do?

Chapter Twelve
Hazen

The familiar wooden door stares back at me with an old eviction notice plastered across the center. I swallow down the bile at the base of my throat, suppressing all the memories from that evening along with it. I shouldn't have come here, but fate has a funny way of forcing you to confront your choices. Laughing at you uncontrollably until it turns into something much more sinister.

Throughout my life, I've always maintained a safe distance from others, never allowing anyone to get too close or evoke any emotions within me. Ever since my father began training me, I've become nothing more than an empty shell. A perfectly groomed member of The Brotherhood. He had a firm belief that emotions were a vulnerability that should be avoided. They would only ever kill you.

He's right. Feelings are the crux of all evil.

Before I can stop myself, I kick the door open and step into the house. Everything's gone, ruined, and damaged. The only thing that remains is the empty shell of what used to be a home. I make my way down the hallway and into a room.

The piercing sound of her cries reverberates in my head, haunting me. I stumble backward, hitting the wall, and everything around me disappears . . .

We arrive at the next house, and it's a red brick one with a tiny wire fence. Lucas and Gage sit quietly next to my ten-year-old self, watching my father with a mixture of fear and admiration. As he turns around in the front seat of the car, his gaze sweeps over all of us.

"Just like I told you. We go in and get them out. If they don't come willingly, we use force. Follow my every order. Got it?" he asks, passing me a gun, then arming the others.

The coolness of the metal against my skin sends a shiver down my spine as I firmly grasp the weapon, my fingers stretching to the other side. I've been using one ever since I turned six, and now, four years later, we finally have the opportunity to use it outside of training for the first time. My palms begin to sweat. I don't know if I can do this for real. Gage's hand gently rests on my knee, and as I look up, he nods in reassurance, silently conveying that we are in this together. No matter what happens, we will always have each other's backs. For better or worse.

My father gets out of the car, and Lucas opens his door and I follow him out. Met with a gust of cool winter air, I instinctively lower my beanie to shield my ears from the cold. With the Glock held firmly in my hand, I trail behind my father, the sound of our footsteps echoing against the gravel road, accompanied by the soft shuffling of Gage and Lucas behind me.

With a loud squeal, the wire gate gives way as it is pushed open, revealing a chaotic scene of scattered toys and play equipment on the front lawn. As we walk through, the long grass brushes against my legs, tickling them gently. Just outside the front door, we come to a halt. The wood bears the mark of an ancient eviction notice. Why didn't they listen and move out? That would have been easier than us having to come and force them out. Wouldn't it? I don't understand but father always says we come by force. That no one will ever listen to us unless we show them who's in charge. Words don't matter, only violence. I have no choice but to trust him.

His boot connects with the front door, causing it to swing open violently and collide with the wall, producing a resounding bang. Echoes of screams fill the home. As adrenaline courses through my veins, my heart accelerates, thumping loudly in my chest. I move into the house, and it's dark and cold. A little girl around our age lets out an ear-piercing scream that reverberates through the air. A fleeting shadow darts past us, dragging a young boy through the living room and disappearing from view.

"Get them," my father yells. Slumped over the couch, the man—who I assume to be the girl's father—remains completely still.

Gage's grip tightens on my arm, urgently pulling me toward the room where the girl and boy vanished.

As I forcefully wrench my arm away from Gage's grip, my fingers instinctively clench around the gun, pointing it forward.

"Fucking gross. How could someone live like this?" Lucas swears and kicks an empty bottle behind me. It flies past me, smashing into the wall and into a million pieces. I roll my eyes. Spoiled little brat, he is, but he isn't wrong. This place is disgusting. With a shake of my head, I carry on walking, feeling the weight of each step.

The dim illumination from the streetlights outside offers us a slight glimpse of our surroundings. Following the cries of the little girl, Gage leads us down a narrow hallway to a small room with a bed in the corner. The girl shoves her little brother into the tiny closet and closes the door, causing my palms to become sweaty. Despite the tremors running through her body, she stands resolute, unwavering in her commitment to protect her brother above all else. My chest tightens and I can't move. Sweat drips down the back of my neck, Gage steps forward, gun raised, aiming it at her chest.

Acting on instinct, I quickly position myself in front of him as a barrier to protect her. Gage's expression turns sour as he slightly lowers his gun.

"What are you doing?" he snaps.

"She's just a kid. We can't," I plea, looking into his eyes. Glancing around nervously, he swallows hard, his eyes darting between me and her before he finally lowers his gun.

"I agree, this isn't okay," Lucas says, coming to stand next to Gage.

With each creak of the floorboards, my father's presence fills the room. With his eyes darkening, he forcefully grabs the back of my neck and swiftly turns me around, making me face the girl. He places his hands over mine, covering the gun. My body starts to tremble.

"No, I can't," I cry, but he doesn't listen. He aims the gun right between her eyes.

"You can and you will—or you'll be next," he breathes into my ear and pulls the trigger.

Her screams pierce my ears until they feel like they are bleeding. Make it stop. Make it go away. As my body trembles, voices fade in and out. In and out. My fingers dig into my scalp as if trying to escape the chaos inside my mind. She's dead because of me. I couldn't save her. I can't save anyone.

The touch of soft hands on mine sends a jolt through my body.

"Hey, it's okay. I'm here. You're safe." A voice cracks through the smoke and the ringing stops.

Coming back into the room, I blink slowly and adjust to the soft lighting. She stares back at me. As though she's looking right into my soul. She isn't afraid of me, which confuses me. Everyone is and should be.

Looking back, I can see now why Dad took us there. That killing was grunt work—something he'd normally pay someone else to do.

That was my training—our initiation into The Brotherhood.

Ever since that day, I became what my father wanted all along. A monster. A killer. Who didn't think twice about it. Who didn't have a conscience. Until today. Being back here has triggered something within me, something I spent so long burying.

"What was that about?" Freya asks, standing and stepping back, creating some distance between us.

I swallow hard, running my hands over my face. "It's best you don't know," I say, pulling myself up and off the ground, unaware of how I even ended up there. "It's as you said. I did this."

She frowns, and before she can ask any more questions, I take one last look at the cupboard door and then leave.

I never found out what happened to the boy in the cupboard, but that's the hope I've held onto for the rest of my life. That at least he got out.

I saved one of them.

Chapter Thirteen
Freya

Without looking back, he walks away while I remain motionless. He's right—The Brotherhood did do this, but the look in his eyes and the way he broke down tells me he didn't want to. Whatever happened here wasn't his choice.

Hazen Hendrix is the devil. Those stories we told each other at sleepovers, the ones that turned into nightmares about being taken and killed—they were about Hazen, lead enforcer of The Brotherhood. However, all that fearlessness I see in his eyes was gone moments ago, replaced by a haunted look. I saw a different person, someone whose eyes reflected kindness and compassion. He regrets some of the shitty things he's done.

I never knew the people who were here before; it's been empty for as long as I can remember. There was talk about a family that used to live here. Their bodies were found hanging over the fence near the railway tracks as a lesson to everyone. If you went against The Brotherhood, if you didn't pay your dues, you died. In my youth, I brushed it off as a rumor, but as I grew older, I realized there was truth to it.

I head back outside and find the shadow of Hazen's figure leaning back against a tree a couple of houses down. As I make my way over, the flickering flame of his lighter casts an eerie glow on his face. With a slow, deliberate motion, he brings the joint to his lips and takes a long, satisfying drag before passing it to me once more. This time I accept, needing something to take the edge off.

I feel a burn in my throat as the smoke hits me and I sink down. We stay in a comfortable silence for a few minutes, looking out into the street. The party is still going strong at the house down the way, the thumping bass reverberating through the air.

"When I was ten, we raided that house," Hazen says, and I freeze, joint midair. My heart races, pounding against my chest. Hazen's eyes are cast down, and I can see the weariness etched on his face as he runs a hand over it. My heart breaks for him. He looks broken, his shoulders slumped and his eyes vacant. Even though I know what he did was wrong, I can't help but feel sorry for him.

He stays silent for a few more minutes, and I don't know if I should ask more.

"I killed her. She was my age, and she's dead because of me." He chokes back a sob, and I find myself moving closer to him until I've pivoted to face him. His body slumps as he leans back against the tree. "I've never thought about this before, but how different would my life have been if I didn't kill her?"

Time slows down and everything disappears, leaving just us. I reach out, tracing my finger along the contours of his jaw, then I gently tilt his head to meet my gaze. His eyes, once as blue as the ocean, now take on a darker hue, churning like a brewing storm.

He embraces me, wrapping his arms around my back, and draws me closer until our bodies make contact. I rest my head against his chest. His heart races, thumping against my ear with increasing intensity. With one hand, he supports my head, while his other hand gently rests on my lower back.

"It was my first kill, and he made me pull the trigger," he breathes out, and tears I never knew I had well up behind my eyes. I know exactly who he's talking about, and anger cuts through the sadness like a knife, stopping the tears from falling.

"I've killed hundreds since without a second thought. I'm a killing machine, just like he made me. But this one still haunts me."

I tremble, and Hazen wraps his arms around me tightly.

"I hate him," I whisper into Hazen's chest, more to myself than him. I hate his father more than anyone in the world. He ruined my family and our life.

I lean back, looking up and into his eyes. He firmly grasps my shoulders, his touch sending a shiver down my spine.

"Do you remember me from when we were younger?" I ask the one question that's been on the back of my tongue from the moment I saw him again.

The slight frown on his face and the way he tilts his head to the side tells me everything I need to know. Pushing against his chest, I manage to pry myself out of his tight embrace.

How could he forget? How could he honestly not remember the day they changed my life forever?

Freya - Ten Years Old

The place we once called home is now a mere memory, erased without explanation. Mom refuses to shed light on its disappearance or the fate of the money, but I can't help but speculate. She's been getting worse lately, and I don't know how much longer we can put up with it. Alec's been disappearing more with The Brotherhood and coming back with money, but it's never enough. He's only eleven—he shouldn't have to, but Mom doesn't care. She only cares about one thing, and that's supporting her habit.

I'm walking down the Hendrixes' hallway, trying to find Mom. She's been gone for ages and we need to pick up Alec. My attention is drawn to movement coming from Dominic's bedroom door, so I step closer. My chest tightens as I watch my mom moving around their room with a sense of purpose.

"Mom, come on, get out of there. Please, you can't do this. What if he catches us?" I beg, reaching out for her hands, but she swats me away. Snarling at me like a dog would at someone it hates.

Stumbling backward, my heart races as I catch sight of her distant, wide-eyed gaze. She's on that stuff again. I wish she never touched it. I don't like her when she's like this, which is every day lately. That blonde who dresses so nicely is always with her, supplying her with more. I just want my mother back—we both do. Alec's been helping when he can, but he's always disappearing with members of The Brotherhood, and when he's back he doesn't tell me much.

She dives back into Dominic and Eveline's dresser, pulling out jewels and wads of cash, shoving them into her duffle bag. My stomach churns with a heavy weight, a sense of dread settling deep within me. The fear of getting caught fills me with sheer terror, and I can't help but shudder at the thought of what might unfold.

Dominic's anger toward us has been escalating, and he frequently directs his outbursts toward my mom and even me. No matter how hard I try, my efforts to be a good girl are constantly criticized by him.

"Help me or fuck off!" Mom yells, and I don't want to help. This isn't right. Even if I don't like Dominic, I don't want to steal from him. It's wrong.

The door to their bedroom unexpectedly swings open, and I lose my footing, stumbling backward and slamming against the wall, my breath catching in my throat. Dominic storms toward my mother, his rage evident in his every step, and without hesitation, he tightly grips her hair and yanks her up. My scream fills the air as I charge at him, but I'm halted by a pair of hands gripping my waist tightly. When I glance up, I find myself captivated by the depth of Hazen's blue eyes. He pleads with me to stop, but I can't. Dominic is hurting my mother.

"What the fuck are you doing, you little crack whore?" Dominic growls, and my mother just laughs.

"You know I've killed people for less. You are done. I can't keep you around here anymore. You are gone," he says, and I break free from Hazen's embrace, running at Dominic. I hold onto his arm tightly as he gazes down at me with an intense, penetrating look, causing my heart to race.

"Please don't hurt her," I plea. He releases my mother, causing her to collapse at his feet. His hand closes around my neck, applying pressure. I can't breathe. Without making a single move, Hazen stands there and watches us. Help me, I try to say, but my voice is blocked by Dominic's hand.

I'm thrown to the floor, my head hits the carpet, and pain echoes in my ears as I struggle to catch my breath. He pulls *out a knife, its gleaming blade catching the light, and I scream.*

I kick my legs, adrenaline surging through my body as I try to stand and run, but he's too strong. My mother remains motionless on the floor. Her eyes are vacant, like windows to a soul lost in another world as she stares right through me.

"Hold her down," he growls, and Hazen doesn't move. "Now!" Dominic yells, and he moves to hover over me. He holds me down and I'm completely immobile. I look up into his ocean-blue eyes, begging him to release me, but he doesn't. He whispers an apology, but it's not enough.

My top is sliced open by Dominic's knife, and I scream once more. My chest rises and falls in a frenzied rhythm, my heartbeat pounding in my ears.

"No, please!"

The moment the knife descends, a wave of intense, burning pain engulfs me.

I'll never forget that pain; my scars are a daily reminder of it. And I can still feel the knife carving my flesh.

"Freya, wait," Hazen yells behind me, but I don't look back. I can't.

All my childhood memories of being with them shatter into a million pieces. Of course, he doesn't fucking remember, but to me those memories will never go away. They are sewn deep in my past, and I've still got the scars to prove it.

I don't stop walking until I'm deep in the party house. People are crowding around me, and I grab a bottle of liquor from the kitchen, unscrewing the lid and chugging a quarter of it. It sears a fiery path down my throat, providing the exact sensation I crave.

The music is so loud that it drowns out all other sounds, making it impossible to hear my own thoughts. I move around, asking a couple of people if they have seen my brother, but their faces remain blank, clueless. Hazen gets lost in the crowd, and I'm glad. I'm done with him for the night. I need to find my brother and get the hell out of here.

Without warning, someone's shoulder collides with mine. I whirl around with my fist cocked back, ready to retaliate, but I come to a sudden halt as I lock eyes with Kai, who greets me with a sly smirk.

"Fuck, that bad of a night huh?" he asks, snatching the bottle from my other hand, and I laugh as he takes a swig.

"You have no idea," I admit with a sigh. "Have you seen Alec?"

Kai shakes his head, passing the bottle back to me. His gaze drifts above me, his eyes growing darker.

"What the fuck is he doing here?" Kai snaps, taking a step forward. I place my hand on his chest before warmth hits my back.

"Chill, Kai, he's looking for Alec," I say, glancing between them both. Kai breathes in and out against my hand and Hazen seems unfazed, even as Zion and Bear come up and surround us.

"You have no business here. Leave now," Kai growls, his hand reaching into his jeans pocket. The silver of his blade catches my eye, and I shake my head. For fuck's sake. All this "my dick is bigger than yours" shit is starting to piss me off.

"Anything going on here is my business." Hazen looks Kai up and down before the corner of his mouth lifts. "Do you forget who runs this town?"

I have to use all my strength to keep Kai from moving forward by pressing my hand against his chest.

"Enough. He's with me so just fucking drop it, Kai," I say, letting out a sigh. "Please."

Kai looks between us before he steps back, snatching

the bottle from me once again, then he turns his back and disappears into the crowd with Zion and Bear behind him.

I whirl around, leveling Hazen with a glare, and he shrugs as if to say, "What did you expect?" And he's right. It's no secret that Kai and the boys from 18 Hood hate The Brotherhood. Hate that they rule everything. They have been trying to take back Daringhood for years, but The Brotherhood just holds too much power here. They control too much. It wouldn't be impossible to kick them out, but it would take an all-out war to do so.

We spend the rest of the night looking for Alec, but no one has seen him. Hazen drops me back at my place in the early hours of the morning.

I reach my door and Hazen clears his throat. I turn around, and he rubs the back of his neck. He opens his mouth, then closes it again.

"I do remember you," he whispers, and my heart breaks in two. "As if I could forget you."

"Have you ever thought you could have saved me, too?" I ask the question that's been on my lips since we left that house. Part of me doesn't want to know, but the other part desperately does.

Hazen steps forward and I step back, hitting my trailer. He cages me in, eyes never leaving mine. "Every fucking day. It's my only regret not saving her." His chest rises and falls. "And you."

I swallow hard, a tear falling down my cheek. Hazen reaches out, catching it with his thumb and pressing it against my lip. I take his thumb in my mouth, licking off the saltiness. He groans, closing the distance between us. His lips press against mine slowly, then he forces his tongue inside, and a flush of warmth spreads through my body. I grip onto his shirt, deepening the kiss and a low noise rumbles in his chest, causing my underwear to soak. I need to stop. I can't do this. I pull away breathlessly and he takes a few steps back.

He opens his mouth, but I shake my head—I don't want to talk about this. I spin around and slowly close the trailer door without saying goodbye. I lock the door and collapse against it, leaning back with a sigh.

Alec is missing. Hazen confuses the fuck out of me. And my head is about to explode.

The house is dark and quiet. My mother is nowhere to be seen, and part of me is grateful that I don't have to put up with any more shit tonight. I just want to go to bed and forget.

Pushing off the door, I head down the small hallway toward my bedroom. My door is slightly ajar and the hair on the back of my neck sticks up. I clearly remember shutting my door when I left earlier; I always keep it closed.

With a kick from my foot, I open the door, flick on the light, and step further inside. Nothing's changed since I left. Clothes are still all over my bed and the floor. A light floral perfume fills the air, and my breathing picks up. Someone's been in here. I quickly check my cupboards, but there's no one here. I remove my shoes, turn off the light, and settle warily onto my bed. Placing my phone on the table next to my nightstand, I tap the screen, and it brightens enough to illuminate the room.

My phone vibrates, startling me, and I grab it within a second. My heart rate skyrockets as I see a text message from Alec.

Freya, I'm so sorry I didn't get the chance to say goodbye. You were right. I shouldn't have started working with them. I shouldn't have gone near their drugs. We both know the damage they can do. I'm so sorry, but I've left without you to start fresh before college starts. I'll message you when it's all good for you and Mom to come. See you soon.

I read over his message again and again, trying to piece together the puzzle.

He left without me? Without us? This doesn't make any sense. We were meant to go together. That was the whole plan—the reason he didn't just up and leave when he first got accepted over a year ago.

Part of me is relieved that he's gone, and he's safe, but the other half is pissed off and skeptical as hell.

He left without me. Now I'm stuck in this town for who knows how long. My brother is gone. And the only person who seems to care is the most dangerous member of The Brotherhood.

Chapter Fourteen
Freya

The front door slams shut, and I jump up from my bed, looking frantically around my room, expecting someone to be there . . . but it's empty. Picking up my phone, I check the screen, and it's six in the morning. What the fuck?

Banging comes from the kitchen, and I throw my head back with a sigh. Cupboard doors open and close, followed by cursing. I follow the noise down the hall, the sound growing louder with each step until I finally reach the kitchen. With a wide grin stretching across her face, Mom grabs a frying pan and gleefully spins in circles.

I lean back against the fridge, observing her as she fumbles around, searching for something. Eventually, she finds a bottle of pancake mix in a shopping bag. She sings to herself and moves her hips as though she's dancing to a beat inside her head.

She's high as a kite, but I don't mind when she's like this, when she comes home with food and cooks for us. It's a rare occasion, those happy highs. It's better than experiencing her hiding in the cupboard, afraid someone is coming to get her and kill her. The paranoia takes her over, and she takes it out on me, on us.

As she turns around, her face lights up with recognition when she finally notices me standing there. A scream escapes her lips before her hand instinctively lands on her heart.

"Fucking hell, Frey, do you want to give me a heart attack?" Her expression quickly shifts from a scowl to a smile in a matter of seconds. I let go of the breath I was holding.

"Pancakes?" she asks, flicking around the spatula in her hand. I smile and nod as she puts the pan on the stove and gets it heating up.

"Did you see Alec earlier tonight?" I ask, moving over to the cupboard. I get out a cup and start filling it with water from the sink.

She continues singing while slipping in beside me to add some water from the tap into the pancake mix bottle. She puts the lid on and gives it a shake before she replies. "I don't think so. I've been in and out."

"He's gone," I say, taking a sip from the cup.

She laughs. "Don't be silly, he'll be back soon."

"No, Mom, it's serious. I haven't seen him and just got a message about him already leaving for college."

She spins around so fast that I jolt and nearly spill my water. The color of her eyes shifts to a haunting, stormy darkness. She crowds closer, and I can't help but feel confined as if in a cage.

"Well, you better fucking find him and drag him back home. I need him here," she snaps, nostrils flaring.

Each week, Alec gave her a small allowance from our earnings, but we both knew it was never spent on food or bills. That's the only reason she's pissed off—her supply chain just dried up.

"Once I've found him, we're leaving," I explain.

She clenches her teeth tightly, grinding them back and forth, creating an audible noise that lasts for several seconds.

"I've told you how many times? I'm not leaving this place. It's home." She huffs.

"Home?" I laugh. "We got booted from the one place we considered home a long time ago . . . because of you."

The moment the words leave my lips, my mother is already on me, her presence looming over me. Her fingers tangle in my hair and she pulls my head back. Intense pain shoots through my scalp like a searing fire.

"Shut your fucking mouth, you ungrateful little bitch," she spits the words in my face.

She lets go of me and I push past her, going straight out the front door. It slams shut, and I start walking without looking back. Through the trailer park, her voice echoes as she desperately calls out my name, but I keep walking. The park is quiet, and the sun starts to peek along the horizon, painting the sky in an orange hue.

I shoot Amirah a message, praying she's up or this jolts her awake. I really need my bestie.

Each beat of my heart reverberates through my body, racing at an alarming pace. *How could you do this to me, Alec? Leave without taking me with you?* Leaving me here to deal with *her*. We were a team, always together and always following our plan. That's why it doesn't make any sense. Why would he leave without me? When I see him, I'm going to hug him tightly, then deliver a swift punch to wipe that smug look off his face.

I keep walking until I reach the edge of the train tracks on the eastern side, far enough away from the crosspoint.

They still keep an eye on this place with cameras, but no one patrols it. Stepping over the first track, I lie down, resting my head against the wooden planks, and stare up into the early morning sky, watching the burnt orange turn into yellow with the rising of the sun.

Time becomes a blur of thoughts, all centered around Alec and his stupid choice to leave me behind. Footsteps crunch against the rocks, and I sit up, heart pounding, but relax when I notice Amirah coming over the tracks. I fall back down, and Amirah joins me.

"What on earth are you doing up this early? And more importantly, why did you drag my ass out of bed?" she asks, resting her arms behind her head.

"Mom," I say, and she huffs.

"What'd she do this time?"

I spend the next hour catching her up on everything. About going away to college for Alec, him leaving without us and working for The Brotherhood. I knew she would find out eventually, but I still struggle to find the right words to tell my best friend I'm eventually leaving her.

Once I'm finished, she sits up with a myriad of emotions flickering across her face.

"First off, I'm pissed that you never told me you were planning to leave. You know I wouldn't have told the boys, don't you?" She falls back down, resting her head next to mine.

"I know, and you have every right to be. I'm sorry. I just didn't want anything to ruin our chance of a fresh start," I explain.

"Secondly, can I come with you?" she asks, and I laugh.

"As if Gage would ever let you leave. He would never stop looking for you, and as much as I want you with me, you can't."

Huffing, Amirah takes ahold of my hand and laces her fingers with mine. I grip her hand tightly and fight back the tears. In my lifetime I haven't shed many tears, but now it feels as if my emotions are on the brink of breaking, ready to engulf me completely.

* * *

Over the next two weeks, I go out of my way to avoid Mom at every opportunity and continue to work my shifts at the diner. Still no word from Alec, but I'm sure he'll reach out when he's ready for us to join him at college. When I haven't been working, I've been on a mission to find anything that can provide a momentary escape from the suffocating anxiety that looms over me. In the moment, everything seems fine, but once it's over, I find myself falling apart once more.

At least one of the guys has been at the diner every day I work, checking in about Alec, threatening me that he needs to show his face. They need to talk to him, and I keep telling them he had to go out of town for a college thing, but he'll be back soon. I'm just buying time until I can leave, but it's getting harder and harder.

With a creak, the door to the diner swings open, and I find myself meeting Gage's intense gaze. He's wearing black jeans and a plain black T-shirt that clings to his muscles. He looks good, which is no surprise. He always looks good—it's just when he opens his mouth that ruins it.

He moves with purpose to the booth right at the end out of sight from prying eyes.

"Kelly, can you service booth seven please?" I ask as she passes me, carrying a tray of drinks. She huffs, rolls her eyes, but doesn't bother arguing.

I can't deal with him or them today. Ever since I received that message from Alec, an immense ball has formed in the pit of my stomach, lingering with every passing moment. I've sent him a bunch of messages and he hasn't read any of them. I just really want to hear from him. So we can make a plan to join him.

Taking some plates from the kitchen, I deliver them to the tables and return for more.

"He wants you," Kelly says, and my body tenses as I instinctively pinch the bridge of my nose.

I don't have to ask who the *he* is she's referring to. I already know, and there's no avoiding him here. I could lose my job, and I need this. It's the only thing keeping me from jumping in the car and driving to Bexley to find Alec myself.

I grab a menu and head over to the booth, putting on the fakest smile I can. Leaning back against the booth chair, he runs his finger along his jawline. He slowly scans me from head to toe. My stomach erupts in a fit of stupid fucking butterflies, and I hate it. I hate how my body reacts to him. How it wants his touch. How it needs it. I can get myself off just fine, but my pussy wants the real deal. Fucking selfish bitch. Gage is off-limits, and he's an asshole.

"What can I get you?" I ask, flipping out my pad and ignoring the way my body is reacting.

Several painfully long seconds pass without him uttering a word, and I'm on the verge of walking away to attend to someone else.

"Your brother," he says, and I roll my eyes, shoving the pad back in my apron.

His fingers clench around my arm and my heart races.

"Did you just roll your eyes at me?" His question hangs in the air, and I lift my eyes to meet his unimpressed gaze.

"Wouldn't take a genius to pick up on that one," I sass back, wincing as a sharp pain shoots up my arm.

"I've been a patient man. Just tell me where he is or I'll have you take his place. We need him back," he says, then lets go of my arm, and I rub my fingers over his grip marks.

"I haven't heard from him in weeks since he left for college. So I have no idea, okay?" I snap, and Gage must see the truth written all over my face because he just nods.

My phone pings in my pocket, and I lift it out without thinking twice. It could be Alec.

It's a message from an unknown number. I open it and all the blood drains from my face.

Unknown - *Your brother didn't go off to college. He's still in town.*

I squeeze my phone to quell the shaking in my hand. What the actual flying fuck?

Chapter Fifteen
Gage

As she looks down at her phone, her eyes widen and a deep frown forms on her face, her grip on the device tightening as if it's her only source of security. She bites down on her bottom lip and my cock twitches, begging to be released so I can shove it down her throat until she can't breathe. Fuck. Why is she the only one who can make me feel like this? Why her, of all the people I could have?

She's all I can think about. It's driving me insane. Having her around is a major distraction, and I absolutely cannot afford any distractions at the moment—or ever.

Work is my number one priority. Always has been and always will be. That's why I've never had a serious girlfriend, because they take me away from what's important. What I've been trained to do before I could even walk.

She shoves her phone into her back pocket, then drops the menu onto the booth between us.

"Did you send that? How?" she snaps.

"Send what?" I frown.

"The message! How would you know—?"

"Show me the phone!" I growl, reaching for her pocket. She stumbles back, shakes her head, then walks away.

She talks to someone behind the counter, dropping her apron off, and then she's gone, hurrying out the front door.

Pushing myself out of the booth, I feel the weight of stares on me as if everyone in the diner is watching my every move. Fortunately for them, I'm not here for that. I'm here cause her brother is causing us fucking problems, and the sooner I find that fucker, the better. He owes us money, and he's meant to be helping with the next supply run. He should know better than to fuck with The Brotherhood. Next time I see him, he'll have a bullet in his head and be hanging from the fence. But, fuck, can I do that to her? Fucking hell, this is exactly why I can't afford to let anyone in, yet Freya's forced herself inside without even realizing it.

She's outside, phone in hand, raising her voice as she speaks into it. She's casually leaning against my Range Rover, a sight that would normally make me furious if anyone else dared to touch my car. She's always had a way of getting under my skin, like an itch I can't scratch. Stripping away layer after layer until only the bones remain. It's a shame she hates me just as much as I hate her.

"What the fuck are you doing?" I ask, coming up right in front of her. She peeks through her thick lashes, hangs up the phone, and curses.

"I have no idea if I should tell you or not," she says with a sigh, her words hanging in the air, and I resist the temptation to make a snarky remark. She needs me and fuck, that feels good.

"What do you need?" I move around my car, then jump into the front seat. She slides into the passenger seat next to me.

"A search party for my brother," she says, and I laugh.

Her eyes lock onto mine, filled with anger, and she reaches over to the door handle. I hit the lock on the doors so she can't run.

"Chill the fuck out. Don't you think I've already sent out a search party? We need him just as much as you do," I say.

"Well, you didn't try hard enough, obviously, 'cause he's still missing. I'm coming with you to Daringville and I'll search myself," she retorts, looking out the windscreen into the bush.

"Isn't he off at college like you keep telling us?"

"I thought so, but I got a message saying he's still here, so now I have no fucking idea," she huffs out.

There's no use arguing with her because when she has her heart set on something, she doesn't back down. If she doesn't come with me, she'll find another way, and it's better like this. She's already on Dominic's radar.

In silence, we start to drive, and she keeps her face pressed against the window as if longing to spot her brother in the distance. I have a bad feeling about why we haven't found him, but I don't want to share that with her. At least not yet.

We fly over the train tracks without stopping for security.

Dominic's name fills the screen on my phone. With a sudden movement, she locks eyes with me, her chest rising and falling against her black T-shirt. I hit answer.

"Meeting at my place," he says, his voice trailing off as tension fills the car. As soon as our eyes lock, she squirms in her seat and turns her attention back to the window. "'Bring Miss Freya LeClair with you."

The moment he hangs up, my grip on the steering wheel tightens, my knuckles turning white from the pressure. Fuck. How did he know she was with me? Stupid fucking question. He knows everything. The sooner he retires and hands the reins fully over to us, the better.

"I can take you back," I say.

She breathes out a heavy sigh. "You and I both know that nothing good ever comes from disobeying him."

I swallow hard, my throat constricting as her words sink in, memories of the scars etched on my skin resurfacing. She has them too.

Neither of us speaks as we continue driving to Dominic's place. Through the security and into the gated community, past Lucas's house, mine, and then turning down the long driveway, Dominic's house sits on the edge of the cliff like all our houses. The sounds of the ocean hitting the steep rock face never get old.

With the car now off, Freya sits silently in her seat, her attention focused on the house, her chest rhythmically rising and falling. Just as I'm about to say something, she rushes out the door and forcefully slams it closed. I don't think she's been back to the Hendrix manor since they left, and part of me wants to comfort her, but the other half has no fucking idea why. She's a big girl and she can clearly look after herself.

I trail behind her as we ascend the concrete stairs, and one of their staff opens the door to usher us inside. Freya's shifting uncomfortably, checking out the foyer. She bites down on her bottom lip and my cock twitches against my jeans.

Footsteps pound against the stairs, and Hazen comes running down but freezes when he sees Freya. He looks at me and I shrug. He obviously has just as much of an idea as me why she's here. The front door opens, and Lucas struts in.

"What the hell?" he asks, eyeing Freya up and down.

"No idea," I reply, shrugging out of my jacket and passing it to one of the staff.

"She shouldn't be here," Hazen says, moving down the rest of the stairs.

"No shit, I'd rather be anywhere else." She shakes her head. "But your father summoned me. You haven't seen Alec, have you?" she asks with a look of hope sparkling in her eyes.

Hazen just shakes his head. His eyes dart between her and me, his nostrils flaring with anger, and I instinctively raise my hands in surrender. It's not my fucking fault.

"He will see you now in his office." The sound of a maid's voice carries down the hall.

Hazen swears quietly before taking the lead. With a gentle gesture, Lucas envelops Freya under his arm, leaning in to share a whispered message that brings a smile to her face. She doesn't push him away, and my teeth clench together watching her with him. She's really getting on my nerves, and it's driving me crazy. Distancing ourselves from her seems impossible, especially with her brother missing. We need her and she needs us.

I step into Dominic's office and a chill runs down my spine. He's the only one who scares me. There is something about him that commands respect and strikes fear in grown men, making them quiver in his presence. Behind his wooden desk, he sits with a cigar dangling from his lips, filling the room with a smoky aroma. His eyes are laser-focused on her, the corner of his mouth lifts, and Lucas removes his arm from around her. Hazen stands on the other side of her, and I stay behind them, closest to the door.

Mia is cozied up on the couch, her fingers delicately flipping through the pages of a book. She looks at me and I frown. What the fuck is she doing here, and why does she look so damn comfortable?

"Little Freya LeClair," Dominic says, his gaze slowly scanning her from head to toe, and I step forward, ready to protect her but think better of it. "My oh my, haven't you grown up?"

She alternates her weight from one foot to the other under the scrutiny.

My fists clench, and the urge to forcefully escort her outside and instruct her to flee overwhelms me. To run as fast as she can. But that would only get a bullet between my eyes and hers.

"Looks like it. Now why am I here?" she snaps, and I let out a heavy exhale. Fuck. She needs to learn to keep her mouth shut.

Dominic laughs, biting into his cigar. "You've got your mother's feisty attitude. I always loved that about her until she ran her stupid mouth too much, and we all know what happened then."

With no response, Freya thrusts her hands into the pockets of her jeans.

"I've heard your brother is missing, and he owes us a lot of money. You wouldn't know where he is, would you, Miss Freya?"

"I thought he went away to college," she says, and the room stays silent for several heartbeats.

"Whatever the case, I need him or the money he owes. I don't give a fuck how you get it, but there better be fifty grand sitting on my desk within forty-eight hours. Now leave," he snaps, and Freya hurries out of the room. "I meant all of you!"

"What?" I ask, frowning.

"This is your mess, too. Now clean it up."

I maintain a composed expression until we exit his office and step outside. We have to help her, not only to get the money back, but also to address the underlying problem. Alec stole from us, and we need to find him.

I slide into my car and Freya, Lucas, and Hazen jump in. We don't talk until we're out of his driveway and heading to Lucas's.

"How in the fuck are we going to get that money?" Lucas curses from the back seat, and I huff.

"We don't have to get anything." I pause, looking to Freya. "She does."

Her lips curl into a scowl, radiating anger from the corner of her mouth.

She's way too easy to play with.

Chapter Sixteen
Freya

The moment I entered his office, my heart started racing and hasn't calmed down since. Being in his presence again was like a painful stab in the chest, reopening old wounds. I never wanted to see him again, ever, after what he did to me and my family. And now thanks to Alec, I'm stuck picking up the pieces. Fucking hell. I can't breathe. And what was Mia doing there in his office looking like she was ready to move in? Does she not care about my brother at all? I never liked her, and now I know why.

Gage pulls up in front of Lucas's house, and as soon as the car stops, I quickly exit. With each step, I inch closer to the edge of the cliff. I stop, then look out into the deep blue ocean. The waves crash against the cliff, one after another. I open my mouth and unleash a deafening scream that echoes around me. The desire to jump like I did two weeks ago, to let the raging waves consume me, lingers within me, yet my legs remain rooted to the earth.

I squeeze my eyes shut, attempting to suppress the flood of memories, but they overwhelm me. Being back in that house, the one place I swore I'd never step foot in again, was like a dam breaking.

Ten Years old.

My cheek stings, and I fight back the tears that threaten to fall. I can't let him see me weak, it'll only push him further. He reaches back and I squeeze my eyes shut as his hand cracks against my face and whips my head to the side. He grips my cheeks and wrenches my head back toward him.

"You fucking open your eyes and show me some fucking respect, you little whore," Dominic growls, and I reluctantly open my eyes. A lone tear falls down my cheek, sliding over his hand.

Three boys surround him in a circle. One with light-brown eyes and blond hair. One with mossy-green eyes and midnight-black hair, and the last boy with ocean-blue eyes and short brown hair. They just stand there, watching Dominic hurt me. I try to plead with them with my gaze, but they don't do anything.

The last thing I see is my mother crouched in the corner of the room with a glass pipe between her lips. She watches us with glazed-over eyes but doesn't move. He squeezes harder until everything fades away into nothing.

I'm going to fucking kill Alec myself when I find him. How could he put me through this? He's my protector. My constant. The only person in this world I can rely on, and now I'm picking up all the pieces and trying to put everything back together.

If he stole that money, he must be hiding at college and that message was wrong. It has to be. I'm not going to stop until I find him.

Footsteps crunch against the gravel, coming up behind me.

"I'm not going to have to follow you in there again, am

I?" Lucas asks, then laughs despite all the shit that's happened tonight.

"No, but I do need to find a way to let go of all this pent-up frustration," I say, mesmerized by the relentless crash of waves against the cliff. The water is sparkling with the bright reflection of the full moon.

"I've got some pretty good ideas on how you can release," Lucas says, wrapping me under his arm. Despite my urge to shove him off, being in his arms provides an unexpected sense of comfort, preventing me from leaping into the icy depths of the ocean.

"Don't you think we have more important things to talk about?" Gage snaps from somewhere behind us, and I straighten my shoulders, shrugging out of Lucas's embrace. Turning around, I start walking toward the house and barge into Gage's shoulder on my way past.

"Let's do it then," I growl.

One of his maids opens the door for me, and it's way quieter than the last time I was here for the grand ball, which feels like forever ago. The night that kicked off this crap. This mess could've been avoided if Alec didn't get caught up with them.

Getting out my phone, I fire off a message to Alec mentioning the money I now have to come up with if he doesn't show his face, hoping he sees it. He will come back now that he knows the shit I'm in. He wouldn't leave me to pick up the pieces. It's just not like him. If I don't hear from him soon, I'm left with no choice but to go to Bexley and find him.

I gaze at the unfamiliar number, puzzled by the cryptic messages it holds. I attempt to reply for the second time, only to have the message bounce back. Fuck.

I text Kai, asking again to let me know straight away if

he sees Alec. My phone vibrates in my hand, and I anticipate Kai's message, but it turns out to be the unknown
number.

Your brother is in deep. Will he return in a heap?

Gripping the phone tightly, a tremble runs through me
as I stare at the screen. In a swift motion, Lucas passes by
and grabs it from my hand.

"Hey," I snap, trying to grab it back, but Lucas keeps it
just out of my reach.

"Who are these messages from?" Frowning, he looks
back and forth between the phone and me.

"I have no fucking idea. The number is unknown, just
give it back. I'll deal with it."

Lucas huffs. "The fuck you will. I'll have a tech guy
look into this for you." He fumbles around with my phone
before passing it back.

"Thanks," I mumble, barely audible as Lucas strides
ahead. I trail behind him, passing through a spacious
kitchen and dining area. He stops in the open living area
with a long bar that overlooks the ocean below through glass
windows.

"What's your poison, little thorn?" Lucas asks, moving
behind the bar.

Leaning my elbows on the wooden ledge, I gaze at the
array of expensive bottles of liquor.

"Whatever one is the most expensive. I'll have that
bottle," I say, and the corner of Lucas's mouth lifts.

"Coming right up."

Gage takes a scotch bottle and divides it into two
glasses. He hands one over to Hazen, who hasn't spoken
since being in his dad's office.

Lucas passes me a bottle and a glass with ice in it. I plop
down on the couch and pour myself a drink. Hazen takes a

seat on the couch beside mine, while Lucas tumbles down next to me. Gage stays standing, leaning back against the bar.

"Do any of you have fifty grand cash sitting around?" I ask, knocking back my drink and pouring another one.

"Of course we do, but if it comes from our bank accounts he will know," Gage says.

"Next question then. How in the fuck do I come up with that kind of money in forty-eight hours?" I say, checking my phone. "Make that forty-six hours."

"There are a few ways, but you're not going to like any of them," Lucas says, placing a hand on my knee, and I don't brush it off.

"The easiest way is to tell us where your brother is and hand him over," Hazen grits out, finally breaking his silence.

Gripping the edge of the couch, I sit up straighter and glare straight at Hazen.

"For one, I have no fucking idea where he is or I wouldn't be here, and secondly, the reason he's in this mess is because of you," I snap, and a pained look crosses Hazen's features for a brief second before it's gone again.

"Your brother chose to work for us, so that's on him," Hazen says, and I hate to admit he's right. My brother did choose this, and now I'm here in this mess.

"Just tell me what I need to do," I say, finishing off another glass.

I hate using a substance to block it all out, but it's the only thing keeping me from running. Running as far away from here as I can.

I find myself in the same situation I warned my brother about, surrounded by three heirs of The Brotherhood. Stuck until I somehow come up with fifty grand. Fuck. I can't do this on my own. I need them and I hate that more than anything. The last time I needed them the most, they didn't protect me. They let him kick us out like trash.

Ten years old

My peaceful slumber is abruptly interrupted as a bag is violently thrown over my head, disorienting me. My screams are muffled by the bag as if swallowed by its suffocating embrace. The more heavily I inhale, the tighter and denser the air becomes, making it harder to breathe. Fuck.

I'm yanked up by my armpits, soaring through the air until I collide with a solid surface. A wave of pain surges through my stomach, eliciting a groan from deep within me. It's still healing from the knife wounds from last night. The memory of the pain is so intense it makes my whole body shudder, and I black out.

An engine humming to life jars me back to reality, and I instinctively reach out for something to steady myself. But before I can react, the vehicle jerks forward forcefully, causing me to lose my balance and collide with a jarring impact against a hard object. Strong hands hoist me upright, and my body quivers uncontrollably.

What's happening? Where are we going? Everything's gone to shit, and I don't know what will happen to us now. Dominic doesn't want us here anymore. I can see it in the way he looks at my mother—he's done with her. Is he going to kill us? I don't want to die.

It feels like we've been on the road forever, the monotony broken only by the occasional rumble of the engine. Abruptly, the car stops, and the doors pop open. I'm yanked out roughly and met with the wind whipping all around me as if it's beckoning me forward. With each step I'm forced to take, the hard gravel road sends a jolt of impact through my feet. I'm pulled forward, and without my sight, I struggle to keep up with the rapid movement. As I trip and lose my balance, a strong grip on my arm saves me from falling.

I am forcibly halted, and the voices around me fade in and out like distant whispers, their meaning lost in the noise. The sound of ringing echoes in my ears, and my body trembles with an intense sensation. I want this to stop. For everything to go back to the way it was before. I don't understand. With a sudden yank, the bag over my head is torn off, and I blink repeatedly to clear my vision.

We're on the edge of the tracks that divide our towns, from Daringville, where we are, to Daringhood—the bad side. Where the poor live, along with those The Brotherhood deem not good enough.

My heart races as Dominic locks eyes with me, and the overwhelming emotions cause tears to brim in my eyes. He scares me, and I hate him. Someone interlocks their hands with mine, and I glance over to see my brother standing beside me, his eye swollen and bruised. No. I try to move, to run, but he shakes his head ever so slightly and I freeze, attentive to his silent command. My brother always knows what to do. He's my protector, my best friend.

Standing behind Dominic are Hazen, Gage, and that blond-haired boy, Lucas, who I haven't really talked to before. They watch, unmoving, with their arms crossed. What's happening? There are those Brotherhood men everywhere, even that blonde-haired lady who looks like Lucas.

"Get her," Dominic snaps to one of the men near the white van across the street. He disappears behind it, and my heart skips a beat as he emerges, leading my mother by the hand. As I take a step forward, my brother's firm grip pulls me back. My mother desperately struggles, her body thrashing against the man's hold in a desperate attempt to *break free. She's wearing a torn white nightgown, the fabric revealing a glimpse of her chest.*

Her gaze shifts between us and Dominic, filled with intense hatred.

"Fuck you," she spits at Dominic, and the other guy pushes her. She lands on her hands and knees between Dominic and us.

"I'm done with you and your family. You are a disgrace to Daringville, and you belong over the tracks. You are nothing but a hood rat," Dominic says with so much hate that my body trembles. With a shake of her head, my mother reaches out to him, pleading for him to reconsider.

I glance at the boys behind Dominic, desperate for their help and hope they can rescue me, but they remain motionless, shattering my heart in two.

As Alec scoops Mom up from the ground, he reaches for my hand, and we venture across the tracks together. I leave behind my old life, desperately clinging to the hope that this will be good for us, for Mom.

Hazen's phone pings, bringing me out of my memories, and he looks from me to the phone.

"Well, will you look at that for timing? A job just came in and it's paying exactly what you need," Hazen says, standing up.

A wave of unease washes over me, settling in the pit of my stomach. Whatever the job is, I'm not going to like it, but I'll do whatever it takes to clear Alec's debt. Then he might come back home if he knows it's been taken care of.

Hazen shows the phone to Gage, who nods in agreement before leaving the room and walking down the hallway. Lucas and Hazen talk in hushed tones at the bar, and I sit there sipping my drink.

"Are you going to tell me what it is or just stand around

gossiping like little teenagers?" I snap, standing up quickly. A momentary dizziness overtakes me, but quickly subsides. No more alcohol for me. Whatever the job is, I need to have a clear head for it.

"We're going on a little bear hunt and you're going to find your prey," Hazen explains, before looking down the hallway, and Gage appears carrying a large black duffel bag. He drops it at my feet and all kinds of guns fall out. I take a step back, shaking my head.

"And kill it," Gage finishes, and a wave of nausea rises as I struggle to keep the bile down.

"No way, anything but this," I say, my eyes not leaving the bag of guns.

"It's a fifty grand reward and time is ticking," Gage insists, his voice filled with urgency. He takes out a small handgun from the bag and hands it over to me, the weight of the weapon adding to the gravity of the situation. With the cool metal in my palm, a rush of emotions floods over me, making me want to let out a scream. I want to run. But there's no running away from them.

"There has to be some other way!" I blurt out, looking from the gun to Gage, Hazen, and Lucas.

"We could rob the diner you work for?" Lucas smirks, and I shake my head.

"He wouldn't have that kind of money lying around. Besides, I can't hurt my boss. Next?"

Gage huffs. "The bear we're finding is bad. He's raped and treats women like shit. You want to kill him. Trust me, Freya, you want this. Just wait and see."

I have to do this. I have to do this for my brother.

Chapter Seventeen
Freya

I've never killed anyone before—or any*thing*, for that matter. The thought of taking another life sickens me to my very core. Here I am, against my better judgment, in a car with three men I made a promise to keep away from. Three trained killers who are taking me to kill some stranger. All to clear my brother's debt. But the only thing that matters is freeing my brother, so he can come home.

The moment I slide into the front seat of Gage's car, my phone vibrates in my back pocket, breaking the silence. My heart pounds relentlessly in my chest. Each time my phone buzzes, I anxiously anticipate Alec's name, only to be met with a wave of disappointment. This time is no different.

Mia - Have you heard from him?

I grimace down at the phone screen. I can't deal with her now, and I should be the one asking her questions. She was in Dominic's office looking way too comfortable on his couch. I don't have time for her little mind games. I knew she was nothing but trouble when Alec first introduced me to her.

Shoving my phone back into my pocket, I stare down at the black gun between my feet. How many people has this gun killed before? What stories lie beneath the surface? A shiver works its way down my spine.

A hand lands on my shoulder and squeezes. Lucas shoves his head between the headrests. "You nervous, little thorn?" He leans in, pressing a light kiss to my cheek, and my stomach flutters.

I nod slightly, unable to form the words. Death doesn't scare me; I've been around it enough in my life. But it's never been at my hand.

Living in Daringhood, if you look hard enough, you'll see violence everywhere. Every person you pass has a similar hardness to their features, borne of survival. They will do anything to survive, and that's exactly why I'm here in this car and about to kill someone for the very first time.

Lucas forcefully grabs my jaw and turns my head toward him. His intense, light-brown eyes lock onto mine, seemingly delving into the depths of my mind, leaving nothing hidden. Everything around us fades into the background until it's just us. My hands ache with the need to touch every part of him, to understand this pull toward him. I've never been interested in anyone, but there's something different about Lucas Fox. I want him, and he wants me, too. His tongue flicks across his lips, and I want nothing more than for him to shove it down my throat.

The car jerks to the left, then right. My head collides with Lucas's and pain explodes. My head throbs with a splitting headache and I squeeze my eyes shut.

"What the fuck, man?" Lucas growls, falling back into his seat and rubbing his head.

Gage meets my gaze, a smug look playing on his lips, and I resist the temptation to smack it away with my palm.

"Sorry, there was a rabbit on the road, and I didn't want to hit it and mess up my baby," he says, patting the dashboard, and I scoff.

"Bullshit," I say under my breath. He knew exactly what he was doing. Gage has never been able to hide his jealousy well.

"Yeah, I agree. That's total bullshit. Next time, warn a fucker before you do it. My head is fucking killing me," Lucas says from the backseat before kicking his foot into the back of Gage's chair.

We don't say anything for the rest of the ride. Lucas stares daggers into the back of Gage's headrest, and Gage taps his steering wheel along to the music. Hazen sits silently behind me, the tension in the air growing with every passing minute. We drove over the tracks ten minutes ago, heading east on the outskirts of town.

We turn onto an empty dirt track that I haven't been down before. I haven't spent much time on the east side of the town—never had to. It's just endless forest, lakes, and wilderness. Everything happens in the middle of town or near the trailer park. People only come out here to camp if they dare. The Brotherhood prefers us to stay in town, and if anyone gets caught out here, they're dead. Stupid politics. The number of bodies that line the forest floor could even make a serial killer squeamish.

Surrounded by trees on both sides, the headlights cut through the darkness, illuminating the dirt road. After five more minutes of driving, we reach a clearing. Just ahead of us, there's a parked car, its lights casting reflections on the lake. Shadows of two people sit in the front seat and movement comes from the back.

I sit up, reaching for the gun, like it's going to save me from whatever Gage has driven us into. What if this was all part of their plan to get rid of me? What if I just walked straight into their trap? Fuck.

Gage turns the car off but leaves his lights on as well. He gets out, then Hazen and Lucas hop out of the back. Hazen opens my door and my fingers curl around the gun like it's my lifeline. Even though I have no idea how to use it.

He offers me his hand and I take it. His large hand engulfs mine, and a shiver works its way up my arm. I'm not sure if it's from the cold or because of the way his warm grip feels.

He lets go and the shivers disappear. I step out into the crisp night. The wind flicks my hair back off my face and kisses my cheeks.

Hazen looks from the gun to me, shaking his head. "You have no idea how to use that, do you?" He knows the answer before I even open my mouth.

He reaches down and pulls something out of his boot. Taking the gun from my other hand, he replaces it with a knife. Its black handle fits my palm perfectly.

"If you don't want to do it, just give me one look and I'll do it for you," Hazen says. "This job isn't just yours to carry. Your first kill will always haunt you, and I'd tell you it gets easier, but you don't need to know that." He looks at me intently before walking off ahead.

I frown, warmth filling my stomach. He'd do that for me?

My heartbeat echoes in my ears, my feet frozen to the spot. Fucking hell. I need to move, to get this over with. To clear this debt for my brother, then he can come home, and I can kick his fucking ass for putting me through this. We'll laugh about it later, but now I have to move.

I continue walking step by step until I reach the space

between Lucas and Hazen. On the opposite side of Hazen, Gage raises his hand in the air. As the car door opens, a man dressed in all black exits the vehicle. Before opening the back door, he acknowledges Gage with a nod, then he pulls out a guy wearing a black bag over his head. The captive thrashes around, yelling, but I can't discern what he's saying through the material.

The other guy pushes him forward until they are standing directly in front of us. The dude from the passenger seat walks over, watching me. My fingers tighten around the knife. Sweat drips down my neck as I wait for them to uncover whoever is under the bag.

If it's someone I know, there's no way I can do this, but chances are if it's someone from Daringhood, I will know them. If not personally, then know of them.

"Leave and get back to headquarters," Gage says to the two men in black, and they nod.

The blindfolded man is tripped by one of them, causing him to fall forward. He groans, moving around in the dirt, but he can't get up. His hands are bound behind his back. The other two leave, driving off down the track. Now it's just us here.

"Freya, will you do the honors of revealing your target?" Gage asks like I have a choice in this. I look over at him and shake my head before heading toward the guy. I flip Gage off over my shoulder, and Lucas laughs.

With my knife clutched firmly in my hand, I come to a stop in front of the masked man and then help him into a seated position. He doesn't fight me, which I'm thankful for. He's a small guy, thin as a stick, so it's easy to move him.

My fingers curl around the fabric of the mask, and I lift it off, then stumble backward.

When his beady eyes meet mine, he throws his head back, and his laughter fills the air.

Well, now this job just got a little easier. I've been dreaming of killing this piece of scum ever since he started whoring out my mother.

Gavin motherfucking McCreed.

Chapter Eighteen
Freya

G avin's face breaks into a wide grin as he looks up at me, and his eyes fill with hope as if I am his savior. The Brotherhood stands behind me, making me seem like the lesser of two evils.

"Oh, Freya! Aren't I glad to see you? Now be a little sweetie and untie me." He tries to stand but falls to his knees again.

I look down at him, my heart racing, and my chest rises and falls rapidly. The nerve of this guy. The amount of shit he's put my mother through . . . and now he's at my feet, begging me to save him.

With a calculated move, I lower myself down, the cold metal of the knife pressing against his throat, and his eyes widen. The sharp tip pierces his skin, causing a trickle of blood to run down his neck. I hate him.

"Please, Freya! I'll do anything you want. I've got money. Is that what you want?" Gavin begs, his eyes glazing over. The strong asshole act is gone, and now he's on his knees, pleading for a lifeline.

Hazen laughs and walks over to stand behind Gavin,

"That's the reason you're here, Gavin. You owe not only your boss money, but in turn, us, and he's put up a reward for you." Hazen forcefully grabs a handful of Gavin's hair. He winces in pain as his head jerks backward.

My throat tightens as Hazen's face takes on a deadly expression. His eyes transform into a mesmerizing shade of deep blue, so dark they seem almost black.

"Do you know the punishment for going behind our backs?" he asks, and Gavin whimpers like a little bitch.

I murmur the word "death," and Hazen gestures toward my knife. I pass it over to him.

"Remember I said earlier that you would be going on a bear hunt?" he asks, and I respond with a questioning raise of my eyebrows. In one fluid motion, Hazen uses the knife to cut Gavin's restraints and then swiftly kicks him in the back. With a thud, he collapses to the ground.

"Freya here is going to count to ten, and you best hope you're a fast runner, Gavin. 'Cause she's fit," Gage says, coming up to stand beside me, his shoulder gently brushing against mine.

I start counting as Gavin lifts his gaze from the ground. "One, two." With a burst of energy, he leaps up and bolts past the shimmering lake, moving straight toward the depths of the forest.

"What are the chances that it's Gavin McCreed, someone I actually hate?" I ask, looking between the three men. Lucas smirks, his eyes gleaming with mischief, Gage shrugs nonchalantly, and Hazen carefully hands me back the knife.

"Looks like you're going hunting, and I'll be right behind you," Hazen says, his voice filled with anticipation.

I pause for a moment to absorb the peaceful sounds of the rustling leaves before following the path that leads me along the lake. The calmness of the outside world is a stark contrast to the turmoil I feel inside. I'm itching to run, to move, to release this fire inside me. Am I really going to find him and kill him? I do hate his guts, but can I actually do this?

With each step I take into the forest, the light from the car becomes more and more distant, disappearing into the surroundings. The wind rustles through the trees, bringing with it the intermittent calls of nocturnal creatures, and I instinctively run my tongue over my dry lips. I hold the knife tightly as if my life depends on it, because it does. The sound of footsteps crunching on the forest floor alerts me to someone approaching from behind. Lucas comes into view and casually drapes an arm over my shoulders.

Gage and Hazen close in on me, forming an impenetrable circle that leaves no room for escape. Their bodies envelop me, pressing close as my body ignites. With their black hoods up, half of their faces are hidden from view.

I shut my eyes and take a deep breath, immersing myself in the forest's refreshing aroma. One second, the warmth of their bodies is wrapped around me, and in the blink of an eye, they vanish into thin air. The cool air brushes against my skin, leaving goosebumps in its wake, then a soft exhale of warmth brushes past my ear.

"Run, little thorn. Run until you get him, then we can play," Lucas whispers into my ear, and my heart races faster and faster. Like I'm about to jump off a cliff or do something reckless.

I sprint into the dark forest, disappearing into the shadows. Trees surround me, and I dodge each one. The light fades the further I run, leaving behind the full moon to guide me between the shadows and darkness.

Slowing down slightly, I become acutely aware of every

sound around me, hoping to detect any hint of Gavin's whereabouts. The snap of a stick to my right startles me, prompting me to continue. Running has always been a favorite of mine, with the exhilarating feeling of my heart about to burst and the subsequent wave of release when I finish. As a child, I had a routine when Mom came home blitzed: I would quickly jump out of my window and sprint away, running until my lungs gave out. Lately, I haven't done that, and I miss it.

I follow the sound of feet slapping against the forest floor and a faint grunting coming from deeper into the woods. Between the trees, a figure moves in an erratic manner, looking around with urgency. With his small, thin body, Gavin zigzags through the dense undergrowth, probably hoping it will shield him from what's to come.

Using the same trees for cover, I stealthily trail behind him, closing the distance with every step. Until I'm right behind him. In a split second, his back straightens and he spins around, but I am already on top of him, forcefully bringing him down to the ground.

His fists swing wildly, and with each blow, a wave of pain erupts across my body, accompanied by Gavin's menacing grin. I roll sideways to avoid his strikes, and he uses my retreat to his advantage.

Gavin propels himself upright and bolts away, his eyes meeting mine briefly, a crazed smile on his lips. He's so busy watching me that he doesn't see Hazen. The impact of Hazen's punch sends him sprawling to the ground like a sack of shit.

Lucas extends his hand toward me, and I grasp it. As I get up, my free arm automatically wraps around my torso where Gavin landed most of his punches, and I bite into the inside of my cheek. Lucas grabs my shirt and pulls it up. He

144

looks down, his knuckles gently grazing over my bruised side, and I take in a sharp breath. His chest swells under his hoodie as he breathes in, then loudly exhales.

With a swift spin, Lucas positions himself above Gavin, his boot firmly planted against the side of his face. The cheerful guy I'm used to seeing is nowhere to be found, replaced instead by the formidable monster who belongs to The Daring Brotherhood. Kneeling, he pulls back his hood and inches closer to Gavin, their faces almost touching. Gavin's body trembles with uncontrollable shakes. I should feel sorry for him and intervene, but my feet remain locked in place. He's a monster.

"I'll do anything you want. Please," Gavin begs, his eyes filling with tears. "I'll suck your cock."

Lucas's lip curls back in disgust before he swings his fist and snaps Gavin's head sideways. "I'm not gay, you piece of shit, and even if I was, I wouldn't let your filthy mouth anywhere near my cock. It's got standards." Not taking his eyes off Gavin, he asks, "Freya, will you do the honors?"

Hazen and Gage flank me, their presence urging me to inch closer. Bending down, I firm my grip around the knife and press it to Gavin's neck. He swallows, his Adam's apple bobbing against the knife's lethal edge. Blood begins to ooze from where the blade digs in, yet his eyes still hold a glimmer of hope as he looks at me. Pleading for me to save him.

The image of my mother returning home in a disheveled state, her skin marked with bruises and her clothes in tatters, is etched in my memory. We were left hungry, with no money to buy food. How many times did she beg him to stop? Or to give her the money he owed her for whoring her out? Too fucking many times to count, and now here he is, begging me to have mercy.

145

"Your mother needs me," Gavin rasps, and tears fill my eyes and fall down my cheeks.

He's one of the reasons she's like this. I hate him so much.

Without another moment's hesitation, I slice the unforgiving steel of the knife across his throat, the sound of his gasp echoing in the silence. Gavin chokes and gurgles on his blood, and I fall backward, landing on my ass. What did I just do? Death has crossed my path countless times throughout my life, yet I have never been the cause. My hands, stained with blood, tremble uncontrollably.

Strong hands pull me to my feet from behind, and thick arms wrap around my waist, pinning me to a hard, warm body. Gage takes the knife from my trembling hands as I collapse against Hazen, his protective hold securing me. Without his support, I'd fall back to the ground.

Lucas aims his gun at Gavin's head and his eyes widen, pleading for mercy while blood gushes down his neck and out his mouth. Gage grips Gavin's shirt and rips it off forcefully, then he brings his knife down on Gavin's chest, etching words into his skin. I can't tear my eyes away from Gavin lying there, all the fight within him gone. I can't move. Hazen's heart pounds against my ear, echoing my own rhythm. Gage finishes carving, then underscores the bottom two words with one last slash of the blade.

Regards, Daring Brotherhood, it reads, and I feel like I'm going to be sick.

Gavin's soft sobs fade away, leaving an eerie silence in the air. As Lucas pulls the trigger, the deafening sound of the gunshot reverberates through the dense forest. Stumbling out of Hazen's embrace, I collapse to my knees and retch, emptying the meager contents of my stomach onto the forest floor.

Someone gathers up my hair, pulling it away from my face.

"And just like that, the debt is cleared," Gage's voice echoes from above, and I shake my head in disbelief.

Just like that.

Chapter Nineteen
Lucas

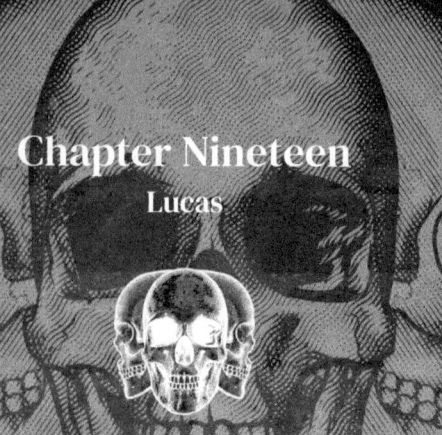

I didn't really know her back when she lived here in Daringville, can't say that I know her now, but I do remember her. My father always kept us away, shielding us from her for reasons unknown.

I saw her at the Hendrixes' house like twice. I remember her hair, neatly divided into two matching pigtails, swaying as she walked with a lost look in her eyes. She smiled at me the first time we met, and I'll never forget the way her smile brightened all the darkness that surrounded me. She brought hope into my life, but then vanished and was never mentioned again until she reemerged alongside Amirah. The desire to catch her and keep her by my side has consumed me completely.

With her head nestled in my crotch, her body trembling nonstop since our exit from the forest, I am determined to find a way to bring her comfort. To take her pain away and replace it with everything she desires. I have no idea what is happening between us, but there's an irresistible magnetic force drawing me toward her that I've become fixated on, and after experiencing just a hint of it, I crave more. I don't think I'll ever get sick of this girl. I want to spend every day unraveling every detail about her, like a never-ending puzzle. Peeling away each layer until there is nothing left. I've never fallen for a girl like this, so I'm in way too deep.

She pulls my hoodie over her shoulders, but the chill in the air still makes her shudder. Fuck. The moment she sliced the knife across his throat, her eyes burned with a deep, unsettling hatred that sent chills down my spine, but her subsequent rush of regret made me question everything. That cut me deep. That feeling—it's like an old friend to me.

The echoes of my first kill continue to reverberate within me. Although the passage of years has made it somewhat more manageable, that initial encounter remains the most impactful. Over the years, I've become adept at burying those feelings of remorse deep within me. Our fathers pushed us through rigorous training designed to detach us from the emotional toll of ending another person's life. Now that I can use it, it's like a light switch that I can easily flick on and off. I want to give her that. So she doesn't have to drown in the suffocating waves of pain. She wanted him gone; I saw it in her eyes. She hated him, but that doesn't take away from what she'll be feeling.

"Are we taking her back to her place?" Gage asks from the driver's seat of his car, and I shake my head.

"She needs to be somewhere safe tonight and I don't want to let her out of my sight," I say, watching her intently. Her soft snores fill the car, and my shoulders drop.

"Father will want her there when we deliver the body," Hazen says from the passenger seat.

"Do we have to do that tonight?" I sigh. "She needs to rest."

Gage catches my gaze in the mirror and frowns. "Oh fuck, Luca boy has caught feelings for the girl."

I scoff. "She has a name, you know."

With a laugh, Gage shakes his head but doesn't respond. He reaches over to turn up the stereo, filling the car with music. Fucking asshole.

"Shut up, you'll wake her," I snap, and she stirs, pushing her head further back into my crotch. Fuck. My cock hardens and I pray it's not digging into her head.

Gage ignores me as he pulls up to Hendrix's manor. Guess we do have to do this tonight. Damn it.

With a gentle stroke of the backs of my fingers down her cheek, Freya lets out a soft groan. I lightly caress her bottom lip with my thumb, and in response, she sighs, her eyes flickering open. Sitting up quickly, she looks around the car with frantic eyes, but her tense shoulders gradually relax.

"This isn't home?" She frowns.

"Nah, little thorn, it isn't," I say, and she yawns.

"Why are we back here? Isn't the job done?" she asks, and Hazen turns around to face us.

"My father will want proof."

She sucks in her bottom lip between her teeth, then nods. "Fine, let's get this over with. Then I can find my brother."

"We may have cleared the debt, but your brother still stole from us," Gage snaps from the front seat, and Freya shoves open the door, scrambles out, and slams it.

I shoot Gage a look, and he rolls his eyes. "What? It's true, and that shit doesn't go unpaid for."

Her brother's been MIA for a few weeks now and that's usually not a good sign around here, but I didn't want to tear down her hope. She loves her brother and I get it. I feel the same about my little sister, and if anything happened to her,

I'd destroy everything in my path. Yeah, she can be a pain, but she's one of the rare good ones here.

Making our way inside, we pass by the staff members without a word and pause right outside Dominic's office. Hazen knocks on the door, and the sound echoes through the quiet hallway.

"Come in," Dominic barks out.

Hazen is the first one to enter, followed by Gage, then Freya, and finally me. She remains by my side, observing everything around her.

Dominic sits behind his wooden desk, the sound of his fingers tapping on the keyboard filling the room, before forcefully closing his laptop.

"Done already?" he asks, frowning.

Hazen approaches and shows him his phone with the transaction to his account, receiving a nod in response.

"Your brother's debt is cleared, Freya, so you're free to go," he says, grabbing out a cigar from his top drawer. He lights it and leans back, puffing out smoke.

Freya moves closer, bracing her hands on his desk, and I widen my eyes. Fuck. What are you doing?

"I'm not going anywhere until you tell me where my brother is," she growls out.

I'm torn between wanting to grab her and leave or staying to see how things unfold. No one ever challenged Dominic, they weren't stupid.

The memories of my teenage years come flooding back, and I can still feel the physical pain from the scars on my back, remnants of my rebelliousness. I learned a long time ago that it's best to follow his orders until he retires and hands over the reins of The Daring Brotherhood to us fully, ensuring our place in the hierarchy. We're practically managing it ourselves, but he still holds the ultimate authority. The sooner he retires, the better, but the old bastard is reluctant to let go. My father retired years ago when he got sick, and it's been the best thing for him as he recovers.

A hush falls over the room and Hazen fidgets next to me. Dominic fixates his gaze on her and then throws his head back in laughter.

"Damn, you remind me of your mother. I miss her."

Her hands tremble as Freya tightly clutches the edge of the desk, her knuckles turning white. "We don't talk about her. Just tell me where he is?"

Dominic blows out a ring of smoke, the pungent smell filling the air, but she stands her ground, unwavering. The tension in the room becomes palpable, and I struggle to resist the urge to grab her hand and walk away. It's a risky game she's playing, and the consequences will leave her scorched. The mere thought of that fills me with intense anger.

"I have no idea where your brother is or you wouldn't be the one here paying off his debt, would you, stupid girl?" He shakes his head and butts out his cigar into a glass tray. "That brother of yours has created a few enemies, so he's probably ten feet under by now, and if you don't want to join him, I suggest you leave. Now."

Freya doesn't budge, staring him down, and my cock hardens—but she's being reckless. Stupid. I take a step forward, encircling my arm around her waist and drawing her toward me. In a sudden motion, she twirls in my arms and forcefully pushes me away. She storms out of the room, with the door slamming behind her.

"If she makes any trouble, it's on you three. Keep an eye on her," Dominic says from behind me.

"Understood, Father," Hazen replies, then we leave.

The hallway becomes a blur as I storm through it, the

sound of Gage's car engine filling the air as the front doors swing open. He sprints out, and I chase after him. Freya drives past, her face contorted with anger as she flips us off from the driver's seat.

Oh fuck, no one drives Gage's car. Ever.

Chapter Twenty
Freya

Gripping the steering wheel tightly, I unleash a series of forceful blows with my fist. He couldn't resist mentioning my mother, that jerk. I want to go back there and smash his face into his desk until he takes his last breath. I hate him. I *hate* him.

It was he who shaped my mother into the woman she has become, tearing her away from us, and now he's repeating the same pattern with my brother. While he insists on not knowing his whereabouts, it is hard to believe anything can happen without his awareness. Without his final say. He's wrong, my brother isn't dead. I'd know if he was. He can't be. No, I won't even think that for a second. He's out there somewhere just waiting for me to find him, then we can leave this fuck hole and start fresh. Just like we planned.

Fuck Dominic Hendrix. Fuck The Daring Brotherhood. Fuck anyone who gets in my way.

As I drive around town, the absence of noise on the streets stands out, especially when compared to the liveliness found over the tracks, making it difficult to locate any sign of Alec. Inside their grand mansions, everyone stays cozy with their heaters and enjoys delicious home-cooked dinners. Fucking entitled pricks. I find myself outside their gated community again, my heart racing. Without hesitation, I snatch the lighter and the bottle of vodka that Lucas left in the car.

With the engine still humming, I cautiously exit the vehicle, bringing the bottle to my lips and taking a long sip. Then I drench Gage's car with the rest of it. This is stupid, reckless, and a little immature, but I need to do something. Anything to feel some kind of release. Tonight was a new level of fuckery. I helped kill someone—someone I hate with a passion, but it still didn't make it feel any better. He had a life, then I took it from him. No matter how much of a lowlife asshole he was, I took it all away.

One second he was here, and the next—gone. Just like that. If I hear someone say those words again, I'll crack.

The gates swing open and blinding headlights pierce through the darkness, revealing a familiar figure approaching.

"What the fuck?" Standing in front of his car, Gage lets out a roar that echoes through the air.

With a loud thud, the bottle slips through my fingers and meets the unforgiving ground, instantly shattering into an intricate mosaic of shards.

Watching the flame flicker in the darkness, I bring the lighter up to my face, its warm glow contrasting with the cool night air. I feel the comforting heat of the flame on my face, and I'm spellbound, completely absorbed in its mesmerizing dance for several heartbeats.

A large shadow appears in front of me. Hazen grabs my shoulders and shakes me, but I can't feel anything. Voices echo in the background, but their words are muffled by the incessant ringing in my ears.

With a gentle touch, he covers my hand, guiding my thumb away from the trigger of the lighter before taking it from me. I let him, losing all the fight I have. With a forceful motion, he throws it to the ground and immediately pulls me into his arms. Collapsing into his embrace, I am surrounded by the soothing scent of sandalwood emanating from his chest.

Our surroundings fade away, leaving only the two of us. I hold on to his comforting warmth as if I'm cocooned in a soft, protective blanket. He gently rubs my back up and down, providing a soothing touch. My body melts into his, and I allow it. Just for now. I need this and I'll use him to give that to me. I hate them, but why are those words becoming harder and harder to believe? Despite being the most feared men in Daring, they somehow manage to make me feel safe. Because I'm just like them. I'm a killer. The once-confined monster has finally been unleashed from its cage. There's no turning back, and I won't give up until my brother is safe.

We stay like this, in silence, for what seems like both a second and a lifetime. While a storm rages inside me, Hazen simply holds me, providing a sense of calm amidst the chaos. I don't want to understand what's going on because that means going deeper, unlocking all the shit I buried so far down inside me. I need to forget what happened tonight. The piercing scream from Gavin as my knife slid across his neck. Watching him take his final breath and leave forever. I have to bury it with the rest of my trauma and forget. For Alec. I have to make him my focus and I can't do that wallowing in regret. It will distract me, and I can't afford to have any distractions.

Eventually, I pull away, and the world around us comes back into focus. Gage has vanished, and his car that I drenched in alcohol along with him. Lucas leans back against his car, his unwavering gaze fixed on me, observing my every move. The lights from the gate and security box cast a bright glow on him and his car.

"You good, little thorn?" he asks as he brings a joint to his lips and lights it up, the flickering flame casting a warm glow on his face.

I shrug. "No one's ever good, but yeah, I feel a little better."

Lucas nods before smirking. "You should have seen the look on Gage's face when you left with his car. He doesn't let anyone drive it, and now he's probably at the car wash getting rid of the mess you made."

Laughter bubbles up from within me, making my chest rumble and tears spring to my eyes. Fuck, that feels good.

"Can you drive me home, please?" I ask Lucas, and he shakes his head.

"You're staying at my place tonight."

"But—"

He hands me the joint and I take it. "No buts. I'm not driving you home tonight—it's late as fuck and I need you with me."

As the smoke hits the back of my throat and my body grows lax, I decide against arguing. I can't be bothered. My only desire is to sink into a soft bed, drift off to sleep, and leave everything behind.

I pass the joint back to Lucas as we get into his car. Not long after, I lean my head against the headrest, my eyelids grow heavy and the world fades away.

* * *

I wake to strong arms encircling my waist, and I am pressed back against a comforting, warm chest. I turn around, groaning, and blink my eyes a few times before finding myself face to face with Lucas. His eyes are closed and his face is relaxed. I frown. What the fuck am I doing here with him?

I'm conflicted because I feel protected with him as if nothing can touch me, and it's messed up. I finally slept through the night without any disturbances; there were no nightmares or sounds of someone attempting to break into the house.

Rolling back over, I lean into Lucas's warm body and close my eyes. It's nearly pitch black in here, and I can't tell whether it's day or night. Since I don't have to work until tonight, I plan on spending the day searching for Alec. I reached out to him last night, assuring him everything is fine, the debt has been settled, and he can come out of hiding so we can go.

He didn't reply.

Why didn't he tell me before he disappeared? I could have helped him.

Lucas shifts behind me, his arm around me tightening, and his touch is warm against my lower belly.

"Morning, little thorn." His words tease the back of my neck.

"Morning," I whisper through a yawn.

"Any requests for breakfast?" His hand slowly descends to the waistband of my underwear. "I'm hungry for your pussy."

His fingers glide underneath the material, down my already wet folds, and my breath hitches.

"I've gotta start looking for my brother," I rasp, even though I don't want him to stop. I need this. I want this. My body wants the enemy, and I can't tell her no.

"Your underwear needs to go."

Lucas gently pushes them down my legs as he rolls me onto my back, and I find myself staring into his captivating light-brown eyes. I extend my fingers toward the waistband of his briefs.

"You next," I say, and Lucas grins.

"Fuck, you are sexy when you boss me around."

He removes his briefs and now he's bare, looking down at me with so much desire that my core begs for his touch. With a firm grip, he lifts the bottom of my top, peels it over my head, and hurls it across the room.

"Fucking perfect," he says, roaming his gaze down over my chest and pussy, now on full display.

With the way Lucas is looking at me, I resist the temptation to hide the scars that mark my stomach. There's an inferno of heat in his eyes as he grips his hard cock. I feel empowered and strong. Wanted.

Taking hold of the back of his neck, I bring him closer, connecting our lips with fervor. He responds with a throaty groan, and our tongues intertwine, moving in sync with each other.

His fingers press between my folds, rubbing my clit faster and harder before he pushes a finger, then two, inside me. My back arches as I grab onto his thick cock, and it feels like silky steel in my hand. His lips never leave mine and we fight for dominance, nipping and tugging. My hand tugs his cock to the same pace until he pulls back, resting his head against mine.

"I want to watch you fall apart until your cum drips from my fingers, then I'm going to fuck you."

My core clenches at his words, and he picks up the pace, driving his fingers in and out. His eyes never leave mine as a shudder racks my body and my stomach clenches, my eyes squeezing shut.

He grips my chin. "Eyes on me while you come," he growls, and I obey, panting through my release.

He smiles, bringing his lips down on mine in a heated kiss. His precum slides down his shaft onto my fingers where I'm still gripping him.

"I need to be inside you," he whispers, pressing kisses along my cheek, and I nod, releasing his cock.

He grabs a condom from the drawer beside his bed, tears the packet, and slips it on. I lick my lips as I watch his movements, and Lucas's eyes darken to a chocolate brown.

"Fuck me, you are the most beautiful girl I've ever met."

I have no idea what to say, so I don't say anything, instead grabbing his cock and lining it up with my pussy. He grins, easing himself inside me, and it takes me a moment to adjust to his size. A whimper escapes at the feeling of fullness, and my walls clench around him.

He starts off slow, then faster and harder. His lips crash down on mine, and I take his bottom lip between my teeth, biting down hard. He groans deeply and I want to hear that sound again. He drives into me, hitting my G-spot, but it's not enough. I need more.

My hands push against his chest, and he pulls out. I flip over onto my stomach, and he laughs, slapping my ass. I jolt forward slightly, and he wraps his fingers around my hair, tugging me back. He lines his cock up and pushes deep inside me. I lay my head down against his pillow with my ass in the air, and he drives into me, hitting my walls again and again. He pulls my hair harder and my back arches. I want—no, *need*—more tension. He slaps my ass and my pussy clenches.

"You love it dirty, don't you, little thorn?" Lucas growls,

and I moan. "Don't you?" he asks again, slapping my ass harder.

I jolt forward, but his grip on my hair pulls me back. Pain erupts across my ass and scalp—fuck, it feels good. "Yes," I pant, getting higher and higher.

He slows down his pace and I curse.

"I'm so close, don't you dare fucking stop," I snap, and he chuckles.

"As you wish."

He pumps in and out faster and faster until I can't take it anymore. My legs become weak, stars dance in my vision, and I release. After a few more thrusts, he pulls out, and the next thing I know, warm liquid hits my back, but I don't give a fuck. My body deflates, my heart thundering in my ears as I try to catch my breath.

He rustles around, his presence retreating briefly, then the bed dips and a towel rubs against my back, removing the cum. He flops down on the bed next to me with a lopsided grin.

"You know I won't ever be able to walk away from you or that sweet, sweet pussy now, right?" he says, tucking a lock of hair behind my ear.

I have no idea how to respond to that, so I don't. I can't get attached to him or them—they are the enemy. But the more I say that, the more I don't believe it, and that scares me the most because I am leaving. Once I find my brother, we are gone, and the thought of growing feelings for Lucas and then walking away is too much.

But it might already be too late for that.

Chapter Twenty-One

Freya

After hastily throwing one last T-shirt into my bag, I make sure to zip it up securely before grabbing my phone and purse. Checking the time, I curse. I've only got ten minutes until the bus leaves. I take one final glance around my room to ensure I haven't left anything behind.

On the way past Alec's room, I grab one of his favorite jumpers and slip it over my head, the soft fabric settling against my skin. His musky scent engulfs me, making it hard to hold back the tears welling in my eyes. I'm going to Bexley, to find my brother and bring him home. We'll clean up this mess together, then leave. I've searched everywhere except for that place because of the puzzling message that threw me off. It claimed he wasn't at college, but still here. It's my last option, and if he isn't there . . . fuck, I don't want to think about it.

Mom's asleep on the couch, her soft snores filling the room. I pull up the blanket that's fallen to the ground, bringing it up to her chin, and press a gentle kiss against her forehead. While she may not excel at motherhood, the absence of Gavin and the disappearance of her supply has allowed her to rediscover her true self. I've been avoiding her when she's coming down because it's not a pretty sight. I have no idea how long it will last this time, but I hope it does.

As I shut the front door behind me, a refreshing breeze caresses my cheeks, leaving them chilled. With my bag securely on my back, I pull the hood over my head and begin my stroll through the park. My feet crunch on the dirt as I power walk to the end of the road. Waiting at the bus stop, I lean back against the pole and listen to the distant sounds of traffic.

Up ahead, a car's headlights beam brightly, forcing me to shield my eyes. Tires screech loudly as it halts in front of me. The moment I withdraw my hand, a stunning black Bentley Mulliner Batur with heavily tinted windows materializes before me. No fucking way.

Gage jumps out of the driver's side and leans against the hood. He runs his fingers through his wet, curly black hair, shaking off droplets of water. He looks all fresh and showered, like he just drove here.

"Get in the fucking car, LeClair," he demands, and I shake my head.

"Not happening. I've got shit to do today that doesn't involve you."

"I know, and we're taking you."

"How the hell do you know? Can you suddenly mind read?" I snap.

"Look, we don't have time for your little games. We're going looking for your brother in Bexley and you're coming with us."

The window of the passenger side slides down, and Lucas pokes his head out.

"Get in the car, little thorn. We're going on a road trip,

and look," he says with a grin. He pulls up bags of candy and chips. "We got snacks."

I fight back the urge to smile. "What if I refuse?" I ask, gripping the straps of my backpack.

"I'll force you inside and I won't be gentle," Gage says before sliding back into the car, and I groan. They won't leave and I can't be bothered fighting them further. I may have better luck finding Alec if they are with me—they may not have any authority in Bexley but their reputation will.

The back door opens, and I slide inside. I put my bag on the seat between Hazen and myself. His mouth curls into a lopsided grin before he returns his gaze to the window.

Gage speeds off just as the bus approaches and pulls into the stop.

Lucas turns around and waves his phone at me from the passenger seat.

"I made us a playlist on the way here. Any requests?"

I shake my head. "Whatever will drown out Gage, I'm all ears."

Lucas starts laughing and Gage floors it, launching us onto the motorway. As I lean back against the headrest, I can already feel the strain in my neck—this drive is going to be a long one.

After four hours, we finally exit the motorway and enter Bexley. The taste of sweetness still lingers on my tongue, but my stomach protests with a dull ache after devouring all the candies Lucas gave me.

As I sit up straighter, I fix my gaze out the window, where I watch the houses whiz by in a blur. Bexley is significantly larger than Daring, more than twice or even three times its size. It's where you escape to if you want an education or just to get out of Daring. Just like we planned. Not many make it here without The Brotherhood's approval.

I'm desperately holding onto the hope that my brother is hiding somewhere in this place, so we can finally reunite and leave this chaos behind.

Out the front of a massive building that resembles something out of the eighteenth century, we park our car in the parking lot. The gothic building casts a shadow over the front quad, with people scattered everywhere, chatting, soaking up the sun, and appearing to be thoroughly enjoying themselves. Jealousy churns in the depths of my stomach.

Alec has been insisting that I join him here to study something, but I've never known what. While he has a scholarship to play ball, I don't have any opportunities. My plan all along was simple: work now, worry about the details later. This move was always for Alec—he deserves the chance at a better life—and for Mom. It doesn't matter what I want to do. Alec's dream coming true and Mom getting sober are the only things that matter.

Once the car engine turns off, I snatch my bag and practically spring out. Stretching my hands over my head, I can feel the tension in my muscles after being in the car for so long.

"Freya, wait," Lucas says, slamming his door shut.

"Thanks for the ride, but I've got it from here," I reply, throwing my backpack on, and I start walking through the quad.

As a hand wraps around mine, I instinctively try to pull away, but Lucas firmly intertwines his fingers with mine, making it impossible to break free. I'm torn between pushing him away and not wanting to. Having him here—and even *them*—makes this easier. More bearable. Where the hell are you, Alec? I glance around the quad, but there are people everywhere.

Gage and Hazen join us. "Let's start with the head office and go from there," Gage says, walking off in front.

As we move toward the building, I can feel the weight of people's gazes on us. As the whispers begin, my eyes dart around, desperately searching for any sign of his whereabouts. Or any glimpse of his black hair. Just show yourself already, Alec. Please. With my phone in hand, I dial Alec's number, only to be greeted by his voicemail, just like every other time.

"Alec, we are at Bexley. If you are here, please come see me," I say, leaving the message for him.

"We'll find him," Lucas says, his voice filled with determination, and I bite my lip, silently praying for his words to come true. If Alec isn't here, then I have no clue where he could be. This is the last possible place I could think of to search. Gage leads the way up the stairs, the stone steps echoing our footfalls throughout a grand foyer.

At the top of the first landing, my eyes are immediately drawn to an old wooden desk that stretches across the vast expanse, and I inhale sharply. A towering bookshelf stretches out behind it, packed with an endless array of books. Wow. It's beautiful. Past the desk and bookshelf, stairs ascend to a higher level.

"Can I help you?" a young woman with black-rimmed glasses asks from behind the desk. Her brown hair is sitting on top of her head in a tight bun.

Gage tries to speak, but I quickly step forward, releasing my hand from Lucas's grasp. I hate to admit I immediately miss its warmth. "Are you able to check your records to see if Alec LeClair is here?" I ask, resting my elbows on the desk.

"We can't look up records without that person's consent. Is he a friend or relative?" she asks.

I reach into my back pocket and pull out my card holder, giving her my ID. "He's my brother."

She takes it and types away on her computer, pausing intermittently to push her glasses up her nose.

"Oh, yes, you're down as his emergency contact. He's registered to start this term, but he hasn't signed in according to our records," she says, and my stomach does a flip-flop, threatening to expel the piece of toast I ate for breakfast.

"Are you sure?" I push, praying she's made a mistake.

"Yes, sorry. Is there anything else I can help you with?" she asks.

If he's not here, then he must be somewhere else—but where? Maybe she'll know the guy that he's going to rent the room from. What's his name? I try to rack my brain to remember. Was it Jeremy? Anthony? I rub my fingers into my temples. Levi, it's Levi.

"Do you know—"

"Gage Ledger. What the fuck are you doing here?" a deep voice asks from somewhere behind us, and I catch the girl behind the desk rolling her eyes before she continues typing away on the computer.

My heart races as I spin around, only to be confronted by three guys closing in on us from all sides.

Chapter Twenty-Two
Gage

Turning around, I'm face to face with Uriah Pierce, Rune Fox, and Aydan Bardot. Uriah crosses his arms over his broad chest, and his blond hair has grown since the last time I saw him, sitting just above his shoulders. With a grin on his face, Rune runs his thumb across his lip and focuses intently on Freya. My stomach stirs, and I fight the urge to claim her in front of them. Despite knowing she will never be mine, the sight of Rune staring at her fills me with anger.

Lucas embraces Freya by wrapping his arm around her, and she doesn't push him away. I'm not the only one who wants to emphasize that she is off-limits. I can't even remember the last time I saw Uriah with a girl, but Rune is a player through and through. He lives and breathes pussy just like his cousin Lucas.

Aydan's face is buried in his phone as he hangs back, his fingers tapping away on the screen, his brown hair falling just above his eyes. I don't think I've ever heard a sound escape his lips. My gaze returns to Uriah.

"You know we like to keep you boys on your feet and do check-ins," I say, and Uriah scoffs.

"You've been trying to recruit us for how many years now?"

I shake my head. "You may not be patched in, but you know as well as I do that we own you and nothing goes on here without us knowing."

Uriah laughs. "Well, apparently, something has. What brings you here?"

As I open my mouth, Freya breaks free from Lucas's grasp and takes a step forward, shaking herself off. "My brother, Alec LeClair, is missing and I'm looking for him. Have you seen or heard anything?"

Closing the gap between them, Rune steps forward until their faces are mere inches apart. Each breath I take is erratic and unsteady, leaving me feeling out of control. I tighten my fists into balls and catch Uriah's eyes moving between me and Freya. Rune reaches out, his fingers delicately brushing a stray piece of hair behind Freya's ear. Before I can move, Lucas forcefully shoves Rune in the chest.

"Don't touch her. She's mine," Lucas growls, and Rune laughs, raising his hands up in surrender.

"Oh, cousin, you know how to pick them, don't you?" He winks, and Lucas grins, bringing Rune in for a hug and slapping him on the shoulder. "We could share?" Rune suggests, and Lucas shoves him backward again. He puts his hands up in surrender with that signature Fox smirk.

Freya huffs. "Have you seen him or not?"

"Sorry, sweetheart, the name doesn't ring a bell."

She pulls out her phone and shoves it in his face. I hold back a chuckle at her forwardness as he shakes his head.

"What about some guy named Levi?" she asks, and Rune nods.

"If it's the Levi I know, then he'll be at the grave tonight," Rune says, and I curse under my breath.

"The grave?" she asks.

"Your boy here knows. See you there." Rune points to me and I roll my eyes. "Oh, and it's dress-up, so make sure you come as your favorite villain or no entry."

For fuck's sake. The grave is a nightmare, and I loathe going, but now Freya has a lead, so there isn't a choice. Alec owes us some answers and needs to pay for stealing from The Brotherhood. If we are going to find Levi here, Rune is right—he'll be at that party.

Hours later, we're at a hotel with bags full of dress-up clothes lying on the bed. Freya takes her costume and slams the bathroom door shut. I pick up my green suit with large purple question marks and shake my head toward Lucas, who's sprawled out on the bed with a snake candy between his teeth.

"You seriously had to go with themed costumes?" I ask, and he grins, biting into the snake.

"You left me in charge, so Batman it is."

Hazen hastily snatches his comically exaggerated Bane ensemble, complete with skin-tight leather pants and a revealing V-neck singlet. He doesn't mutter a word as he gets dressed. He's been quiet pretty much the whole day, and I have no idea if it's because she's with us or if something else is going on.

I begrudgingly slip into the foolish suit, adamantly refusing to wear the matching green hat, which I leave untouched on the bed. The bathroom door opens, then closes, and I look up . . . fucking hell. The room is completely silent, and I can hear my heart pounding in my ears.

Freya is now wearing the Harley Quinn outfit chosen by Lucas, and I take back all my previous statements. Lucas picking these outfits is a blessing in disguise, or a curse, because my cock is begging to be touched by her and her only.

In fishnet stockings, and red and blue shorts that ride up her thighs, she turns to grab a glass from the kitchen cupboard, showing off half of her perfectly shaped ass. God damn. Her dark hair is in pigtails and her eyes are painted with heavy eye makeup. A small heart rests on her cheek. She's got a gold collar around her neck saying "Joker," and the tight white T-shirt makes my cock twitch. She's fucking perfect.

The bed squeaks and Lucas rolls off it, moving across the room like a predator stalking prey. Grabbing the back of Freya's neck, he claims her lips. She tries to shove him away but eventually gives in. I wait for the pang of jealousy to hit me, but it never comes. There's no denying I want her, and the more time we spend together, the further I fall—but I can't. She's better off without me and without us. The sooner we find her brother, the better, and we can all move on with our lives. However, the more I say that the more it doesn't feel right.

I turn away, catching Hazen watching them intently. Does he want her, too? I see the way he looks at her, more than he's ever looked at a female before. He's been with girls before, of course, but he's never shown any interest beyond hook-ups. Not until her. I get it, I really do, but we can't get attached to her.

My father always used to say that women were mere distractions and to never let anyone get close to your heart because they will rip it out at any chance they get. According to him, women only had one job: to look good for appearances. But even then, if my mother looked too good, father used to punish her. If anyone looked at her for too long, it was her fault for making them. Then, when she got sick, my father took off and left her to fend for herself. It was apparently too much for him to see her like that—a shell of a person—but I knew better. He didn't want to look after her; she was useless to him. And the funny twist was he ended up dying before her.

Every girl I've ever met and spent time with only had one use for me: to get my dick wet. And I never let them get close, just like father always taught me. But Freya is like an itch, and no matter how much I scratch, it won't go away. She's an infection that I can't shake.

Freya isn't the type of woman to just look good for appearances. No, she's someone who fights beside you. She's an equal. If my father was alive now and heard me say that, I'd have a bullet to my head.

"Harley Quinn needs her Joker, doesn't she?" Lucas says, kissing her neck, and Freya swats him away playfully.

There's a knock at the door and Hazen looks through the peephole before opening it and taking a couple of pizza boxes from the delivery driver. He places them down on the table and Freya digs in.

Lucas starts getting dressed in his ridiculous Joker outfit, complete with vibrant purple pants and a flamboyant green coat. I get now why he chose these, so he could be her Joker. I shake my head, trying to resist the temptation to wipe that self-satisfied grin off his face.

We eat in relative silence, and Freya keeps checking her

phone. Like she's counting down the seconds until we leave for the party. I get it. I didn't say anything to her or the guys, but if Uriah, Rune, and Aydan haven't seen or heard about Alec, then I didn't like our chances of finding him, but hopefully, this Levi guy has answers for us.

Whatever the case, we need to wrap this up quickly and get back home. I don't like being away from Daring for too long because that's when shit goes down, and some people think it's okay to break the rules. The clean-up is never pretty.

For the next couple of hours, we sit on the couch, mind-lessly eating snacks and flipping through mind-numbing TV channels, while I observe her growing more and more restless. Her fingernails must be worn at the buds from her constant biting. She's on the king-sized bed next to Lucas. With the last-minute plan, the hotel only had one room left with one bed. I don't plan on staying long, but if we need it, it's here.

"Can we go already?" she asks, rubbing her eye and smudging some of her red eye makeup.

"Soon. Party doesn't start until late, little thorn. I've told you this already," Lucas says.

"Make time go quicker," she snaps, and I snort.

"We will get there soon enough. You think I like being dressed up in this stupid-ass outfit?" I ask, running a hand down my pants. The more I look at the bright green, the more my eyes bleed.

"I think you love it," she replies, raising her eyebrow.

"Let's fucking go," Hazen snaps, pushing back the chair opposite mine. He storms out, slamming the door shut. Well okay then.

Freya doesn't have to be told twice—she's up and out

the door within the next second. Lucas takes his time rolling off the bed.

"What's up with Hazen?" I ask.

"Beats me." Lucas shrugs.

We follow them out and jump into my car. The drive out to the grave is silent. Freya taps away on the door handle, pushing the window up and down until I can't stand the sound any longer. I hold my breath, not wanting to start anything. We need to keep close to her tonight if these parties are anything like I remember.

I pull down a dirt road that leads into the forest, coming to a stop outside a rusty set of gates. There are a couple of men guarding it, and one comes over. Winding down my window, I make eye contact with him, and he freezes. His mouth opens, then closes before he motions for the other guard to open the gate. Smart move.

Continuing on the dirt track, the car jostles and bumps along, sending vibrations through the steering wheel. The trees grow thicker and more tightly packed together, forming a natural barrier around our car. Up ahead, a large fire casts flickering light, dancing into the dark night. We reach a small opening where several cars are parked together. I pull up next to a worn-down pick-up truck and pray that no one touches or hits my baby. I'm not looking for an excuse to spill blood tonight.

As soon as I switch off the car, Freya is out the door and gone. I curse—there goes the plan of not losing her tonight. I slide out, holding Hazen's door for him, and before he takes one step I grab onto his elbow. He looks up.

"You good, bro?" I ask, and he nods, then rips free of my hold and storms off after Freya. Apparently not.

Lucas falls into step beside me. There's a large bonfire up ahead casting shadows into the night. A few people surround it, talking amongst themselves. They're all dressed in different villain outfits, just like Rune said. Freya starts talking to a few people and flashing her phone screen at them. She moves quickly before disappearing again up ahead. It's going to be a fun night babysitting her ass.

Beyond the fire, there's the entrance to the graveyard— an old, worn-down fence—then grave upon grave. Rather than being disturbed, I find comfort in the midst of the deceased; it's a welcome relief. At least the dead know how to be silent.

Chapter Twenty-Three
Freya

Hazen sticks to me like glue as I navigate through the crowd. I urgently question every person I come across about the whereabouts of my brother, flashing them the last photo I took of him at the diner, cooking burgers with a playful grin on his face. Tears well up in my eyes, their sting threatening to spill over, but I fight back the urge to cry. I can't. Tonight, my mission is to find Alec, no matter what. At this point, I've reached my limit, and I'm going to make sure my brother comes back with me.

We move further into the graveyard, but it becomes quieter. The fading light makes it increasingly difficult to see, but the faint strains of music still reach our ears from somewhere to our right. Hazen lifts out his phone, its bright torch illuminating the darkness.

"From memory, the actual party is underground. I just can't remember which one's the entrance," Hazen says, then something catches his eye and we move toward it.

As we get closer, the bass of the music reverberates through the air, growing more intense. We come to a halt in front of an imposing mausoleum, guarded by two sturdy iron doors. With a determined stride, Hazen steps forward and applies pressure to the door, and it opens with a reluctant squeal. As he slips away into the shadows, I follow him without any second thought.

I am surrounded by darkness as it wraps around me tightly. The unmistakable sound of footsteps crunching against the dirt floor reaches my ears, followed by a hand grasping mine. My scream escapes, but I quickly clamp my hand over my mouth to stifle the end of it.

"Shh, just me," Hazen whispers.

I cling to his intertwined fingers like my life depends on it—because it does. I'm with one of The Brotherhood members in a dark chamber in a graveyard. Stupid move.

My heart hammers against my ribcage, threatening to burst. As we walk further, the bass of the music reverberates through the air, growing increasingly louder. We follow it through the dark tunnel, the musty smell of damp earth getting stronger with each step. A faint light finally begins to erratically dance and twirl across the walls, and we hurry forward until a burst of brightness blinds me, stopping me in my tracks. Shielding my eyes with my other hand, I blink a few times until my vision adjusts.

The tunnel leads to a spacious cave filled with people dancing and chatting. A DJ is set up and music pours from the speakers. I was not expecting this at all.

"Wow," I breathe.

Hazen leans down closer to me so I can hear him over the music. "Yeah, the guys know how to throw parties here. Pretty sick."

Something lands on my shoulder, and I jump. Whirling around, I find Lucas grinning at me. Hazen drops my hand instantly, and I miss the warmth. Lucas wraps me under his arm, and I can't help but lean in, relishing the comforting heat he provides.

"Anything yet?" he whispers in my ear, and I shake my head.

"Come on, let's get a drink and ask around," he says, and we start moving through the thick crowd. A few people get out of our way, but others don't budge until Lucas makes them.

I lean my elbows down on the black gothic-looking bar with imprints of skulls on its surface. Lucas orders us some drinks while I turn to the girl next to me, tapping her on the shoulder. She offers me a warm smile and I lean in, practically yelling in her ear so she can hear me over the music.

"Do you know where I can find someone named Levi?"

"Levi Asher?" she asks, and I nod, guessing that's his last name because I have no idea.

"Yeah, he's working behind the bar." She spins around, pointing at a guy behind the bar with a bald head. "That's him," she says.

"Thank you so much."

Lucas shoves a shot glass in front of me and I raise an eyebrow. The corner of his mouth lifts before he clinks it with mine and downs it. I follow suit. It burns as it makes its way down my throat, and I put the empty glass back on the bar.

I move through the crowd to the other side of the bar where Levi is pouring out shots. I squirm through two guys and pop up in front of him. He hands off the shots, then leans over the bar.

"What can I getcha, cutie?" he asks in a smooth tone.

"Answers," I say, and he cocks his head to the side. "Have you seen my brother, Alec LeClair? He was going to rent a couple of rooms from you."

Levi frowns, looking over my shoulder as warmth fills my back, and I don't have to turn to know who's there. Lucas lands his arms on either side of the bar, caging me in, and leans his head on my shoulder.

"Answer her. Now," Lucas growls, his breath tickling my ear and sending shivers down my spine.

Levi raises his hands up before leaning over the bar. "Huh, you don't look anything like your brother, apart from your eyes." He frowns before shaking his head. "I haven't seen him since he checked out the place a couple of months ago."

My heart sinks, and everything around me fades away into the background. If Alec isn't here, then I have no idea where he is. The last bit of hope I held of finding him shatters into a million little pieces.

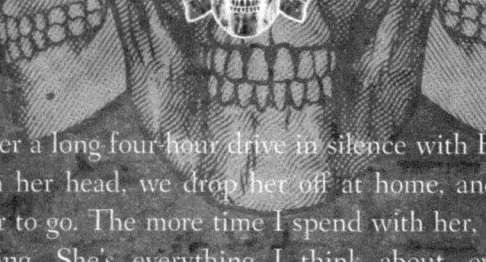

Chapter Twenty-Four
Lucas

After a long four-hour drive in silence with Freya lost in her head, we drop her off at home, and I don't want her to go. The more time I spend with her, the more I'm falling. She's everything I think about, everything revolves around her. I want to be near her every second of the day, and it's making me crazy. Like a lovesick puppy. I've never been like this with anyone. Girls flock to me like bees to honey, and I used to love the attention, but now I don't care for it. I want more—but only with her.

"I don't think we'll be finding Alec alive. Not now we know he isn't in Bexley," Gage says, pulling up to my place.

"Just don't go opening your big mouth around Freya. She's still holding out hope," I say, shaking my head.

"One thing I don't understand is why we haven't gotten any information yet. We know everything going on here," Hazen says from the backseat.

"We'll keep looking, and one way or another, we will find him. Let's hope for our sake, and hers, he's still alive," Gage mutters, then pulls out his phone and starts typing away.

"See you tomorrow for training," I say, before slipping out the door.

I walk up the front steps. The door opens and my mother's there, leaning against the frame, her silk nighty wrapped around her body. Fucking hell. I just want nothing more than to go to bed.

"Where have you been?" she asks, ushering me inside.

It's sad that I'm twenty-three, still living at home, and getting grilled by my mother about where I've been. Fuck my life. Dominic may be a distant father, but it's better than coming home to this and a father who's practically dead.

"In Bexley with Freya, helping her look for her brother," I say with a yawn. She crosses her arms over her chest.

"What have I told you? Keep away from that girl. She's nothing but a distraction." She sighs, walking over and placing a hand on my shoulder. "You've got to keep focused on the endgame: ruling over The Brotherhood. Now that your father is on his deathbed, I'm counting on you. We need to keep up appearances, and all of this"—she gestures up and down her body, then around the house—"doesn't pay for itself."

"I know, Mom," I say, biting back any smartass remark. It's late and I can't be bothered.

All she cares about is what effect my father's dying will have on her lifestyle. My father's been in and out of treatment for years and my mother never checks on him. She's just waiting for the day he's gone. Their marriage has just been for appearances. There's no love there, never has been. It's why I never believed in it either until Freya came back into my life. Her claws have tightened around my heart and there's no releasing them. But I still love my mother, and as far as parents go, she's got my back.

"I'll try to stay away," I reply because what harm will a little white lie do?

"Good boy," she says before kissing me on the cheek, and part of me clings onto that approval from her. She might drive me insane, but I do love her and the way she protects me. It feels good to know someone cares enough about me.

I take the stairs two at a time, holding back the scream I want to release. I reach my door but stop. Faint music and light comes from across the hallway in my little sister's room. Turning around, I knock on the door before slowly opening it. Her small body is engulfed in her king-size bed, and she's got a book in her hands. She looks over the top of it and smiles.

"Lucas," she says with a big smile, and all my anger from moments ago vanishes.

I move over to the other side of her bed and jump in. She cuddles up beside me, passing me her book.

"Hey, princess. Whatcha reading?"

"A fairytale about a long-lost princess who finds her prince charming. Are all boys like the princes in my fairy-tale books?" she asks.

I don't want to break her eight-year-old heart, but I also don't want her thinking about boys—not now, not ever. I'll spend my whole life protecting her from them. My father signed a contract about marrying her off to another Brother-hood in another state. Over my dead body will that ever happen.

My family has only ever cared about what use we are to them and how we affect their reputations. My father raised me to be a ruthless member of The Brotherhood. He taught me to never let my emotions get the better of me, and to never let anyone close because they are just distractions.

They take our attention off our duty of making everyone fall at our feet as the upcoming leaders of Daring. He always said love was for the weak. I used to believe it all, take everything in like a sponge, and I never liked disobeying him or my mother. I wanted their approval—I craved it. But since Freya's been around, everything has changed.

My father was right about one thing: emotions are distractions. Because every thought I have is of her. Wanting to be around her and needing to gain her approval. But he was wrong about saying love is for the weak because the love I feel for my sister, Layla, isn't weak. It keeps my heart beating on the bad days. Those days when everything is too much, when I remember every evil thing I've done to be part of—and eventually lead—The Brotherhood.

"Some are, Layla, but some are like those villains you read about. They aren't good people," I say, and she frowns, leaning further into my body and wrapping her arm over my chest. I don't tell her I'm one of the bad guys, that I'm a villain, because she wouldn't believe me. That's the problem—villains aren't easy to find, they hide in plain sight.

What if Freya is a villain and she's been playing us this whole time? Maybe she's the one who got rid of her brother? What if this has all been a ploy to get close to us? I shake my head. Fuck no, she's been too distraught over her brother. The pain's written all over her face; there's no way she's that good at acting. I know real pain when I see it.

"So, I just need to find the good ones?"

"Why don't you leave that to me?"

She screws up her nose but doesn't argue with me. "Read to me?"

I read to her until her eyes droop, and she falls asleep with her head against my heart. Her soft snores are like music to my ears. She's so young and innocent, and I just wish she was born into a different family, into a different world. Her future isn't pretty, but I'll do everything in my power to change that. When I'm in charge, things will be different.

As quietly as I can, I sneak out of her room, shutting her door behind me and heading into mine. Darkness surrounds me, broken up by the faint light of the full moon coming through my window. I grab a towel from the bathroom cupboard, shuck off my clothes, and step into the shower. The hot water drowns the last of my lingering tension, and I'm finally surrounded by soothing white noise. All the questions I have about Freya and the things I want come flooding in.

The way her body looked in that Harley Quinn outfit, the way the fabric curved against her ass. Fuck. I grab my cock, stroking up and down. Closing my eyes, I fall back against the shower wall.

I can still taste her lips on mine and remember the way her tongue danced alongside mine. I yearn to wrap my fist around her long, dark hair, pulling it back until her scalp burns and her eyes stare into my soul. I want to watch her lips swallow my cock. My breathing gets heavier and heavier. Her teeth will scrape against my shaft just enough to feel the burn, then her tongue will lick me clean. Fuck. Shit. Damn! Cum shoots from my cock and lands on the shower door. Holy hell, I'll never get over this girl.

I finish my shower in a daze, towel off, and drag my tired ass out of the bathroom, leaving the cum for the maids to clean up because I'm just that kind of guy.

Chapter Twenty-Five
Freya

I spend every available moment outside of work over the next week searching for Alec and hoping to find any leads, but it seems nobody has any information. Well, that's at least what I'm uncovering. There is information that someone is withholding, but no one is willing to share it. The longer it takes, the heavier the knot of worry becomes in the pit of my stomach. No matter how many leads I pursue, they always end up at dead ends.

I've never gone this long without seeing or speaking to my brother. It's killing me, but I won't give up. I can't. I will find him—I have to.

I've been coming and going from Lucas's and Gage's places, and they have been helping me where they can. The more time I'm spending with them, the more I'm finding out about them and their roles within The Brotherhood. I've always known it's run by the three founding families: the Hendrixes, Ledgers, and the Foxes.

The grail is getting passed down to them soon when Dominic finally retires. The rules are that everyone has to retire before handing it over. Lucas's father, George, retired years ago; he's got cancer and isn't doing well. Lucas doesn't talk about him much. Gage's father, Julian, died years ago, and Amirah didn't even shed a tear. She hated him and what he did to her and Gage. I met him once, and that was enough. The guy reeked of evil, and he never smiled or showed an ounce of emotion. The stories Amirah shared with me still haunt my dreams.

"You've been spending a lot of time over here lately, and with Gage," Amirah says, dropping a set of blue jeans and a top onto her bed. I sit up, leaning back against her pillows, and cock my head to the side.

"Is this you asking if I'm fucking your brother again?"

"Yeah?"

"No. There is nothing going on between Gage and me. I still hate him, but they are all helping me find Alec. They may want him found for different reasons than me, but I'll use all the help I can get," I say, pinching the bridge of my nose as I try to fight off the headache pounding between my eyes. The lack of sleep is starting to take its toll on me. My thoughts are tangled and chaotic, making it impossible for me to focus.

"Okay. We will find him. Promise," Amirah says, sitting down on the edge of the bed next to me.

"Don't say that. No one can make that promise." I sink into the soft pillow, gazing up at the pristine white ceiling above me.

"Have a little rest before Gage comes back." Amirah throws a blanket over me, and my eyes become heavy.

I can't afford to sleep—Alec is out there, and he needs me. I have to spend every minute looking for him. My thoughts eventually wander and become distant . . . then everything disappears.

My phone vibrates against my leg, and I jolt up, the

room coming back into view. Amirah is next to me on the bed, her Kindle in her hands.

"You still snore like a suffocating dog." She laughs, and I roll my eyes.

Lifting my phone out, I glance down at a message on the screen from an unknown number. My heart beats faster and faster. Is it Alec?

Tick tock, tick tock. Better run quick, sighting at Magick.

I sit up straight, gripping my phone as I read the words over and over again. I still have no idea who is sending these messages. Lucas's guy is having trouble tracking down the owner. Whoever it is, they are good at keeping their identity hidden. But it doesn't matter because this is a lead at least, and I'll take whatever I can get.

"Is Magick Club still open?" I ask Amirah, jumping off the bed, and she frowns.

"Yeah, why?"

"We're going out tonight," I say, shoving my phone in my back pocket and moving toward her closet.

Amirah comes up behind me as I hastily search through her clothes, finally finding a black denim skirt.

"Not that I'm complaining, but why are we suddenly going out?" Amirah moves in behind me and her eyes immediately lock onto the skirt. She heads to one of the drawers and retrieves a red lace bralette. She gives it to me, and I begin to pull my shorts down.

"I just got a lead."

Her brows furrow. "From that unknown number again?"

I nod, and Amirah presses her lips together. "Should we trust some freak who's sending cryptic messages?"

"That's all I've got, so yes." I slip into my outfit, and Amirah pulls out a black leather dress.

We spend the next thirty minutes getting ready before heading down the stairs. With each step, the sound of my knee-high boots echoes through the foyer as they click against the smooth marble. The front door creaks open and slams shut. I glance up and meet Gage's gaze, and for a brief moment, time seems to stand still. My heart dances a silly rhythm inside my chest. He's wearing black running shorts and nothing else, exposing his bare chest. Fuck. There's no denying the way his body makes me feel, but it's his mouth that usually ruins it all.

"Where the fuck do you think you're going looking like that?" he snaps. Case in point.

"Excuse me?" I walk down the last few steps, with Amirah right behind me, and straight up to him.

His eyes remain fixed on mine, and I can't help but notice the gentle rise and fall of his muscular chest.

"You heard. Where are you two going?"

I open my mouth, but Amirah beats me to it. "Fuck off, Gage. We are going out. That's all you need to know."

"The fuck you are," he growls, folding his arms over his chest, his jaw clenched.

Swiftly sidestepping him, I make my way toward the front door, eager to escape him. I'm done with this shit. We got a lead and we've already wasted enough time.

Moving at lightning speed, Gage swiftly blocks the front door, bringing himself inches away from my face. Beads of sweat glisten on his sculpted torso, making it hard for me to focus. Alec needs me.

"Move out of the way *now*, or else," I grit out.

"Or else what?" He raises an eyebrow, and I squeeze my hands into fists.

"Just move, Gage, we need to go," Amirah pleads from somewhere behind me.

"I'm coming with you."

"The hell you are," I say, my head pounding, and I squeeze my eyes shut, then open.

Gage steps aside as the door pushes open. Lucas and Hazen come in, and Lucas gives me a slow, suggestive whistle.

Amirah uses the guys' distraction against them by grabbing my hand and pulling me out the open front door.

Gage yells something behind us, but we ignore him. A car's already waiting for us, and we slide in.

"Step on it, Phillip," Amirah says from the backseat.

I look back through the window, and Gage is standing at the front door with his phone to his ear, his eyes never leaving mine. He'll find out where we are going, but at least we have a head start. I don't need any distractions tonight, and those three guys are nothing but.

We make it to the nightclub on the elite side of town within minutes. There's a line down the block, and I curse under my breath. Phillip opens my door, and I step out, meeting Amirah on the curb.

"We'll never get in," I say, and Amirah laughs. Fuck, maybe I should have let Gage tag along to get us in before I ditched him.

"You still underestimate my family name." She takes my hand and walks us up to the front of the club. The security guard takes one look at her, then lets us through.

Vibrations from the music reverberate off the corridor walls, engulfing me. We continue walking until the corridor ends, opening up into chaos. In the middle of the room, there is a bustling bar, surrounded by a lively crowd of people. There's a stage with a DJ set up in the middle, and people dance and sit at tables scattered around.

Amirah grabs my hand, pulling me toward the bar, and she wedges herself between two guys. I pull up a photo of Alec on my phone and show it around to a few people nearby. Each person either shakes their head or doesn't even give me the time of day. Fucking assholes. Imagine if one of their loved ones went missing? Surely they would be out doing the same thing.

Looking out into the crowded dance floor, I catch a glimpse of a familiar face. Mia is sitting back against the wall, her face in her phone.

I turn back to Amirah. "Mia is here," I say, and Amirah's nose screws up.

"Let's go." Amirah grabs my arm, pulling me through a sea of people toward Mia.

Mia looks up, then smiles and pulls me in for a hug, but her body is stiff against mine. I've never liked the girl, but my brother did, so that means something.

"What are you doing here?" I ask.

"Have you heard from him?" She completely ignores my question.

"No, have you?"

She shakes her head, looking past me. "I've never gone this long without talking with him. I'm worried," she says, her eyes filling with tears.

Amirah scoffs and I elbow her.

"Me too. What were you doing in Dominic's office the other day?" I ask the question that's been at the back of my mind.

Mia shifts uncomfortably, and I step forward, closing in on her. She looks everywhere but at me.

"He was helping me with some research papers for an article I'm writing," she says, and Amirah scoffs behind me.

"It seemed to be a little more than that. You looked awfully comfortable on his couch," I say, raising an eyebrow.

"It's not what it looked like—I love Alec," Mia pleads, reaching out to grab my hand, but I pull it away, taking a couple of steps back. I don't believe her, but I need to keep looking. I won't get anywhere standing here talking with her. We say goodbye, and I promise her I'll message as soon as I hear anything. Amirah and I head back to the bar, and I tap on a large guy's shoulder. He turns around, towering over me. He smiles, and it works to make him appear slightly less intimidating.

I motion for him to lean down, then whisper in his ear so he can hear me over the music, "Have you seen this guy?" I show him the photo and he takes my phone from my hand.

He taps out something on it before handing it back to me. The messages app is open, displaying a message to an unknown number.

Meet me near the bathroom.

I look up, frowning, but he's disappeared into the crowd. It's stupid meeting a stranger in a quieter place, but it's the first lead I have. The *only* lead, actually, so I have to do this.

Amirah turns around, handing me a glass with something pink inside.

"I'll be back. Just got a lead," I say, and Amirah shakes her head.

"I'll come with you."

"No, it's fine. Just find us somewhere to sit and I'll be back soon," I say, moving into the crowd before she can argue any further. Bringing the straw to my lips, I take a drink, and before I get to the bathroom sign, I finish it.

Handing it off to a passing waiter, I make my way through the crowded corridor, the dim lighting casting shadows around me. Leaning back against the wall, the guy from before looks up and flashes another warm smile. It's quieter down here and I can actually hear myself think.

"What do you know?" I ask, standing directly in front of him.

He lets out a low chuckle. "Straight to the point. You don't muck around, do you?"

I don't have time for pointless chit-chat. "Just tell me," I snap.

He glances down the hallway, searching for something or someone. "I could get killed for this, but you should know I saw your brother the night of the ball," he says, his gaze darting around.

"And?"

His eyes grow wide as he firmly clutches my shoulder. "Fuck. I can't. They will kill me. Sorry," he mutters before opening the emergency exit and fleeing.

I look back, and Gage, Lucas, and Hazen are storming toward me. What the hell? I don't think, I just follow after the guy, and the sound of their hurried footsteps fades into the distance. He's got answers and I need them.

Chapter Twenty-Six

Freya

Stepping out into a dark alleyway, I yell out to the guy running away. "Stop, please!"

He glances over his shoulder, a pained look in his eyes. The door behind me slams shut, and I whirl around. Gage has his gun raised and pointed toward the guy. When I look back, there is no sign of my informant. Fucking hell.

I turn to go back inside and come face to face with Gage, Lucas, and Hazen. "What the fuck is wrong with you?" I spit out, glaring at Gage.

He lowers his gun, nodding toward Hazen, who takes off after the guy.

"Leave him alone," I yell after Hazen, but he doesn't stop, ignoring me completely.

"What did he tell you?" Gage snaps, crossing his arms over his chest, his muscles bunching and shifting under his white shirt. Damn it. Can't get distracted.

I frown. "What are you hiding from me?"

A gust of wind sweeps down the alleyway, sending shivers down my spine and goosebumps across my skin. Lucas shrugs off his suit jacket, moves toward me, and places it over my shoulders before pressing a kiss against my forehead.

"Let's go home, little thorn," he says, wrapping me under his arm. I shake him off, stepping forward until I'm right in Gage's face.

"Tell me!"

"Ain't nothing to tell," Gage says, glaring.

"And you're a fucking liar," I throw back, barging past him toward the club's back door.

I've lost my sole lead, and they completely messed it up. I was starting to trust them, building something that I didn't quite understand myself, and now that's all gone up in flames. It pisses me off that they know more than me. He's my brother. How could they keep information from me? Because they are The Brotherhood and that will always come first for them. I was foolish to think I could compete with that.

"Freya, wait," Lucas yells, but I flip them both off, then drop his jacket to the ground before opening the emergency exit door and slamming it in their faces.

I find Amirah at the bar, chatting with a couple of older guys.

"You okay?" she asks, pulling me next to her, between her and one of the guys.

"No, your brother is an asshole, and he ruined my only lead."

She rolls her eyes. "Tell me something I don't already know."

She hands me a shot, and I quickly gulp it down, feeling the warmth spread through my body. With a grin, she hands me one after another, causing my head to spin. I sense my trio of stalkers' gazes upon me and a chill runs down my spine, but I choose to ignore it—and them.

Amirah grabs my hand, and we navigate through the crowd and onto the dance floor. Moving my body to the beat of the music, I give myself a few minutes to unwind and forget about the chaos around me.

The heat of a body presses against my back as hands roam freely around my waist, and I give in. The stranger spins me, gripping the back of my neck, and without hesitation, I kiss him. His sloppy kisses have no effect on me, so I quickly pull away, wiping my mouth with the back of my hand. Oblivious, he moves closer and yells in my ear.

"Want to take this to the backseat of my car?"

A laugh escapes me as I shake my head. With a frown, he tightly grasps my arm, causing excruciating pain as I struggle to escape, but his grip is too powerful.

"Listen here, gutter slut. If I ask you to drop to your knees and suck my cock, you will. Now come with me."

With each forceful tug, he guides me through the sea of people, my anxiety intensifying as Amirah disappears from sigh. Fuck. No one stops him, and before I know it, we are out the front of the club. Moving back into the alleyway, he tightens his grip on me. With a strong push, he pins me against the building, the impact reverberating through my body as my back slams into the hard surface.

"Get down on your fucking knees, slut."

I remain frozen in place as he pushes me forcefully to the ground. The gravel bites into my knees, sending a jolt of pain through me. He lowers his pants, revealing his small, limp dick.

"Suck."

He grips my hair, forcing me forward, his cock hitting me in the face. I hold back the urge to vomit all over him. Oh shit, I can't. I empty everything I've drunk tonight all over his cock. He curses and laughter bubbles up from deep within me. His hand tightens around my throat, cutting off my air supply and leaving me gasping for breath.

A gunshot rings through the night, the grip disappears, and his body falls on top of me, knocking me onto my back. I scream. Blood covers my skin, and his lifeless, open eyes stare into mine. I continue screaming until his weight is lifted off me and then a pair of black shoes appears in my line of sight.

"Take her home. I'll finish off here," someone says from close by.

Someone grabs me under the arms, pulling me up. My knees buckle, and I fall, but he catches me and pulls me into his chest. I look up, and Hazen's blue eyes stare back at me. He pulls me closer, and I relax into him. The fight within me is gone.

"I'm taking you home," he says.

"No, I can't go there." If Mom sees me like this, she will freak, and I haven't liked being there without Alec. Too many memories.

Hazen's chest rises and falls against my ear.

"Take her to mine," Gage says from somewhere behind us.

"No! I'm not going anywhere with you. Where's Amirah?"

"Shut her up," Gage growls, and I want to punch him, but all my energy is gone. I melt further into Hazen's chest and my eyes close.

I must fall asleep because when I wake next, I'm in Gage's bathroom. Hazen places me on the edge of the vanity, but I don't want to turn my head and catch a glimpse of my own reflection. My arms are drenched in blood, its metallic scent filling the air.

Moving between my legs, Hazen lifts my head by running his finger along my jaw. His eyes clash with mine.

"I'd kill that fucker again and again for touching you like that," he says, his gaze intense.

Swallowing hard, I can't help but notice the undeniable truth etched across his expression.

"I know," I sigh out, and he runs his thumb over my cheek.

"Now, let's get you cleaned up. That fucker's blood needs to go."

As I ease myself down off the vanity, Hazen's hands glide over my stomach and my scars. I suck in a deep inhale, and he meets my gaze. He leans down, peppering kisses over my scars, and my heart swoons. He comes back up, pressing a light kiss against my lips as he raises the fabric of my bralette. Just as I turn around, he deftly unhooks the clasps, and I let it drop to the floor. Next, my denim skirt is gone along with my underwear.

The shower turns on and I spin around, getting an eyeful of Hazen's cock. I swallow hard—fuck. I shouldn't be seeing it, let alone lusting after it. My head is spinning with what happened tonight, and I feel like I'm drowning in a whirlwind of emotions. I want to leave because of what they did. After chasing away my only lead, they killed that guy without hesitation. He deserved it for what he did to me—but still.

I enter the walk-in shower with Hazen, and the drain soon fills with red-tinted water, the distinct scent of blood permeating the air. Collapsing against the tiled wall, I hold myself tight as tears blend with the flowing water.

Hazen remains silent as he reaches for a loofah and body wash. He approaches me and begins to wash the remaining blood from my skin. I don't move, frozen in place as I allow him to clean me. Tracing my jawline, his fingers guide my gaze up to his piercing blue eyes. His tongue touches his lips.

"I'm sorry," he whispers, then his lips gently claim mine. Before I can comprehend what's happening or kiss him back, he pulls away and rests his forehead against mine.

"Why?"

"Maybe one day you will understand why we have to do what we do, but until then you have to trust me. Okay?" He eases back further, but his hand remains on my chin, and his thumb comes up to rest on my bottom lip.

I open my mouth, but nothing comes out. I can't trust him or them. Trust doesn't come easy to me when I've spent my whole life being betrayed by people around me, including the one person who's meant to be there for me no matter what. I can't. The only people I trust are Alec, Kai, and Amirah.

"Where's the guy from the alleyway who had information for me?" I ask, and Hazen shakes his head.

"I'll deal with him—don't worry about it."

I shake my head. "I want the information he has."

"And you'll get it once I'm done with him," Hazen says just before a door slams shut somewhere nearby, and he pulls back, taking his warmth with him. There's someone shouting outside the bathroom.

"Fuck," Hazen bites out, stepping out of the shower and wrapping a towel around his waist.

Gage bursts into the room, slamming the bathroom door behind him. He looks at my dripping-wet, naked form, licks his lips, and my legs instinctively close. I'm disappointed by how my body responds to him.

"You have about fifteen seconds to get out before Amirah storms in here."

I step out of the shower and receive a fluffy white towel from Hazen. I quickly wrap the towel around my chest, the plush fabric soft against my skin.

Gage reaches for the door.

"What are you hiding from me? Do you know where Alec is?" I ask and Gage stops, hand on the handle.

"Nothing is as it seems, Freya," he says, then he's gone before I can figure out what that even means.

No wonder I can't trust anyone here when all they do is talk in riddles.

Amirah bursts through the door and rushes over to me, embracing me tightly. She withdraws and examines me.

"Are you okay? What the hell happened?" she asks in a rush.

"I'm fine. Let's go to your room," I say, and she tightly grips my hand, shooting a piercing glare at Hazen, who casually leans against the vanity.

Seated on Gage's bed, Lucas springs to his feet the moment we emerge from the bathroom. But with a simple shake of my head, he halts in his tracks, a pained look in his eyes.

As we make our way down the hallway, I let Amirah lead me into her cozy bedroom, and I'm ready to fall onto her bed. She retrieves a set of silk pajamas, and I change into them. Joining Amirah on her bed, I quickly twist my damp hair up into a bun.

At her urging, I recount what happened at the club after we were separated, and with each word that leaves my mouth, she becomes angrier and angrier.

"I love my brother, but when it comes to The Brotherhood, no one ever comes before that. They signed their lives away years ago, and I'm stuck here, too, until they figure out what Dominic wants to do with me." Amirah sighs, falling back onto her pillow. "What are you going to do?" she asks, and I shake my head.

"I think it's time to go to the police."

I've held off going to the local police, but I don't have any other choice. Alec has been missing for weeks now, and they might know something or could even help me find him.

Amirah sits up, looking down at me. "But they are corrupt and in The Brotherhood's pocket."

"I don't have any other choice. Maybe they know something I don't."

"Just be careful. I'll come with you," she says, and I nod.

My phone vibrates next to me, and when I pick it up and unlock the screen, my stomach sinks.

You could have saved your brother, but you're too late.

Chapter Twenty-Seven
Hazen

H is piercing screams reverberate through the shed, creating an eerie echo that bounces off the walls and back into my ears. The little bitch has been screaming like a little girl for hours but still hasn't muttered a word. I'm about ready to kill the fucker for wasting my time and energy.

"Next finger will be this one," I say, placing the vice around his index finger and pushing down.

He screams, tears falling down his pathetic face. "No! I told you everything I know."

"Bullshit. Where is he?" What I have managed to extract from him is absolutely useless; I already know it all. With so many men at our disposal, it's not necessary for me to be involved in this, but there's a special circumstance that sets it apart. This is personal, and I want to hear the truth fall from his lips. I want answers.

I've had enough. With a tight grip, I exert pressure until his finger separates, joining the other three on the bloody ground. Despite his wailing and thrashing, the restraints hold him firmly in the chair.

It's frustrating that he's still refusing to speak; he was ready to share something with Freya before, but now he's not playing ball. Looks like he doesn't give a fuck about his fingers. Next is his face.

I make my way to the wall where my tools are stored and pick out a carving knife. I run my thumb along its edge. I can't help but smile as I watch a drop of blood drip down my thumb, and I savor the metallic scent in the air.

The door creaks open, and Gage's eyes widen in horror as he takes in the sight of me, covered in blood. A shudder runs through his body. It's comical that he's so unnerved by the sight of blood, especially considering our occupation. Whenever he gets any on him, he has to spend hours cleaning it off.

"Any luck?" he asks, moving around the tarp that's surrounding the guy. He's being careful not to get anything on his shoes.

I shake my head, twirling the knife between my fingers. "I'm about to go Picasso on his face. Wanna watch?"

"Fuck no."

He departs with a forceful slam of the door, leaving me alone with my target. Just how I like it. No distractions, just me and him.

"Time to play a game, Jeremy."

Moving closer to him, I carefully step over his legs and settle down on the chair, which groans in protest. Tremors run through his legs as I lift the knife toward his face, carefully sliding it beneath his eye. I refrain from pushing too hard just yet, despite the blood trickling down his cheek.

He screams pitifully.

"I'm going to paint a picture on your beautiful face. One that even the famous Harry Potter can't compete with."

"Please, no!"

"It can all stop if you just tell me what you saw."

"I can't or he'll kill me."

"Who?"

"Please . . . no."

I chuckle. "You're dead either way. It's either at my hands or his. Take your pick."

The knife digs in further, and I start carving a star into his cheek.

"Stop," he yells, so I pause, pulling the knife back slightly.

"Talk."

"I saw Alec LeClair talking with your father at the ball. He was in his office. That's all, I swear."

"This would have been so much easier if you just talked first, but then again, we wouldn't have got to play this little game, would we?" I rise up, taking my weight off him.

"Just let me go please?" he begs, tears rolling down his cheeks and mixing with the blood.

"Can't do that. You're a dead man either way, best at my hands."

Without hesitation, I slide the knife along his throat before he can utter another word, and a rush of blood drenches my chest, creating a vivid crimson canvas. His bloodshot eyes glisten with moisture as he gargles before they slowly glaze over.

I casually toss the knife into the sink, its sharp blade clinking against the cold metal basin. His words continuously repeat in my mind. Why was Alec in my father's office? The Daring Brotherhood shares no secrets, but my father doesn't follow our rules.

I head into the bathroom at the back of the shed to shower, leaving the mess for one of the soldiers to clean up. Scrubbing vigorously, I clear the blood from my skin, then lean back against the shower wall, feeling the cool tiles against my back and the hot water cascading over me.

If Alec was talking with my father behind our backs it had to be about him working with The Brotherhood. We've never worked with anyone other than those inside our chain of command, but Alec was different. He already patched in at an early age before he and his family were forced to leave. He's a soldier, and it's the only reason we allowed him to come back and work for us. No one knew apart from the founding families.

Going behind my father's back and bringing him back in to work for us was maybe not the smartest idea, since he's now gone. Lost. And when you get lost here, there's no finding you.

I couldn't find it in me to break the news to Freya, but I suspect she already has an inkling. With each passing day, the probability of her finding him diminishes. Alec, driven by desperation to earn extra cash, has now paid the price for wanting to work for us again. Gone in the wind.

I've learned the hard way to never let anyone get close to you because people can use that against you. Use them to manipulate you. It's a weakness, but that doesn't stop me from thinking about Freya. She's all I can think about. I want to protect her, hold her close, and have her beside me as the one I come home to. But, fuck, that can't happen. I won't allow it. She's better off on the other side of the tracks where she's out of sight and mind. But. That fucking word will be the death of me. There's a selfish part of me that won't let her get away again.

When she asked me if I remembered her, fuck, my heart —what I have left of it stopped. How could she ask me if I remember her? Of course I fucking do. Even back then, there was something about her. The way she stood up for herself and her friends in a world where men rule and women do as they are told. She knew the rules, but that didn't stop her.

Eight years old

I watch her sitting on the forest floor, playing with Amirah. The doll Lucas found for them sits between them. Amirah picks it up and starts moving it around, unsure of what to do with it. If father knew they had that, it wouldn't be a pretty sight to see. I don't know why Lucas gave it to them. He found it in one of the abandoned houses and insisted on keeping it. We aren't meant to play with toys. They are for the weak, father always says. We are meant to live in the real world—not some make-believe one.

Pain erupts against my cheek, and my father stands in front of me with an angry scowl on his face. Oh no.

"What have I told you about paying attention? Don't fucking disrespect me again, boy," he growls before stepping back. He looks into the forest, catching sight of the girls, and before I think, I step in front of him, trying to stop him.

His fist hits my nose with a crack and tears well in my eyes. I'm not allowed to cry but I want to. Blood drips down my lips, and the tangy taste burns down my throat. Gage and Lucas stay still beside me. They know better than to react.

My father moves quickly through our backyard and into the forest. Footsteps follow behind me, Lucas and Gage hurrying to catch up.

Freya stands up and pushes Amirah behind her back, protecting her from him. My heart beats faster and faster like it always does when she's around. I don't understand it. Girls are bad. Father says we aren't meant to show them any love because they don't deserve it. They are meant for one thing only: to be at our beck and call. But I like her and my best friend's little sister. I don't want to treat them badly. Like my father did with my mother. She always had sores on her, and I wanted to make them better, but she didn't let me.

"What the fuck is this?" My father grabs the doll and rips off its head. Amirah gasps and Freya's nostrils flare.

"Give it back," Freya yells, and my chest tightens like someone is grabbing it and squeezing. She steps forward, trying to reach for it.

I see it coming, but I can't stop him. The back of his hand lands on her cheek, and she falls to the ground. My feet move, and before I can think about the consequences, I fall to the ground, grabbing onto her shoulders. She looks up, her ocean-blue eyes filled with tears, and I want to hug her. Make all her pain go away.

A hand grips onto my neck and her eyes widen. She tries to reach for me, but it's too late. My father pulls me up, spins me around, and his fist comes straight for me. Her screams ring in my ears before everything goes black.

That was the last time I protected her from him and us. I have to keep my distance from her, but the more time she spends with us, the closer she's getting—and I don't know how to keep her away anymore.

Our worlds are tied together with black ribbon, and I can't seem to cut the tether no matter how much I need to.

Chapter Twenty-Eight
Freya

Amirah takes me to the police station on their side of the tracks and drops me off.

"Are you sure you don't want me to come in?" Turning down the stereo, she then puts the car in park.

"It's fine, I'll message you later." I unbuckle my seatbelt and reach for the door handle as Amirah grabs my hand.

"Just be careful with them. They may look like cops, but they are Brotherhood through and through."

I know she's right, but this is my last resort. I don't want to leave any stones unturned.

"I will, promise," I say, and she lets go, waving goodbye.

When I shut the door, the engine of her car roars to life, gradually fading into the distance as she departs. Despite the presence of a couple of cop cars in the parking lot, an eerie quiet hangs in the air. The sun slowly descends behind the building, momentarily blinding me with its brightness. Putting one foot in front of the other, I head inside.

With an eerie creak, the station door swings open, drawing the attention of the older man behind the counter.

He momentarily breaks his focus from the computer, his gaze fixating on my chest for an uncomfortably long moment.

"You're a little far from home, aren't you, darlin'?" he asks before I can even open my mouth. I shove my hands into my pockets.

"My brother, Alec LeClair, is missing. I want to file a report," I say, ignoring his stupid question.

"People go missing all the time here. You should know that. He'll show up one way or another." He shrugs, looking back at his computer, and starts typing away.

Is he for fucking real? I forcefully slam my fists down on the counter with a loud thud that echoes through the room, and he responds with a piercing glare.

"Please, tell me if you've heard anything," I beg, but he ignores me. I'm about to lose my shit.

"I want to know everything that you do about my brother, and now!" My voice is raised, and a cop who looks younger than me peers through the door leading to the back. I've seen him before, but I can't recall where.

The older guy behind the desk shakes his head. "Look, kid, you're wasting your time here. He's probably dead and he'll show up somewhere. Just move on and keep to yourself."

My shoulders tense and I grip the counter, my fingers turning white. The desire to lunge forward and eliminate the smug look on his face overwhelms me. How dare he say that?! My brother isn't dead. No, I'll never believe that. He can't be. I've come to the one place that's supposed to help me, and they won't. Before I make a huge mistake and assault a cop, I reach over, grabbing a piece of paper and a pen. I hastily jot down my name and number, then slide it toward him with force.

"If you hear anything, please call me," I say, and head back out the front door.

As the sun sets on the horizon, the sky is bathed in a warm, orange glow. Lifting my phone out of my pocket, I navigate to my contact list, and my finger hovers over Amirah's name before scrolling down further to find one of the guys' numbers to arrange for a ride, but I hesitate. When did I start relying on them so heavily? With each passing moment in this place, the lines between their actions and identities blur, causing me to forget who they truly are. I just want my brother to come back, then everything will be solved. We'll leave this place behind and start fresh. Just like we always planned. However, with every passing minute, my desire to leave diminishes, and a sense of longing settles in my stomach, making it increasingly difficult to walk away.

A whistle cuts through the otherwise quiet parking lot. As I spin around, my eyes catch sight of a figure emerging from the building, waving me over. It's the young guy from before. He looks around and starts walking into the forest. I follow him without hesitation. The tall trees loom overhead, casting long shadows that send shivers down my spine. I wrap my arms around myself, tugging my hoodie's sleeves down to shield my fingers from the chilly air.

When we are far enough away from the police station, he stops and turns around.

"I didn't want to say anything in there because you know it's flooded with Brotherhood, and nothing happens without their approval, but I saw the pain in your eyes, and it reminded me of a time I needed their help too." He pushes his hands into his pockets and averts his gaze, focusing on the forest floor beneath his feet.

"What happened?" I ask, noticing the pain etched on his face.

"My sister went missing and they did nothing. I had to solve it myself and it's the reason I wanted to become a cop. I'm Drew by the way."

"Sorry to hear about your sister. Do you know anything about Alec?"

He raises his gaze, and his eyes grow wider. He turns around and takes off.

"Wait, please!" I chase after him, and he grabs my arm, looking at something behind me.

"Don't trust them," he says before running off deeper into the woods.

Trust who? The sound of a snapping twig startles me. I spin around and meet Gage eye to eye. He's wearing a long black top and jeans. His hair is all wet and wavy like he just got out of the shower.

"What the hell are you doing here?" I snap, and he storms over.

He stops right in front of me. "I could ask you the same thing. What did he tell you?" He glances past me to where the guy disappeared.

"Not to trust you," I scoff. "Which I already knew."

"Come on, we're going." He snatches my hand, and our fingers lace together. I peek down to where his huge hand grips mine, and I freeze, not sure if I should let go or hang on. Nothing makes sense. That guy is right; I can't trust them. I can't trust anyone. Only myself.

I pull free, taking a couple of steps back, but my foot catches on something and I fall, landing on my ass. Gage rushes to my side as pain courses through me, leaving me breathless. His gaze travels over my body as he kneels. My chest rises and falls at a rapid rate. I need to get out of here. I need to run. To do something reckless.

Gage's fingers lightly graze my cheek as he gently tucks a strand of hair behind my ear. A stirring sensation ripples through my stomach, and a comforting warmth spreads across my skin.

"You don't trust me now," he whispers before leaning down. His lips are only inches from mine. "And you never will."

As he pulls back, a chill runs down my spine and goosebumps appear all over my skin. A conflicting desire arises within me—to have him back but also to create as much distance between us as possible.

I push myself up and take one last look at Gage. He watches me with intense scrutiny, his expression betraying no emotion on his flawlessly handsome face. Spinning around, I start running, feeling the wind rush through my hair. With each step I take, the forest seems to tighten its grip around me, making me acutely aware of its presence. As sweat beads on my skin, I continue to press forward, relishing the searing sensation in my legs. Pain. Hurt. Release.

Up ahead, I see a clearing, my eyes locking onto the tracks that serve as a boundary between our worlds. The looming, massive fence adorned with barbwire has never been an obstacle for me, and it won't be this time either. As I start climbing, my fingers find purchase in the small holes, providing me with a sense of stability. I reach the top, my muscles straining as I hoist myself over. The wire bites into my skin, but the pain brings relief.

My feet hit the ground, back in Daringhood and I'm off again, stepping onto the tracks. I stop and lie down, looking up into the almost black sky. My heart rings between my ears.

Stars stare back at me, sparkling against the increasing darkness. A train could come at any second and that's why I love doing this. The thrill of not knowing when I'll have to jump and run or just let it take me. Life has never been easy, but I've always held on to our dream of escaping and living far away from here. Now as each day, hour, minute, and second goes by without hearing from Alec, it fades a little more.

Somebody knows something, but every time I get close, one of them shows up and I get nothing. The only way I'm going to get answers is by being around The Brotherhood. Nothing happens here without their approval or say. If I'm going to find Alec, it's with them. As much as I want to push them away and run for the hills, I can't.

That message still replays over and over in my head. *You could have saved him.* What did they mean, and who's sending them? Alec is still alive—he has to be. I can't even bring myself to think about the alternative. I will find him, and we will leave. Together.

I have no idea how long it's been, but the moon rises into the night. There's a distant rumble of a train and the tracks start to squeak. My phone vibrates against my leg, and I pull it out, reading over the text message. My stomach drops, and the ringing in my ears returns.

His body hangs from the wire, and you will pay for the liar.

A horn blasts from behind me, but I can't move. I can't breathe.

Chapter Twenty-Nine
Freya

Everything else fades away into nothingness. I can't tear my eyes from my phone screen, the words becoming etched into my mind as I read them over and over. It can't be Alec. It has to be somebody else. The horn gets louder and closer. The frantic voices around me grow more incessant, drowning out all other sounds bar the train, while I remain immobile, trapped in my own stillness. What if it's him? What if he's gone? No, I won't accept it. He's still alive. It's not him.

Rough hands suddenly seize me, forcefully lifting me and tossing me over a strong shoulder. Everything that surrounds me is drowned out by the ringing in my ears. I hit the ground with a thud, and I don't move, letting myself sink deeper into the ocean of numbness. A figure hovers over me, I can't help but feel a sense of detachment, my gaze passing right through them.

My phone is taken from my hands. "Freya!" a voice yells, and a hand lands gently against my cheek.

"Come back to me." Soft lips touch mine, and I blink,

slightly taken aback. The light-brown eyes lock onto mine, pulling me in and holding me captive. A small smile tugs at the corner of his mouth.

"Thank fuck for that." Lucas sighs, shifting back slightly. "Now, what the hell were you doing?"

Swallowing hard, I sit up quickly, my elbows digging into the gritty dirt. Lucas moves backward, resting on his knees.

Hazen hovers nearby, while Gage stands next to him with his hands in his pockets, watching me closely.

"She has a death wish," Gage snaps, and anger bubbles up inside me.

I can't deal with him. I have to find my brother.

Lucas extends his hand to me, and I accept, wiping off the dirt from my ass. He passes me my phone, and I put it in my back pocket.

"Thanks," I say before taking off along the track.

"Freya, wait!" Lucas yells behind me, but I don't stop. I can't. I need to see who's hanging from the wire. The Brotherhood utilizes a section of the fence to hang dead bodies as a lesson for us. Those who disobey pay the price.

I refuse to accept that it's my brother. The message has to be about somebody else. The faster I run, the more my legs burn. The crunch of footsteps on the dirt trails behind me, but I am determined to keep moving without slowing down. The closer I get, the more sweat drips down the back of my neck. The moonlight provides enough illumination for me to see a little, although I am familiar with this area. Spotlights become visible in the near distance, and I can't bring myself to look. I lower my head until I'm facing the wire fence.

My feet carry me across the tracks. Someone grabs my arm, and I stumble backward.

"Freya. Don't look up," Lucas begs, his voice laced with worry.

I break free from his hold and glance upwards. I'm met with the lifeless gaze of my brother's eyes.

I scream until my throat feels parched and devoid of moisture. No. It can't be. No, please! Suddenly, my legs give way beneath me, and I find myself on the ground, kneeling in a puddle. Every muscle in my body quivers and shakes uncontrollably. Why him? His body slumps over the fence, his white shirt covered in red. His hand is outstretched as if it's waiting for me to grab it. To save him. But it's too late. He's gone, and whoever sent those messages was right. I should have saved him.

Tears stream down my face. It should have been me. Alec had a future outside of here. I didn't.

Strong hands wrap around me, lifting me effortlessly and bringing me close to a comforting, warm chest. I pull back before my fists relentlessly pound into his stomach, each blow delivering a jolt of pain. The moment he catches me, my legs turn to Jell-O and my chest heaves, struggling to find air. All the fight leaves me. I can't. My cheek rests against his chest, tears flowing freely and soaking into his shirt.

"I'm so sorry," Lucas whispers, pressing a kiss on my head.

This has to be a nightmare. Please. I can't live without my brother. He's my everything. My best friend. The one person in this world who loved me no matter what. Who protected me from everything. I can't go on without him. It's all too much.

I find myself slipping out of the warm embrace and falling backward. My hands instinctively shield my ears, trying to muffle the piercing ringing inside them. My heart pounds relentlessly, and I struggle to catch my breath. I can't move.

"It should have been me!" I scream into the night.

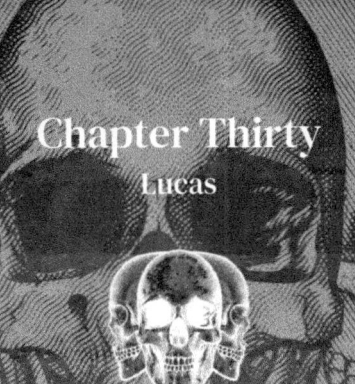

Chapter Thirty
Lucas

As Freya crumbles before my eyes, my heart shatters into fragments. I want to make it all better, to take away the pain. I collapse onto my knees in front of her, the sharp fragments of rocks and other debris piercing my skin. She throws herself at me, and I catch her in my arms, bringing her against my chest. As she wraps her arms around my neck, I hold her close, feeling the warmth of her embrace and the weight of her body against mine, reminiscent of my mother cradling me in her lap when I was young.

She clings to me desperately, believing I have the power to make it all go away. I want to, but *fuck*, this is a low blow. He's dead, and I have no fucking idea how. Nothing goes on in our town without us knowing about it, but this did. Directly in front of us.

Hazen storms off along the tracks with his phone to his ear, and Gage stares at her brother in disbelief. Freya's sobs reverberate through her small body, and I run my fingers up and down her back, providing a comforting touch. The air is tainted with the unmistakable scent of decay—a smell I'm used to.

Gage kneels in front of us, gently wiping away the tears that trickle down Freya's cheeks, but she remains motionless.

"I'm sorry, Freya," he whispers, and she turns away, shoving her face into my chest.

Footsteps crunch against the ground and Hazen reappears. "We gotta go. Clean-up is on its way," he says, running a hand over his short, clipped hair.

With a sudden burst of energy, Freya moves out of my embrace and jumps up. I follow her.

"No, you can't take him. No. Please. I won't let you take him away," she yells, standing in front of her brother to block him from us.

Hazen takes a step forward, and she growls. He raises his hands. "I'm just getting him taken to someone I know to examine him. To find out who did this."

"You did this," she accuses, pointing directly at us. Her gaze lingers on mine, and a heaviness settles in my chest. "All of you."

"We didn't do shit," I snap, vigorously shaking my head.

She can't believe that we did. We've been looking for him, too. Wanting to find him to get our money back. Why the hell would we kill him?

"It's your fault. Everything is."

I want to grab her, to never let her go. To make it all better, to take the pain away. But I can't. She's right. This is on us. If not us directly, then The Brotherhood, and we are them.

Car headlights shine, temporarily blinding me. The vehicle screeches to a halt on the other side of the fence, followed by the sharp sound of car doors slamming shut. Two of our men emerge.

Hazen points to Alec's lifeless body, dangling precariously from the edge of the fence. They come over to our side and Freya turns around.

"No! You can't take him!" she screams, but they don't respond. While they are pulling him off the barbed wire, Freya desperately tries to climb up by digging her fingers into the fence.

I look at Gage and Hazen. Gage's face remains emotionless as he watches her attentively. Does he even have a fucking heart? Hazen curses and swiftly wraps his arm around her waist. Even as she thrashes and screams, Hazen refuses to let go, holding her firmly.

They get Alec's body down off the fence and quickly place him in the back of the van. As Freya's foot makes contact with Hazen's, he stumbles backward, his curses filling the air. Then she's off. With a swift and agile movement, she effortlessly scales over the fence and gracefully lands on the other side. The van pulls out, and she runs after it.

"Go get the fucking car," Gage yells at me.

It takes me ten minutes to run, get my car, and pull up on our side of the tracks. By the time I return, Hazen and Gage are back on our side, leaning against the fence. Gage's head is down, his focus on his phone as he madly types away, and Hazen stares off into the distance.

Hazen slides in the back and Gage into the passenger seat.

"Where is she?" I ask, looking between them, and Gage slams his door shut.

"Just fucking drive. She's gone, and I've got the fucking bite marks to prove it," he growls out, showing me his wrist.

I snort. "Well, fuck. The girl does have bite."

"Shut up. I need a drink or something heavier to figure

out what the fuck just happened and why we didn't know about it," Gage says.

I drive off, going slow and looking out the window in the hopes I'll catch a glimpse of her.

She just found out her brother is dead, after all this time, and all I want to do is hold her and tell her it's going to be okay. But is it? If I lost my sister, my world would come crashing down, and I'd have no idea how to rebuild from that.

I want to take Freya's pain away and replace it with love and hope. For a better time and place. Everyone grieves in different ways, and I have no idea if she will ever be the same again.

In the backseat, Hazen sits in silence, his gaze fixed on the passing scenery. His phone starts ringing, and I catch his eye before he answers it. I don't need any guesses to know who it is.

"Dominic," he says, and my fingers tighten around the steering wheel.

There's only one person in the world who scares me, and it's Dominic. I hate the power he still has over us and can't wait for the day he retires—or better yet, dies. Then the noose he has tightened around our necks will be free. We will run The Brotherhood how we want to and won't be dictated to by him. My father thought differently to Dominic. He wanted different things for The Brotherhood, but it always went Dominic's way. Now my father is retired, cancer slowly eating away everything from the inside out, and there's nothing he can do.

Pressing his fingers to the bridge of his nose, Hazen listens attentively to his father. Then he ends the call and slams the phone down on the seat, muttering a string of curses under his breath.

"He knows about Alec's body and wants us to clean it up."

"Question is, did he arrange the hit or was it someone else?" Gage asks from next to me.

"Nothing goes on without him knowing about it," I say, stating the obvious as I look out at the dark, empty road.

Hazen shakes his head. "She won't trust us now."

"She never did," Gage says.

Chapter Thirty-One
Freya

My lungs burn, begging me to stop, but I can't. I have to follow him. This can't be happening. My brother is dead. No, I don't accept that. He can't be. He's my everything. Without him, without my best friend, what am I? Nothing.

I keep urging my legs to move faster, desperately trying to catch up to the van as it gradually slips farther out of reach. As the brake lights fade away, I tumble onto the road, the asphalt scraping my knees. The salty taste of tears on my lips matches the ache in my heart.

Images of his lifeless body hanging over the wire flash repeatedly in my mind, his vacant gaze haunting me. If he didn't get involved with The Brotherhood, none of this would have happened. He would be going off to college soon and everything would be as it should.

Headlights illuminate the road, and the rumble of a car comes up behind me, but I don't move off the road. I can't. My body feels like cement. Car doors slam, hands wrap around me from behind, and I let them. I lean into a warm chest as voices carry through the wind, but I can't understand them. It's all too much.

I want to yell and kick at them, but all the fight within me is gone. Warmth surrounds me, and we're moving into the car. I'm positioned across two bodies in the backseat, with my head resting in Hazen's lap and my feet in Lucas's.

"Take her to mine," Lucas says, pulling my feet closer to his lap.

"No," I mumble into Hazen's stomach, pushing slightly so I can look up. He stares down at me with a mixture of sorrow and something else that I can't quite put my finger on.

"Where do you want to go?" Hazen asks, brushing my hair out of my face, then his fingers gently caress my cheek. Warmth fills my belly, and I lean into his touch for a second before remembering that this is his fault. Their fault.

"Your place," I say, and he frowns, shaking his head.

I don't want to be anywhere near them, but they have all the answers. The Brotherhood is involved in this, and I'm going to find out who killed my brother. Even if it gets me killed in the process.

"No fucking way."

"Please. I have to find out what happened, and nothing goes on without your father knowing." Hazen watches me intently before he curses.

"Fine, but you don't leave my side. Got it?"

I nod, my attention drawn to the intricate patterns on the car's ceiling above me. Repeatedly tracing the crisscross pattern with my eyes, I tune everything else out until we eventually come to a stop. With the sound of the door opening, I swiftly rise from Hazen's lap and scramble out of the car. As I take one step forward, Gage grabs my hand, bringing me to an abrupt halt. I whirl around, my heart pounding, ready to swing, but freeze when I meet his glassy eyes.

"I'm so sorry, Freya," he whispers before letting go and jumping into his car next to Lucas's. He's gone before I can process what just came out of his mouth.

Part of me wants to believe they did this—Hazen, Gage, and Lucas killed my brother—but it doesn't make sense. They were looking and helping me find him. If they knew he was dead this whole time, then *fuck*, they deserve an Oscar for that performance. I want to hate them, to blame them, but I can't. My only hope of figuring this out lies with them. I know I can't do this alone—even my stubborn self realizes that.

Hazen gently clasps my hand, intertwining his fingers with mine. The front door opens, revealing darkness before us. I have no idea what the time is, but it's late. We move up the stairs in silence, down the hallway, and into his room.

As he turns on the light, a king-sized bed captures my attention, as it's placed prominently in the center of the room. My mind is racing a million miles per hour, but my body is begging for sleep to come. Sleep will be impossible for me.

"I'll run you a bath," Hazen says, letting go of my hand.

I instantly miss his touch. A bath is the last thing I want —I should be storming into Dominic's bedroom and demanding answers, but that's reckless and will result in a bullet to my head. I can't avenge Alec if I'm dead too. Rest first, then come morning, I'm demanding answers.

I enter the spacious bathroom a minute or two later, following after Hazen. A large bubbling jacuzzi tub sits in the corner, overlooking the ocean. Without any hesitation, I shed my clothes and drop them on the cold tiled floor. His eyes leisurely scan my figure, growing more intense with every passing moment until they lock with mine. As his throat bobs, I ascend the steps. When I slip into the water, I let out a sigh as it embraces me, its warmth enveloping my body like a cozy blanket.

"I'm so—" Hazen starts, but I shake my head.

"Don't, not tonight. I just want to forget," I say, leaning back against the jets.

Hazen nods, then removes his T-shirt in one swift movement, followed by his pants. His thick, jutting cock stares back at me, and this time I'm the one swallowing hard. He hops in, the water swirling around his mesmerizing body. He sits down opposite me and my broken heart beats at a crazy stupid rate. I wanted a distraction, and he's it.

My feet take me closer to him, then my hands find his knees, and they move higher and higher.

"Are you su—?" Hazen says, and I cover his mouth with my hand.

"Make me forget," I say, fisting his cock with my other hand and slowly moving it up and down.

I remove my hand from his mouth and wrap my fingers around the back of his neck, pulling him to me, then his lips crash into mine, and our tongues collide.

He grabs my ass, lifting me, then breaks away from my lips to place me on the edge of the jacuzzi. His hands land on my knees, pushing them apart until my pussy is completely bared to him. He slowly licks his lips, and I can't take it anymore. Gripping the back of his neck, I shove his face between my legs.

The breath from his chuckle tickles my clit, then he swipes his tongue between my folds and my eyes slam shut.

My fingers grip the edge, and I push my pussy further into his face. He doesn't need to be told twice; he eats me out like I'm a five-star meal. His mouth works me over, expertly bringing me to the edge again and again.

My head falls back, a deep moan falling from my lips as I finally fall apart, and he laps up every drop. When he comes up for air, his eyes clash with mine.

"Fuck me so I can forget, b-but just . . . for tonight," I stutter, trying to catch my breath.

He picks me up and spins me around. Water splashes around us, hitting the bathroom floor. He lowers me into the water, then slowly onto his hard cock.

My eyes slam shut as I adjust to his length. My head rests against his, my knees landing on the jacuzzi seat giving me leverage to move up and down on his cock. He keeps his hands on my hips but lets me fuck him.

He fills me, hitting the right spot over and over, climbing me higher. My hands rest on his shoulders, and he takes my bottom lip between his teeth, biting hard. The tangy taste of blood fills my mouth, and he licks my lip clean, then claims my mouth.

In the next breath, he releases me, lifting me off his cock, and spins me around so my ass is facing him.

"Hold on," he says in a husky voice.

I hold onto the edge he has maneuvered us to, lifting my ass in the air. In one swift motion, he fills me again, and I jerk forward. Oh my God.

He fills every inch of me, splitting me open, and it's too much but not enough at the same time. He grips my hair, wrapping it around his fingers and yanking my head back. Fuck. He builds me up and up.

"I'm gonna come. Fuck," I say breathlessly. He doesn't

stop, fucking me harder and harder until I release all over his cock, and he follows right after with a deep groan.

After a few languid thrusts, he pulls out, and I fall backward into the water. He catches me, pulling me into his chest. I'll regret this tomorrow, but it's exactly what I needed. A moment to forget. We remain in our embrace until the churning water makes everything else fade away.

Chapter Thirty-Two
Freya

My bare feet sink into the forest floor, the rough ground biting into my skin. Voices carry around me, getting louder and louder. They can't catch me. I push harder, ignoring the pain shooting up my shins. I have to make it. I have to save my brother. He needs me. I'm the only person he's got.

A shadow jumps out in front of me, and I scream, skidding to a stop. A neon-red skull mask stares back at me. Then another, then another, until I'm surrounded by glowing skulls. One of the masked figures steps forward, coming closer until they are only an arm's length away.

"Let's play a game," a robotic voice says. "If you beat me, your brother will be saved."

"And if I don't?" I draw in a sharp breath.

"Then you die with him."

I'm off running again before the person in the mask can react. His footsteps crunch against the forest debris, getting closer and closer. No, I have to move. The forest opens up and train tracks stare back at me. Keep pushing. Figures surround me, closing in. No, I'm so close. I make it over the *train tracks and to the fence. I look up and scream. Alec's lifeless eyes stare back at me.*

His head jolts, his eyes open. "You could have saved me."

I scream until my throat becomes dry. As my body trembles, I force my eyes to open. Ocean-blue eyes collide with mine.

"Just a nightmare. You're okay." Hazen holds my gaze for several heartbeats until I look away.

"Is my brother really gone?" My voice is quiet, just below a whisper, and I don't know if I'm asking him or myself.

Hazen rolls onto his back, the bed dipping, and he pulls me under his arm. All the energy in me is gone, so I don't fight him.

"I'm sorry." He rubs his hand up and down my arm, but I barely feel a thing.

My brother is dead. My whole body feels numb as though I'm hovering above it. I can't move. I just want this nightmare to be over. If only I could build a time machine, so I could bring my brother back and switch places with him. So he can fulfill his dream of attending college. I don't have anything good to live for; he deserves this life more than me. I need this to be a fairytale where I find a witch to cast a spell and, *poof*, it's all okay. But that won't happen— this isn't a fairytale, and witches aren't real.

Time seems to vanish, and I have no idea how long we lie there in each other's arms. I wait for the regret of last night to come, but it never does. I feel safe in his arms. Protected. Which is something I don't understand. He's the bad guy, a demon in disguise, but the more time I spend with him and the other two, the more my disdain toward them fades. They might be the most feared men in Daring, but to me, they have soft spots. My body wants them, my heart is falling for them, and I don't have any power or say in it.

The bedroom door opens and shuts softly, and I look up. With silent steps, Lucas makes his way to my side of the bed. I ease out of Hazen's embrace, and he mumbles something in his sleep, then rolls over to his other side.

"You hungry?" Lucas asks, tucking a piece of hair behind my ear. I nod, my tummy rumbling.

Shifting off the bed, I look down at the plain dark-gray T-shirt I'm in, remembering that Hazen gave it to me last night to wear. His masculine sandalwood smell still surrounds me.

Lucas's eyes move up and down my body before he shakes his head. "You shouldn't be allowed to wear that. All I want to do is rip it off to see what's underneath." My usual smartass remark stays lodged at the back of my throat. Without saying a word, he pulls me close and guides us out of Hazen's bedroom.

Voices come from an open door down the hallway, and I freeze when I spot a young boy and girl who look to be around four, playing dolls together. The boy plays with one of the dolls, doing everything the girl demands. My heart breaks in two. My brother used to do the exact same thing. No matter what, he just wanted to make me happy. So he played with my dolls instead of his toys. We made up stories and dreamed of a better life. Like those fairytales he used to read to me.

The little boy looks up, his eyes widening as he catches us. Staring back at me are eyes as blue as the ocean, just like Hazen's. As Lucas approaches, his face lights up with a smile, and he excitedly waves. Tears stream down my cheeks, leaving a salty taste on my lips, and I find myself paralyzed under the child's curious gaze until Lucas steers me away.

I'm a mess. My heart aches and these tears won't stop. I've never been a crier, always keeping my emotions locked up inside, but since last night, that box has been opened and it won't close. No matter how hard I try. I don't want them to see me in this position. Vulnerable. Weak. I just want to go back to the safety blanket of Hazen's bed and sleep forever, but that won't bring my brother back. That won't help solve his murder. I need a distraction—I need revenge.

We head down the stairs in comfortable silence. Lucas flips his black cap backward, his blond hair fanning out underneath. He gets to the last step and reaches out his hand, and I take it, his large hand engulfing mine.

We move through the foyer and into the large open kitchen. On the bench lies a banquet of food fit for an army. Fruit, pastries, eggs, bacon, and my God—pancakes. This is insane.

"Tell me this is not just for us?" My eyes widen, taking in all the options.

"Just for us." Lucas chuckles, leading me to a chair that overlooks all the food. He piles up a plate with everything, then places it down in front of me.

"Jesus, she's not going to be able to eat all of that," Hazen says, moving through the kitchen. He's dressed in casual stone-colored cargo pants and a black top. I wait for the awkwardness to come from what we did last night, but it doesn't.

"No, she might not, but I will," Lucas says, stacking his plate double the size of mine. We eat in a silence. Each bite tastes bland, and I don't know if it's because of the flavor or my appetite is gone.

Once I'm finished, I take my plate and start washing up.

Lucas turns off the faucet and takes the plate from my hands.

"That's what we pay people for," he says, and I roll my eyes.

"Come, we've got something to show you, but first you need to get dressed." Lucas takes my hand in his and I let him guide me, not having the energy to argue and demand to know where we are going.

Ten minutes later, I'm showered and dressed in one of Hazen's plain black tees that's tied and sitting above my high-waisted black cargo pants. Moving down the staircase, I run my fingers through my hair, fanning it out.

Hazen meets us at the bottom of the stairs with a warm smile, and then he wraps me under his arm in a protective hold. I lean into his chest, inhaling his earthy scent reminiscent of a cozy embrace. I have no idea when the lines blurred from enemies to friendship, then feelings, but I don't want this to go away. They are my anchors; without them I'll drown.

The front door opens, and Mia comes walking in. Her eyes widen when she sees me, and I freeze. Does she know? And what's she doing here again? I've got a million questions she needs to answer, but now isn't the time. I have to tell her about Alec.

"Alec . . . he's, he's—" The words stumble out of my mouth, and I can't bring myself to say it. She comes up to me, takes me out of Hazen's embrace and pulls me in for a tight hug.

"I already know," she whispers, her voice breaking. She pulls back, wiping away her tears, her mascara running down her cheeks. "I'm sorry," she says before disappearing through the foyer.

I go to follow her to find out what she knows or if she

wants to talk about it, but Lucas and Hazen guide me out the front door. The bright morning sun blinds me for a second, then we move around the side of the house and the manicured grass is soft beneath my feet as we make our way toward the line of trees. They could be leading me into something deadly, and yet here I am allowing it, lacking the energy to question them or fight.

The towering trees create a canopy that shields us from the harsh sunlight. I spot movement in the clearing ahead, and as we approach, I reach out and grab Hazen's hand for moral support.

The crunching of leaves announces the approach of someone, and as I look around, Gage's gaze collides with mine. From his jeans to his T-shirt, he is clad entirely in black. He comes to a halt in front of us, extending his hand, and I accept it. I don't understand what's going on, but I just go along with it. They could be leading me to my death for all I know.

My heart starts pounding harder as we near the clearing. I clutch onto Gage's hand as if it's the only thing keeping me grounded. When we step into an open space near the cliff's edge, I come to a halt. There's a large hole dug, dirt surrounding it, and a couple of people standing close, but I can't see them. Everything around me becomes blurry. If I take another step, it's truly the end. If I see my brother there, that means it's not a dream—he's gone and never coming back. My fingers clutch around my necklace as though I can somehow feel him within it.

I collide with Gage's solid frame, relentlessly pushing against him to make him budge. Despite my attempts to make him move, he remains in my path. He embraces me and I surrender. The strength drains from my body, and I latch onto him, clutching his neck for dear life. If I release my grip, I'll plummet and be lost forever.

He presses a kiss on the top of my head and whispers into my ear, "I'm so sorry."

"How did you do this?" I ask, my voice breaking.

"I wasn't going to let him take this from you."

Tears stream down my face and soak into Gage's shirt, my body shakes, and I ache with so much pain. I want to go back to where this all started and change everything. To never have gotten involved with The Brotherhood or to never have even been born here. For my mother to not have developed a habit. To Alec never needing the money for college. We should have moved away years ago. If we did, none of this would have happened. Alec would be living his dream at college—we could have made it work.

Time blurs, and I have no idea how long I stay there in his arms, but eventually, Amirah appears next to us and takes me from Gage's warm embrace.

"Let's give your brother the farewell he deserves, then we'll avenge him. I promise," Amirah says, squeezing my hand. I nod, unable to form the words.

Today, I'll say goodbye to my brother, and then tomorrow I'm going to get answers.

Chapter Thirty-Three
Freya

The front door opens, then slams shut, and I practically jump off the couch. In a flash, Hazen moves, standing up and swiftly placing himself in front of me.

Dominic rushes past the living room, his voice booming as he yells into the phone pressed against his ear. As I turn back to Hazen, I catch his frown, but he quickly dismisses it with a shrug and plops down in the seat beside me. Now that I've laid my brother to rest and said my final farewell, I need to find out if Dominic knows anything more about Alec. He's still in charge of The Brotherhood and nothing happens without his final say.

"Where's the bathroom?" I ask, and Hazen cocks his head to the side, studying me for a beat too long.

"Go left, and it's the first door."

With a nod, I leave the living room and follow Dominic. The echoes of his voice reverberate through the foyer, and I vaguely recollect that his office is down the corridor. Guided by his voice, I stop outside a set of large double doors made of dark wood.

Pressing my ear against them, I can make out Dominic's voice. I keep my ear to the door as I look back the way I came, making sure no one catches me.

"Kill the cunt if you don't get answers. He's dead to me anyway." He pauses, and I freeze. Shit. Did I breathe too loud? My heart pounds against my ribcage, loud and relentless. "Yes. The LeClair situation has been resolved."

Is he talking about my brother or me? My phone vibrates against my leg.

"Deal with it." His words are clipped, and the sound of footsteps grows nearer and nearer. Fuck.

I stumble backward, my hands desperately searching for something to steady myself, and I finally reach the bathroom door and enter, slamming it shut. I fall back against it, then reach for my phone hidden in my underwear.

There's another text from the unknown number.

Revenge sounds like healing, doesn't it? Find me the killer or you're next 💀

My stomach churns, and I can taste the remnants of breakfast rising in my throat. But at least I have an idea of who the killer could be now—the only man with motive.

Dominic.

He must have hated having us hood trash working with his heirs. He's always looked at us with such disdain, and Alec did owe him that money. Oh God. Is he the one sending those text messages, too? Everything is one big head fuck and I'm going to get to the bottom of it.

I need to break into Dominic's office and find answers, even if it kills me in the process.

The day drags on painfully slowly as I anxiously keep an eye on corridor across from the living room, hoping Dominic will come out of his office. The weight of Hazen's scrutiny is palpable as he frowns, his words seemingly trapped on the tip of his tongue.

I lean back into the couch, leveling him with a raised brow. "Just ask."

"Why do you keep looking down the corridor?" he asks, and I contemplate if I should tell him or not. Without his help, it will be hard but not impossible to find what I need. If we do get caught, it will make it easier to get out of it if he's there, but if it's just me, then I'm gone. There are no second chances with The Brotherhood.

I motion for him to come over, and he reluctantly rises from his recliner and plops down beside me, his knee brushing against mine. I turn and am captivated by his piercing blue eyes that mirror the vastness of the ocean.

"Promise me you know nothing about what happened with Alec?" I ask, and he frowns.

"We've already been over this. I told you we have no idea what happened. Otherwise, we wouldn't have been searching for him with you. That would have been pretty fucked up if we knew the whole time, wouldn't it?" He takes my hands in his, and I glance down at his large ones clasping my much smaller ones. "Look, I have no idea what's going on between us, but what I know to be true is I want to be near you every second of the day. I want to help you avenge your brother's death. But I'm not a good person —I play with death every day, and mostly at my own hands. I live and breathe The Brotherhood. That always comes first, and you need to know that." He pleads with his eyes, even though his admission is harsh.

I nod and squeeze his hands. I get it. Blood in, blood out kind of thing.

"Whatever is going on between us . . . this"—he lets go

of my hands and points from himself to me—"I want. Do you?"

His question catches me off-guard for a moment, but I find myself saying, "Yes."

His lips curve into a smile, the first one I've witnessed from him, and it takes my breath away. His hands roam up my arms, igniting a fire within me. In one swift motion, he pulls me toward him, his lips crashing against mine in a powerful, unforgettable kiss.

His fingers tangle in my hair as he presses his tongue further into my mouth. My stomach churns with a swarm of menacing butterflies, their wings fluttering violently, while my chest tightens and releases in rapid, uneven breaths. I want more, I need more. I shuffle forward, feeling the heat of his body as I wrap my legs around his waist and press myself against his firm crotch. He groans into my mouth, and I have to stop before I pull down his pants and fuck him here in the open-planned living room.

I pull back, resting my head against his. "What about Lucas and Gage?" I ask the question that's been on my mind ever since the feelings started to become blurred. There's no denying I want them all.

"We are The Brotherhood. You have one of us, you have all of us," he says like it's a normal thing for three guys to share one girl.

"Okay, I want all of you," I declare, more to myself than him.

He smiles, wrapping his hands around the back of my neck, and claims my lips once more.

He eventually shifts his focus, peppering kisses along my neck, and I press my hands on his chest, leaning slightly away. "I want to break into Dominic's office. He's hiding something about Alec, and I want to find out what." It feels like several heartbeats before Hazen replies.

"There's a party tonight. Let's do it then," he says.

I frown. "Let's?"

"There's no way you are going in there alone. You're one of us now, and we work as one. I want answers, too—we all do."

I stare at him in disbelief.

* * *

After having a long hot shower, I exit the steaming bathroom and pad into Hazen's bedroom, a soft towel wrapped snugly around my chest. The room is empty and there's a gown laid out on the bed. It's a gorgeous blue silk with a low-cut bodice. I glide my fingers across the smooth fabric. It's beautiful. Beside it, there's a blue lace bustier set that matches. When I lift the top half, I confirm that the cup size is perfect for me.

The bedroom door opens, then closes.

"Do you like?" Lucas asks, eyeing the lacey set between my fingers.

"You got this for me?"

"Of course. I need to see you in it." His voice sends shivers through my body. He's been by my side nearly all day with Hazen, keeping me busy and distracted. I thought I'd hate having someone around me all the time, but with him, and them, it's nice. I don't feel so alone. It hurts a little less.

Lucas grabs the pretty undergarments and helps me put them on. The brush of his fingers against my skin sends sparks of desire racing through me, leaving me burning with need. Wanting and needing more.

Once it's on, he steps back. "Fuck me, you are breathtaking."

My heart soars and my cheeks flame hot.

Lucas sneaks up behind me, his warm breath tickling my ear as he gently traces his fingers up my arms. My chest rises and falls as goosebumps spread.

He grabs my shoulders and spins me around, trapping me with his captivating honey-colored eyes.

"So beautiful," he sighs out, biting into his bottom lip. His gaze moves over my body, lighting up every part of me. I need to feel something real. Everything has felt so numb, and I need him to anchor myself. To take away the grief.

He falls to his knees, his tongue swiping over his bottom lip, and I can't control myself anymore. My fingers fist his blond hair, and I push him exactly where I want him. His hot chuckle dances over my lace-clad pussy. He hooks his fingers around the strings of the skimpy underwear and brings them down my legs until they fall to my feet.

He rests one hand on my belly before he buries himself between my legs, his tongue destroying me from top to bottom. My eyes close, head falling back. He licks me like I'm his favorite dessert, his tongue flicking my clit over and over again. His other hand trails up my inner thigh and teases my entrance before he fills me with two fingers. Fuck.

My legs start to wobble, and Lucas helps ease me back onto the bed without missing a beat. The man clearly takes eating out seriously.

The bedroom door opens, then slams shut. I turn my head toward the noise and freeze. Gage's eyes widen before narrowing into slits, and he looks to where Lucas is face-deep between my legs, then back to me. Lucas doesn't stop, and I moan, no longer able to suppress it.

"What the fuck?" he roars.

Lucas laughs against me, the vibration and his puffs of breath sending me over the edge. My thighs clench as my fingers grip his head, encouraging him to lick up every last drop of my release. I ignore Gage completely.

Lucas pulls himself up, presses a kiss against my cheek, and disappears into the bathroom.

I glance over to Gage, who doesn't move and doesn't speak. He runs his finger across his jaw, watching me intensely. Warmth spreads across my chest. I'm waiting for him to yell at me, to be pissed off, but there's nothing but silence between us.

I hop off the bed and retrieve my underwear from the floor, then turn to pick up the dress. Warmth hits my back, and his hand snakes around my waist. The heat of his palm burns my skin.

He moves my hair off my shoulder, his fingers running across my nape and sending shivers through me. His lips brush up my neck.

"Don't you dare put those on." His husky voice makes my knees weak. I release my grip on the dress and panties.

"So bossy," I say, glancing over my shoulder.

His fingers twist into my hair. "You haven't seen anything yet." He cranes my neck using his forceful grip, and pain rips through my skull, but then he claims my lips in a demanding kiss and the pain is replaced with desire. I try to twist my body around so I'm facing him, but his hand lands on my hip, holding me in place.

He breaks away from the kiss, and I instantly want him back. Releasing my hair, he skates his hands down my back, then he undoes all the hooks of my bustier, and it falls to the ground, leaving me butt naked. My nipples harden, begging to be touched, and I nearly take matters into my own hands.

It's not the first time Gage has seen part of me, but it

feels like it. The first time was a hate fuck, quick and angry. He didn't see me completely naked. This feels different. I want him and he wants me. I have no idea when the lines started to become blurry between hate and love, but they have.

He slowly turns me around until I'm facing him. His clothes are now gone, discarded on the floor between us. His hard cock is in the palm of his hand, and I swallow hard, having forgotten how big he is. His gaze drifts over every inch of my body, and I stand proudly, even as wetness pools between my legs. I need him. Now.

I step forward, pressing myself against his rock-solid body, then drag my fingers up his legs until his cock is firmly in my grip. I stroke up and down his length a few times before falling to my knees. Glancing up, I bat my eyelashes, and his stare is feral, his chest rising and falling.

"Don't play with me. Put that filthy mouth on my cock, now."

Jesus. I take him in one go, running my tongue along his shaft, then pull back, my teeth lightly grazing over his hot, silky flesh. His deep groan sets my belly on fire. The control I have over him is empowering.

The door to the bathroom opens, and Lucas emerges, but I don't stop.

"Fuck yeah, about time," he says from somewhere behind Gage.

"Fuck off," Gage growls, and Lucas laughs.

"Hell no. I'm here to watch. This is way better than porn."

Gage's answering grumble morphs into another deep groan, his hand twisting into my hair, and he forces my head back and forth. His cock hits the back of my throat again and again, and I fight the urge to gag, breathing through my nose. I watch Lucas from the corner of my eye as he drops his towel to the floor and grabs his cock, watching us—watching *me*—intently as he jerks himself off. Fucking hell.

It's not long before Gage's cum hits the back of my throat, and I swallow every last drop. Then I slide my lips over his length one last time and let him pull out of my mouth. He grabs my hand, helping me up, then claims my mouth in a searing kiss.

He pulls back to rest his head against mine, ignoring Lucas still working himself over.

"So fucking hot," Gage whispers.

Before I can take my next breath, he spins me around, forces my head to the bed, and his weight presses against my back. He spreads my legs with his and runs his finger between my soaked folds.

"So wet for me," Gage says.

"'And me,'" Lucas pipes up, but Gage continues to ignore him as he slides his finger inside me. I jolt forward, my face pressing into the mattress. Another finger fills me, joining the first one as they move in and out. I want more. I need more.

"What do you want?" Gage asks as he leans forward and wraps my hair around his hand.

"You. Inside. Me."

His fingers disappear, leaving me empty and aching, then a drawer opens and closes. There's the tearing sound of a wrapper, then a brief pause before he yanks my head back at the same time he slams his cock into me. A deep, animalistic groan falls from my lips. My back arches, pain searing through my scalp from his grip on my hair, and it takes a few seconds for me to adjust to his size.

His hand lands on my ass, the slap echoing through the bedroom. He keeps the grip on my hair tight, his body shifting over my back, and his finger disappears between my legs. He flicks my clit to the rhythm of his thrusts, but I need more.

Covering his hand with my own, I force his finger to go faster and faster. My skin flushes hot as pleasure builds and builds, but before I can finish, Gage removes his hand and pulls out. I'm spun around so fast, my body sways and my vision clouds.

He drops me back onto the bed and I land with a huff. Then he grabs one of my legs, lifts it high and fills me again. My eyes squeeze shut.

"Eyes on me," Gage growls. "I want to see you fall apart."

The bedroom door slams again, and my eyes clash with Hazen's. His mouth is hanging open. "Fucking hell" is all he says.

Gage's fingers wrap around my throat and my gaze snaps back to his.

"What did I tell you?" Gage huffs.

"Eyes on you," I reply huskily.

His grip tightens until I struggle to breathe, then he loosens for a beat before squeezing again. He touches every last part of me, mastering my body, and I can't take it anymore. With his, Lucas's, and now Hazen's eyes on me, I — *Fuuuck.*

My cries fill the room as he thrusts in and out so fast my vision starts to blur, but I don't dare shut my eyes. My gaze locks with Gage's in an intense stare, and we both orgasm fiercely at the same time, with me literally seeing stars.

He pulls out after a few languid thrusts of his hips, then removes the condom and drops it on the floor. His chest rises and falls to the same rhythm of my own. Just when I think he's going to storm out of the room, regretting every second, he surprises me by leaning over my body and pressing a gentle kiss against my cheek.

"Just as perfect as I remember," he whispers, and butter-flies fill my stomach.

I'm totally done for.

Chapter Thirty-Four
Freya

Hazen holds my hand as we descend the staircase together. He looks breathtaking in his dark-blue three-piece suit that matches my dress perfectly. The way he, Lucas, and Gage have been there for me these past few days has been everything. I haven't been alone since finding Alec, and part of me doesn't want to be because it hurts so damn much. With them around, it hurts a little less.

Lucas and Gage are at the bottom of the staircase, wearing the same suit as Hazen. My heart almost breaks through my chest. Gage leans in, pressing a kiss against my forehead and then Lucas swoops in, claiming my mouth in a passionate, knee-wobbling kiss. A loud gasp reaches us, and I pull away.

Amirah breaks us apart, pulling me into a hug. She whispers in my ear, "Whatever is going on between you and them"—she looks behind her at the guys—"I approve."

I cock my head to the side, the words stuck on my tongue.

"Yes, even my brother," she answers for me.

"I should have asked before, but are you okay?" She grimaces, then shakes her head. "Stupid fucking question. Sorry."

Her arms draw me in, and I respond with a warm hug. Words clog at the back of my throat. I have no idea what to say. I'm not okay and nothing will make it okay until I find out who did this. I need to know who took my best friend, and the only person in my family who cared about me.

The foyer echoes with voices that reach all the way to the backyard. Amirah releases me and I find myself falling into Hazen's arms, his embrace wrapping around my waist as I lean into him. Pulling strength from his body. He eventually shifts and tucks me into his side, and Amirah joins me on my free side as Gage and Lucas hang back a bit.

Leaving the foyer behind, we venture into the backyard. It's a sea of people in expensive suits and fancy dresses. They sip champagne from crystal glasses and talk in hushed tones. Pushing past the crowd, Amirah heads straight for the bar.

"Lucas, darling." Lucas's mother, Nadine, moves toward us with confidence. The bright pink, skin-tight dress she's wearing showcases her hourglass figure and makes her white blonde hair radiate. She's beautiful. She brushes past me, wrapping her arms around Lucas, and presses a kiss against his cheek. Amirah comes back, passing me a glass of bubbles, and I take it, downing it in one gulp.

Nadine chuckles. "If I didn't know you were from the other side of the tracks, I do now."

I press my lips together in a smile and fight the urge to roll my eyes.

"Nadine, you need to fix your lipstick. It's smudged," Amirah says with a smirk.

I try to hide my laugh with my glass, and Nadine glares at Amirah before she plasters on a fake smile.

"Sorry to hear about your brother, Freya. Such a shame." She clicks her tongue before leaning in closer, her perfume hitting the back of my throat. "Do you have any idea who did it?"

"I have my suspicions," I reply, and she stares at me with a little sparkle in her eye.

"And I have mine." Her gaze travels over my shoulder, and I follow, leading me straight to Dominic.

I whirl back around, cocking my head to the side. What does she know? If she thinks so, too, surely my suspicions are right.

Nadine reaches into her cleavage, then glances around before she discreetly brushes her fingers with mine, handing me a key. "You seem to mean something to my son. I'm risking everything—but I'll distract him. You go in. Find some kind of proof to bring him down for good."

Just as I'm about to inquire further, she moves into the bustling crowd, making a beeline for Dominic. I squeeze the key between my fingers—this is our one and only shot.

I watch as Nadine takes Dominic's hand, leading him over to the seat by the fountain, out of view. The guys follow my gaze and I pass Hazen the key.

"Nadine?" he asks, and I nod.

Lucas frowns but doesn't say anything.

"We have to break into his office. Now," I say, placing my empty glass on a passing tray.

"You what?" Amirah asks, glancing between the four of us before she shakes her head. "I have no idea what's going on, but I'll be the lookout."

I smile. "And that's why you're my best friend."

We make our way back through the foyer and toward

his office. Hazen uses the key to open the door, flooding the room with light as Gage and Lucas enter, then me, while Amirah remains by the door.

She closes the door behind me, and I take a deep breath. Hazen is already searching through Dominic's drawers, while Lucas lights up one of his cigars.

"What the fuck are you doing?" Hazen growls, snatching the cigar from between his lips.

"Hey, I need that," Lucas whines, and I roll my eyes.

Hazen slowly opens the window before chucking it outside. "We're supposed to be discreet, not leave evidence, you idiot."

Lucas shrugs while Gage sifts through the papers on Dominic's desk.

We spend the next ten or so minutes going through everything with a fine-tooth comb. With every passing second, my heart races uncontrollably, and I'm anxious that Dominic might walk in through the door. We have found nothing.

After slamming a drawer shut, I cringe at the loud noise and hastily pick up a fallen pile of paper, handing it to Hazen from under the desk. Moving the last piece of paper, I do a double take. There's a phone underneath it. I pick it up, showing it to Hazen.

"Is this his?" I ask, handing it over to him.

He studies it, then presses the on button. It comes to life, and Hazen grins. "Yep."

He tries to open it, but it's password-protected. Hazen curses. He tries multiple combinations, but nothing works. It won't be long until it locks him out, then we are fucked. This is all for nothing. We haven't found a single fucking useful thing.

He tries one last code and then *bam*—the phone lights up.

"Unbelievable," Hazen whispers.

I raise my eyebrows at him. "What was it?"

"My birthday."

Hazen shakes his head, and I snatch it out of his hands and start going through Dominic's messages. Nothing catches my eye, just business shit, but then one name stands out. Mia. What the fuck? My finger hovers over her name for a second before I click on it, then a bunch of messages load, and my breath catches. I lower the phone to the desk. Nude photos of Mia stare back at me.

"What the fuck?" Hazen snaps from beside me, and Lucas leans over my shoulder.

"Holy shit, isn't that Alec's girlfriend?" Lucas asks, stating the fucking obvious.

What the fuck? How long was this going on? Did my brother know? Is that why he's dead? A million questions filter through my head. Then it all clicks. That's why she was so cozy in Dominic's office, and why she seemed so comfortable waltzing into his house. I've been so naïve and distracted that I didn't put it all together before.

Picking the phone back up, I read every single text message dating back months ago. My thumb freezes on Alec's name. *We need to get rid of Alec.* My stomach twists, and I think I'm going to be sick. The phone drops from my hands, landing on the desk with a thud.

"Um, Freya, isn't this yours?" Gage asks, pulling something from between the couch cushions. The silver catches my eye, and I move toward him. There in his hand is a necklace identical to mine. My fingers instinctively clutch at mine around my neck.

"That belongs to Alec," I whisper. Tears well up in my eyes and my chest constricts, making it hard to breathe.

Gage approaches me, his fingers lightly touching my neck as he fastens the necklace, allowing it to rest against mine. When my legs give out, Gage catches me, and I hold onto him tightly for support. Like he'll take all this pain away.

With the necklace in Dominic's office and the affair with Alec's girlfriend, Mia, there's no denying he killed my brother. He took him away from me.

A subtle knock echoes through the office, and I freeze in Gage's arms. Fuck. We have to get out of here. Gage lets me go, and I take several deep breaths.

My phone buzzes against my hip. Lifting up my dress, I pull it out. There's a text from Amirah.

Dominic is on his way over here. Get out now. I'll try to distract him.

Part of me wants to just stay here and confront Dominic, but the other part of me values my life. He will deny it all, and then I'll have a target on my back. I need to play this smart and figure out what to do with the information I have.

Moving back to the desk, I pull out my phone and take photos of the text messages, then my hands start to shake uncontrollably. My breathing comes in and out at a rapid rate. I place the phone back where we found it, under the papers.

"We need to get out of here. Now," I say, and Hazen takes the lead. I follow behind him with Lucas and Gage trailing behind me.

When Hazen opens the door, Amirah is no longer there, and we come face to face with an enraged Dominic, who is accompanied by four intimidating security guards.

Dominic smirks, and I picture him holding a gun right in Alec's face, then pulling the trigger and taking him away from me.

Anger roils inside me, and I finally snap. Taking two steps forward, I cock my arm back, ready to deliver a punch to Dominic's face. Fuck the consequences.

Chapter Thirty-Five
Hazen

Coming through the door from my father's office, I immediately lock eyes with him, his stern expression giving away nothing. There are only a few people in this world who can scare me, and my father is one of them. He has that power to bring me to my knees, to make me feel like a little boy who can't stand up for himself. I fucking hate it, and I hate that I let him do it. That I feel like I have no control.

He killed Alec. Part of me knew it but the other part didn't want to believe it. Death isn't something I'm shocked about; it happens every day for me. I'm surrounded by death. But he took away someone who means something to me because of her. Before her I didn't believe in love—it didn't exist for me. I had no idea what it even meant or how it felt. The only glimpses I've had are from my little brother and sister. They rely on me to protect them and care for them. Now she's who I want to protect.

With lightning speed, Freya rushes past me, ready to confront my father with clenched fists. I position myself in front of her, preventing her from reaching him. With a strong shove, she tries to move me, but I stand my ground. From behind, Gage grabs hold of her, pulling her backward, but she fights back by clawing at his arms. There is a predatory look in her eyes, a longing to do him harm, and I can't fault her for it. He murdered her brother, the only family she could rely on. I'd do anything to protect my little brother and sister—and I do. I keep them away from him.

Dominic's laughter resonates from behind, his breath caressing the back of my neck, and my body tenses.

"Best get a leash for your girl, Hazen, before she causes a scene and ends up like her brother," he says with a slight chuckle, but I know him well enough to know when he's not joking.

"No, Dad, this time you've gone too far," I say, folding my arms over my pounding heart.

"You will all pay for this, starting with you." He points at Freya, and I step forward.

"It was my idea and I—" It all happens so fast that I don't have a chance to react.

I am being forcefully dragged away by someone with their arm wrapped around my neck. Despite my fingers digging into the security guard's hand, he maintains a firm grip on me. As he tightens his grip further, my lungs beg for air, and I gasp for breath. Everything becomes a hazy blur as my vision fades, but I can still hear the chilling scream that Freya lets out and our eyes lock in a moment of shared panic. She struggles against Gage's tight embrace, but he refuses to release her. I did this, I broke into my father's office, and I'll take the blame for it—not my brothers, and definitely not her.

* * *

Pain rips through my stomach, over and over again. My eyes blink open and he's there, standing over me. The bright lights of the shed blind me, and I want to shut my eyes again and go anywhere else—but that's weak.

My father spits, and it lands on my cheek, rolling down my face.

"How fucking dare you sneak into my office without my permission! I should kill you for this. All of you," he growls, kicking his boot into my ribs.

My body jolts backward and I swallow down the pain. He never hits me in the face because he doesn't want anyone else to see heirs of The Brotherhood looking weaker than them.

"I know you killed Alec," I say, staring up at him and he laughs.

"Believe what you want, boy. It doesn't mean shit to me. That boy got himself killed, doesn't matter who did it."

"It matters to me," I say, and he laughs, moving back a step.

"Fucking hell, son. Have I taught you nothing about women?" He shakes his head. "Pussy makes men weak. The Brotherhood always comes first."

"What about Mia?" I ask, biting back.

It's no secret to my mother or me that he cheats. She's caught him multiple times, and somehow, it's always her fault. My mother just puts up with it. She'd rather be in The Brotherhood by my father's side than outside and thrown to the other side of the tracks. She plays the perfect wife—just like he's played the perfect murderer.

My father scoffs. "You wouldn't understand. She's nothing, just like Freya is and will be to you. You need to get rid of her before it's too late. You are already looking weak, running around town with her and playing the hero. Remember who you are and what's at stake here."

My breathing picks up and I manage to find my feet. I wobble from side to side, and my father's smug face is all I can see. He opens his arms wide, teasing me to hit him because he knows I won't. He knows I wouldn't dare hit the last standing leader of The Brotherhood—and once he would have been right, but not anymore. He's wrong. He's dead to me now, and the sooner he's gone, the sooner we can take our rightful place as leaders and run The Brotherhood how it should be run.

I take another step forward and my fist connects with his jaw with a satisfying crack. He stumbles back a step, then a cruel smile splits across his otherwise emotionless face. Blood stains his teeth, and he runs his thumb along the corner of his mouth, wiping off the damage.

I stand as tall as I can, my ribs burning with pain, and wait for the beating of my life. I welcome it, knowing he will eventually get what he deserves. My brothers—Lucas and Gage—won't stand for this, just like I wouldn't either. As soon as I get back, we will plan our revenge. We will come for him.

And it's not going to be pretty.

Chapter Thirty-Six
Freya

I haven't slept since Dominic took Hazen away, and Gage carried me kicking and screaming out of the house and brought me to Lucas's. I'm pacing his bedroom for the millionth time, wondering if Hazen is okay. Is he alive? Fuck.

"Will you just chill out?" Lucas groans from his bed. I glare over at him. He's kicked back with his hands wrapped around his gaming controller.

"Why are you so chill about this? Hazen could be dead for all we know," I snap, and Lucas shakes his head, dropping the controller onto the bed.

"Come here," he says, and I huff, moving over to stand next to the bed. He takes my hand, pulling me so I fall on top of him. I shove against his chest until I'm sitting on his hips, glaring down at him.

"Hazen will be fine. I promise. Dominic won't let it get that far. Hazen's an heir of The Brotherhood; he can't kill him. Okay?" he says, and I nod.

I move off Lucas and settle in next to him, watching the

door closely and waiting for Hazen to come back. The door opens, and I sit up, but curse when it's just Gage.

"Sorry to disappoint you," he says, swirling his keys around his finger.

"Have you seen him?" I ask, and Gage shakes his head.

"But he messaged me. Let's go for a drive."

I roll over Lucas in my haste to get off the bed, and my knee collides with his balls, making him groan. But I'm in too much of a rush to apologize.

Gage drives us out of the private estate and through the streets of Daringville. He turns down a dirt road with nothing but forest surrounding us on either side.

"Where are we going?" I ask, sitting up straighter in the front seat as I watch the trees fly past my window.

"Just a place that we head to when we need to talk privately without anyone else around. No one knows about this place but us," Gage says, and I hear the warning in his tone.

Bringing me here is a risk, but it also means I'm one of them now. They trust me, and that means everything to me. Now that Alec's gone, having them by my side makes me feel less alone. Never in a million years did I think this would happen—working with and falling in love with the enemy—but fate has other plans.

We drive down the dirt road for a good ten minutes until a black motorbike comes into view, with a familiar guy leaning against it. He takes off his helmet as Gage brings the car to a stop, and I'm out the door in a second, running toward Hazen. He looks up just before I crash into his body. He groans and I pull back, checking him over. Part of me can't help noticing how good he looks in a leather jacket and jeans.

"I'm so sorry. Are you okay?" I ask, taking his hand in mine.

"Yeah, I'm fine," he says, but I can see past his bullshit answer. His breathing is raspy, and he's leaning against his motorbike for support. My fingers curl around the hem of his T-shirt and I lift it up, taking in a loud inhale. Deep blue and black bruises line his ribs.

"I'm going to kill him," I growl, lowering his top back down as gently as I can.

"You can't," he sighs out in defeat.

"But we have to do something," I say, taking a couple of steps backward and hitting a wall of muscle. Hands grab my shoulders, holding me in place.

"I'm going to the cops," I say, folding my arms over my chest.

A rumble comes from Gage's chest behind me. "What's the point of that? They're all in Dominic's pocket."

"Not everyone is. I know a good cop. You guys are going to get initiated and become leaders, yeah?" I ask, looking at Lucas, then at Hazen across from me.

"Yeah, but not until Dominic is retired," Hazen says.

"If I can get Dominic out of the way for at least a little bit, can you speed up that process and do it now?" I ask.

"But we need Dominic to hand over the reins. That's how it works," Gage says from behind me, and Lucas chuckles.

"Actually, The Brotherhood law states that if a leader is dead or out of action, and that includes being locked up, a past leader can do the initiation," Lucas explains with a grin.

I lick my dry lips. "Who? Who would help us do this?"

"My father," he replies.

"He wouldn't go against Dominic," Hazen says.

"He would for this. To have his son as a leader. And my mom is already worried about Dominic going too far. Besides, my father hasn't got much time left before death takes him. Trust me, he'll do it," Lucas says.

"Your mom did help us earlier, so it seems like she's on our side," I admit, and Lucas nods.

"She will do this for me."

"Well, it's settled then. Tonight we become the leaders of The Brotherhood," Gage rumbles at my back, then he spins me around and claims my mouth in a hot, demanding kiss.

Lucas hollers, clapping his hands together, and I grin against Gage's mouth.

Checkmate, Dominic.

* * *

I'm back in familiar territory, and it feels like a lifetime ago since I've been home. Everything's the same, yet everything's different. Everywhere I look, I see him. The hill he took me down when we stole a bike, and he taught me how to ride by shoving me head-first down that same hill. When I fell off, with grazes across my knees, he was there with an ice cream, making it all better.

My feet carry me through the park that used to feel like home, but now it just feels like a distant memory. Without Alec here, this side of the tracks doesn't feel like home. It never really did. Anywhere he was, was home. The closer I get to our trailer, the further I want to run back. Is she home? Does she already know? How's she going to take it?

I stop just outside and take a deep, heavy breath in, then let it out. Just get it over with. Twisting the door handle, I step inside, and a figure jumps in front of me, pulling me into a headlock. I shove her off and she falls to the ground. Her wide eyes, the size of saucers, stare blankly up at me before a smile claims her mouth, and she laughs.

"Oh, Freya, it's just you. Thought you were that slut, Harriet." She shakes her head, then starts mumbling under her breath. She slaps her head, throwing her hands around. Yep, high as fuck. This is going to be fun.

I reach out my hand and she smacks it away.

"Where the fuck have you been?" she asks, lifting herself up and off the ground. She moves into the kitchen and starts pulling out drawers, throwing the couple of pots and pans we have onto the ground.

"Around," I say, coming to stand on the other side of the kitchen counter so that the door is easily accessible. "Mom, Alec . . . he's . . . he's . . . ." The words get stuck in the back of my throat.

She doesn't stop, doesn't hear a word I'm saying. I squeeze my hands into fists and bang them down hard against the kitchen counter. She jumps backward, holding a glass in her hand. Her eyes are wild and staring right through me.

"Alec's dead, Mom," I say, and she doesn't blink, doesn't move for several heartbeats. Nothing crosses her features and my heart breaks. "Did you hear me?" Tears well up in my eyes. "Alec is dead."

"You're a fucking lying cunt. You little—" she screams, throwing the glass toward my head. I duck just in time, and it smashes into a million pieces against the wall behind me. She moves like lightning, coming straight for me, and I manage to dodge out of her way. I bolt straight for the front door, slamming it in her face, and I run.

"Don't you ever come back here, Harriet, or I'll kill you," my mother yells after me. She doesn't even know who

I am. Fuck. There's no saving her, is there? The dream that Alec and I once had of escaping here and creating a better life for her is gone. Shattered. And I don't think I can save her because she doesn't want to be saved. Drugs are her life, and I'm nothing to her anymore.

The streets are quiet as the sun crests over the row of run-down shops. A loud whistle comes from across the street, and Kai steps out of one of the shops, shoving something into his jeans pocket.

"Where the hell have you been?" he snaps when he gets closer.

"Around," I say, avoiding eye contact. Does he know about Alec?

"I haven't seen you in ages, and that's not like us. I haven't heard anything about Alec—no one's peeping a word. Have you?"

My chest squeezes tight. I open my mouth, but the words won't come out. Kai moves closer.

"Ah fuck. Just tell me."

"He's gone," I say, and Kai frowns.

"But we'll find him," Kai promises, and *fuck*, I can't.

I squeeze my eyes shut. "He's dead, Kai."

Silence greets me. Then a bird screeches from above, and I open my eyes, but Kai's gone. He's halfway up the street, and I run to catch up. When I reach him, I yank on his arm, but he won't stop.

"They're dead," Kai growls out, staring off ahead toward the train tracks.

"It's not them," I say, standing in front of him with my hands on his chest, forcing him to stop.

"Like fuck it isn't. Don't fucking tell me you're with them now? Is that why you've been spending so much time over there?" His chest rises and falls against my palm.

"You know I've been looking for Alec, and they've been helping me," I say, swallowing the words I really want to admit. That yes, I've fallen for them.

"You've fallen right into the enemy's hands, Frey, and they killed him." The way he says Frey almost brings me to my knees. Alec always called me that. Fuck. Everything is too much. My hands fall from Kai's chest.

"I've gotta go deal with this shit, but it's not them. It's Dominic, and he's going to pay," I say and start walking off toward the cop shop.

Kai follows me, falling into step beside me.

"Go home, Kai."

"Fuck off, little one. I'm coming with you, or I'll be storming over those tracks and killing every motherfucker. You know this could start another war, right?"

"Yes, but I've got a plan. So don't fuck this up for me," I say, and Kai sighs, not uttering another word. My best friend knows when to shut his mouth. I have no doubt in my mind that he'd go to war to avenge my brother, but then it would only get him killed, and I can't lose someone else.

"Does ya mother know?" he asks.

"Yeah, I told her this morning, but she didn't believe me. She's high as a kite," I say, kicking a rock along the road.

By the time we walk across town, the cop shop is open. Kai waits out the front, refusing to come in, and begs me not to go to the pigs. He hates them just as much as I do, but I'm hoping that one guy I spoke to earlier will be able to do something.

The lady behind the desk greets me. "Can I see Drew please?" She smiles and disappears through the glass door.

"Back again?" Drew asks, meeting me in front of the desk.

"Yeah, I've got some information about my brother. Can

we do this in your office or?" I ask, staring through the glass door behind the front desk at some other cops in uniform watching me. There are dirty cops everywhere, in The Brotherhood's pocket. If what I'm about to tell this guy gets to Dominic before they take action, I'm fucked.

"Ah, yeah, follow me," he says, moving down a hallway and into an interrogation room. He shuts the door behind him, and I take a seat behind a large table.

"What is it?" he asks, dropping into the seat opposite mine.

"My brother is dead." Pain rips through my chest, and I don't think it'll ever get easier saying those words. I swallow hard, trying to force down all the emotions swarming inside me. "And I've got evidence that Dominic Hendrix did it."

The cop stares at me for several painful seconds before he runs his fingers through his curly black hair. "Show me what you've got."

I spend the next twenty minutes showing him the texts from Mia and the motivation for killing my brother.

"Where's the body?" he asks.

"A white van came and took it off the fence. He's buried on the Hendrix property."

"You've got something here, but I'm just not sure if it'll be enough."

My fingers clutch onto his necklace in my pocket. "Wait, I forgot this," I say, placing the necklace on the table.

"What is it?"

"My brother never took this off—we've got matching ones. I found this in Dominic's office. Can't you test it for blood or something?"

"Ah, yeah, we can try, but with your DNA on it, too, I'm not sure if we'll get a hit. Let me grab some papers so you can write down your statement, and I'll take that in for testing." He leaves, and a little of the weight on my shoulders lifts.

He returns with some papers and takes the necklace, putting it into a Ziplock bag. I write out my statement and sign it, handing it back to him.

"What happens now?" I ask, praying that they can just go and arrest him.

"We'll go over all the evidence. It's enough to arrest him as a suspect, but I'm just not sure if it will stick. I'll do my best," he says, and I smile.

"Thank you, and if you can keep him here for as long as you can, that will help."

"Do I want to know what you have planned?" he asks, collecting the papers and standing from his chair.

"Nope," I say, shaking his hand, then I head back out the front door to meet Kai.

"All good?" Kai shoves his phone back into his pocket and hops up off the curb.

"Yeah, I think so. Things around here are going to change. Hope you're ready."

Kai side-eyes me, shaking his head. "I'm ready for a war, kid."

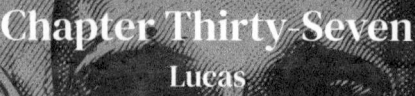

Chapter Thirty-Seven
Lucas

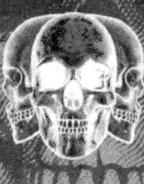

Hazen slides a glass across the marble bar, and I grab it before it falls off the edge, my fingers wrapping around the heavy crystal. Then he does the same for Gage after filling it with two fingers of scotch.

"To new beginnings," Hazen says, raising his glass, and I follow suit. As I bring it to my lips and toss it back, the whiskey sears a path down my throat. I slam the glass down and Hazen pours another.

The deafening sound of a loud bang fills the foyer, its echoes reaching the living room. My shoulders immediately tense up and I lift my gun, pivoting toward the source of the noise. Gage and Hazen are right behind, keeping a close distance. Shouts echo and footsteps clatter across the marble floor. I spot a cop in all black, fully geared up, and quickly hide my gun in my waistband.

As police occupy Hazen's home, we find ourselves in the archway between the foyer and living room. She's done it. We haven't talked to Freya since she left earlier this morning, and part of me wasn't sure if we could pull it off, but now seeing the police here, it's real. Fuck.

The cop forcefully pushes Dominic forward with his hands restrained behind his back. Holy shit. More cops come back through the foyer with Dominic's security, who are all in handcuffs and being forced out the front entrance. Looking over at us, Dominic's eyes light up, and he licks his lips.

"Hazen, get my lawyer," he snaps, yet Hazen doesn't respond or react. When I look at him, he is motionless.

"On it," I say for Hazen, and Dominic nods before getting led outside. As they all go, the house is left in complete silence.

"Fucking hell, she did it," I say, and Gage slaps me over the shoulder.

"Did you really doubt she would?"

"I mean, I know what she's capable of, but this is crazy. Are we really going to be the top dogs?" I ask, eyes widening.

Gage laughs. "We've waited our whole life for this and now it's time to make it official."

Hazen remains silent, watching the front door intently.

I snap my fingers in front of his face. "You all good, brother?"

He blinks a couple of times. "Yeah, I think so, but we don't have much time. Go get your father and meet us at the graveyard in thirty," Hazen says before heading to the stairs, climbing them two at a time. As I watch him go, a nause-ating sensation settles in the pit of my stomach.

"He'll be all right," Gage assures, and I give a nod. I fucking hope so because he needs to be.

I've heard about what happens during these initiations. My father used to tell me bedtime stories about it, and I'd have nightmares because they weren't just stories—they were descriptions of a real event. Now we're about to go through the process, and I just hope to God we all come out the other side for her.

* * *

"This is the day I've been waiting for. My son taking over The Brotherhood and being the ruler I raised." Mom pulls me in for a tight hug, plants a kiss on my forehead, and I close the front door. Apparently, news spreads like wildfire around here. Jesus.

"Thanks, Mom, but Dad has to agree first," I say, letting her go, and she laughs and pats me on the arm. "Don't worry about your father, dear. He'll do it."

She's right, I doubt he'll refuse initiating his son to lead, but I'm still worried. Do I want to lead The Brotherhood? Yes, this is what I've been training and waiting my whole life for. I'm eager to shake things up and have a say in what goes on in our town. We're already the most feared ones, but now it's official.

Sometimes I wonder what life would be like without The Brotherhood, without all the stress, just living with my best friends and Freya. It'd be all right at first, but then I'd start missing all of this. The authority, the will to make people fall to their knees in front of us, the action and shit that goes on every day.

I was born into a world of chaos, and I never want to leave. But now I want Freya by my—our—side. She's the missing puzzle piece for us, and I just hope to fuck she'll say yes. I'll force her to if she doesn't. She's one of us now, and that means she doesn't get to walk away. She can try, but I'll bring her straight back and land her where she belongs: on my cock.

I follow Mom into our mansion's elevator and ride it up

to her and my father's level. Then we exit into the long hallway and come to a stop outside his bedroom. She refused to have his machines and everything in her room, so he's been here, rotting away. I take a deep breath and force back the tears that prick the backs of my eyes when I think of him dying someday–someday soon. My father may not be a good man, but he has always gone to great lengths to protect me.

He's never told me he loves me or shown any affection at all, but he's always put me first. Gave me the most treats as a kid, gave me the deadliest knife on my fifth birthday, and taught me how to kill someone in one move. For as long as I can remember, I've admired him, but in the past few years, I've watched him slowly lose himself. Fuck, it hurts.

Taking one, then two steps inside, I freeze just inside the door, struck by the sight of my father, who looks pale and translucent, like a washed-out ghost. In the corner of the room, he sits up in a chair while a nurse stands before him, carefully examining him. She is holding a needle as she looks for veins. With a soft click, I close the door behind Mom and me, and he raises his eyes to meet mine, a subtle smile forming.

"Son," he says in a husky voice, and I move over to his side. The nurse finishes her work and goes away. Watching us intently, my mother takes a seat on his bed.

"Hey, Dad, how are you?"

He chuckles before coughing. "Well, they haven't managed to kill me yet, so that's good."

"Listen, Dad, I know Dominic's meant to initiate us in, but he's been arrested."

He frowns. "What for?"

I look at Mom and she shrugs. Clearly, she hasn't filled him in about Alec. "Killing Alec LeClair," I tell him.

My father's eyes widen, and he exchanges a glance with Mom, silently communicating something. "He didn't do it."

"What do you mean?" I ask, kneeling beside him.

Mom springs off the bed and is standing in front of him in just two quick strides. "We don't have much time. Will you initiate them or not?" my mother asks, grabbing my father's hand.

He takes a few deep breaths, inhaling and exhaling slowly, before nodding. "Of course I will."

"What were you—?" My words are cut off as Mom claps her hands together and ushers me out of the room. I look back at my father, and his mouth is slightly ajar as if he wants to say something, but then the door slams shut, trapping him inside.

What did he mean, Dominic didn't kill Alec LeClair? How would he know that and what did he want to tell me? My mother forcefully pulls me down the hallway, heading toward the stairs.

I yank my arm free, and she stops. "What the fuck was that?" I snap.

"Just forget it. He said yes, so we have to do this now. You go to the graveyard, and your father and I will meet you there." Before I can ask her more, she quickly spins around and disappears back into his room. I should follow her and demand answers from my father, but I don't want to jeopardize our initiation while Dominic is detained. Who knows how long they'll be able to hold him?

I take the stairs two at a time, slam the door to the garage so hard it shakes, then slide into my black Ferrari 812 GTS. Reversing out of the garage, then switching gears, I rev the engine and speed down my driveway, using voice commands to get my phone to call Gage.

"Is it done?" he asks by way of greeting.

"No, hello, or how's your day, sweetie?" He grunts and I laugh. "I'd like a warm welcome before you fuck me, brother."

"Just answer the fucking question," he snaps, and I scoff. Someone isn't in the mood for a little banter.

"Yes, I'm on my way, and they will meet us at the grave-yard. You guys there?"

"See you soon," he says, then hangs up. Fucking grumpy asshole.

Turning up the stereo, "Bad Things" by I Prevail fills the car, and I tap against the steering wheel. Are we really going to take over leading The Brotherhood? Am I ready for this? I thought we'd have more time before this happened, but it feels right. It's time for change.

I roll into the dirt parking lot next to Gage's Range Rover twenty minutes later. Slamming my door shut, I follow the familiar, well-worn trail into the forest that leads to the graveyard. Here, in this sacred ground, all members of The Brotherhood find their final resting place, regardless of their rank or role. This is our private estate, where all signifi-cant meetings are held.

The imposing wrought-iron gates tower above me, and my hand hesitates on the handle. This is the moment—once I step inside, a new chapter begins. A new era. And I'm fucking ready for this.

I steel myself, then cross the threshold into the graveyard.

Gage and Hazen are already waiting outside the famous arched entryway of the tomb of our great, great, great grand-fathers, who created The Brotherhood. They look over us now and will be part of the initiation.

"Can you believe this day is finally here?" Hazen says as he heads through the archway, with Gage by his side and me following closely. As we move further into the tomb, the darkness becomes suffocating, wrapping around us like a thick blanket.

"It feels like I've waited my whole life for this moment," Gage says, flicking his lighter and lighting the candles in the sconces one by one, so we can see where we are going.

"Just didn't think it would be like this. With my father in jail and everything a mess," Hazen says.

My phone rings, and I pull it out of my pocket, seeing Freya's name.

"You okay?" I ask.

"Yeah, where's the graveyard?" she asks in a hurry, and I give her the directions, then she hangs up without saying goodbye. I frown, shoving my phone back into my pocket. I hope she's okay. It's not tradition for people outside of our families to watch the initiation but fuck the rules, I want her by my side on the biggest moment of my life.

The tomb opens up into a large area, the air heavy with the scent of aged stone and candle wax. Rows and rows of headstones stretch out before me, each one a solemn reminder of the important members of The Brotherhood who rest here. Nestled in the middle, an imposing grave-stone pays tribute to the legendary founding fathers: Nicolas Ledger, Herold Hendrix, and Julius Fox. The entire area is blanketed in moss, and three skulls are perched on top as if they are staring directly at us. Fucking creepy, but cool.

We carefully traverse the space and stop in front of the center gravestone. Gage drops some twigs and logs into the fire pit that lies in front of the skulls. With a flick of the fire starter, Hazen directs sparks onto the kindling and the fire takes hold, marking the start of the ceremony.

For years, we've immersed ourselves in the stories of the

initiations, delving into the rich history of our ancestors and the sacred ritual. Now standing here, on the threshold of going through it, everything feels surreal.

The flames of the fire flicker and sway, casting eerie shadows on the walls of the tomb. I pull my hood up to cover my head as Gage takes out the branding iron and places it into the fire. I fist my hands to mask the tremor that runs through them. Fuck, this is really happening.

The sound of hushed voices precedes my parents' arrival, then they enter the chamber and make their way over to us.

My mother pulls me in for a tight hug. "I'm so proud of you," she whispers into my ear.

She releases her grip, and my father shakes my hand, then he limps over to the gravestone.

"Welcome, sons, to your initiation," my father yells, his voice echoing off the walls and it's the strongest his voice has sounded in weeks. "It's your time to take over the reins, to sacrifice yourselves to the founding fathers and rule over The Daring Brotherhood."

He lets go of his walking stick, handing it off to Mom, then he places both hands on the gravestone and bows his head. He murmurs something that I can't fully comprehend before approaching me and standing in front of me.

I lower my head, the hood concealing my face, and stretch out my hands. He takes them in his.

"Do you, Lucas Julius Fox, vow your life and the life of your brothers to The Daring Brotherhood until your dying breath?"

"I do," I say without any hesitation.

I signed my life away to them when I was first initiated in all those years ago. This is my life, and nothing stands in the way of The Brotherhood. Freya's face appears in my mind, and it kills me, but that applies to even her. She's one of us, and I love her like I do my brothers, but they and The Brotherhood will always come first. I've signed away my heart, soul, and spirit. She has part of me, but not everything. It's just the way it is. The Brotherhood is my life.

"Do you agree to lead The Daring Brotherhood in the path of justice and be the voice of our people?"

"I do."

"So be it," my father whispers, letting go of my hands.

I take off my hoodie and T-shirt, placing them next to me. My nipples harden as the cool air gently brushes against my skin. When my father steps aside, I am fully aware of the next move to make.

I carefully stand on the gravestone of our ancestors and lie on their skulls, feeling their sharp edges against my back, yet I remain still. The fire comes close to my legs but doesn't quite touch them. The sound of metal hitting the fire pit is painfully loud in my ears. Beads of sweat trickle down my forehead and back, and the real pain hasn't even started. Fuck.

With the branding iron in his hands, my father leans over me. Chanting softly, he gradually lowers it.

"Fathers of The Daring Brotherhood, open your arms and welcome in your new leader." He pauses as the hot iron sears my stomach and I bite down hard on my molars, holding in the screams. The smell of burning flesh fills the air. "Lucas Julius Fox!" my father's voice booms, and loud clapping and cheers fill the cavern.

"And so be it," my father finishes, taking my hand. He helps me off the tombstone and brings me into his waiting arms. He allows our heads to rest together briefly, then withdraws.

I lower my eyes to the engraved marks above my heart.

The letters *DB* that I got when we were first initiated in are there, but now, down my stomach is the symbol only the leaders wear. At the top of an hourglass are the words *Daring Brotherhood*, with three skulls inside.

I raise my gaze, locking eyes with my brothers, and we become united.

Chapter Thirty-Eight
Freya

Without any objections, the guards grant me passage back to Daringville; it seems my photo is on the approval list. When I step over the tracks, my shoulders relax a little, which confuses the fuck out of me. Although this isn't home, it now feels like it. The trailer has never felt that way—home was only ever Alec. *He* was that comfortable place where I could just be myself, and he never judged me or told me to act differently. Fuck, I'll never get used to the fact that he's gone. My heart feels like it's completely shattered and I'm trying to put a million pieces of it back together.

Having the guys by my side has been precisely what I needed, but the thought of going home and feeling lonely is not what I want. I want to be with them and that's fucking crazy. Never in my life did I think I'd be back over these tracks, falling for the most feared members of The Brotherhood who are getting initiated as I wait. Those same men I warned my brother about. Despite the lump in my throat, I continue walking through town toward their private estate.

I arrive at the guard's box and request access.

"Sorry, ma'am, but I'm not authorized to let you in," a younger guy says before shooing me away. Fucking asshole.

I kick a rock on the ground, then sit on the curb opposite the box.

As I reach for my phone to call Lucas, I mistakenly open my photo app and find a picture of Alec's face. He took a selfie one time when he stole my phone. He's sitting on the toilet with his tongue out and holding up two fingers in a peace sign. Tears fall onto the screen, and I don't bother wiping them away. He's really gone. They could have taken anyone else—hell, even me.

The gates open and a car drives out, but it's not until the car door slams that I bother looking up. I frown as Lucas's mom, Nadine, kneels in front of me.

"Oh, sweetie, are you okay?" she asks, her eyes the same brown as her son's.

My head shakes involuntarily as I struggle to express myself, the words eluding me. My life is a mess, and I can't think straight.

"Do you want something to take away the pain?" she asks, opening up her purse and pulling out a bag of powder.

My eyes widen. "No way! That shit only causes more headaches."

Nadine kneels in front of me, placing her hand on my knee. "Are you worried you'll end up like your mother?"

"She made her choice. I'm not weak like her."

Nadine blows out a laugh. "No, sweetie, you aren't, but once or twice won't make you an addict. You're strong, your mother is weak."

I shake my head. There's no way I'm touching that shit no matter what she says.

She places the bag in my lap. "My boy needs a strong woman in his life, and with this, you'll have the power to

277

take on the world. Just think about it." Before I have a chance to utter a word, she's gone, effortlessly slipping into her car and driving away.

I raise my gaze and spot an older man in the backseat of the car. His face presses against the window, and my mouth drops open. I feel like Alec's ocean-blue eyes are looking right at me. In a flash, they're gone, the car zooming away down the road.

I stare at the bag of powder in my hand and shake my head, throwing it to the ground. My phone buzzes in my other hand and a message appears from the unknown number.

Looks familiar, doesn't it?

Why did she give me drugs? What does the text mean? Why would it look familiar? I reread the text over and over . . . and then it clicks, just as another message comes through.

Your mother didn't become addicted to drugs by accident.

All the blood drains from my face, and I think I'm going to be sick. My phone drops out of my hand, and I lean forward, spewing up bile. Memories flicker in my mind of Mom back when we lived in Daringville, back when things were happier. She'd been fine for so long—but what if someone gave her drugs, too?

Nadine's the mother of the man I'm falling for—but what if she's not what she seems? Jumping up, I retrieve my phone and wipe my mouth with the back of my hand. She's *dead*.

I hit dial on Lucas's name, and he answers straight away. "You okay?"

"Yeah, where's the graveyard?" I ask in a hurry, and he

gives me directions before I hang up without saying goodbye.

The gate opens once more, and without pause, I sprint through it toward Hazen's estate, evading the guard's attempt to halt me, and I don't stop until I'm outside his place. The garage is open and there's a guy cleaning Hazen's dirt bike right outside it. I peer around while leaning against the side of the house. After five minutes, the man stops, dropping the rag into the soapy bucket, and goes inside the garage. Before I can second-guess myself, I sprint toward the bike, swing my leg over, and start it. I feel the vibration as it stirs, rumbling between my legs.

"Hey," the guy yells and races back out, but before he can reach me, I'm flying down the driveway, onto the road, and out of the estate through the still-open gate.

With the wind blowing past me, I feel as though my cheeks are being showered with a million kisses. Hazen will likely be furious with me for taking his bike, but I don't care. Nadine is going to pay.

If what the messages say is true, Nadine started my mother's habit all those years ago and got us kicked out of Daringville. I always thought it was Dominic, never her. It changed our lives forever. I need answers, and I'm going to get them from that bitch's mouth.

Leaving the bike next to Gage's car, I run down the trail into the forest. The sun dips behind the trees, casting shadows all around me and turning the sky a marshmallow pink. I continue walking until I finally arrive at a massive pair of wrought-iron gates, the entrance to the cemetery, and push them open.

Before me, there are countless headstones arranged in perfect rows on the grass. I stick to the paved pathway that leads me through the rows of graves as the sun dips farther beneath the horizon. Soon it'll be dark, and the thought of experiencing this place at night fills me with an eerie sensation of excitement and nerves that runs through my entire body.

Movement catches my eye up ahead, and I catch a glimpse of Nadine's long blonde hair disappearing through the large archway of an imposing mausoleum-type structure. I hurry the last hundred yards across the graves and follow her inside the building. Ahead is a dimly lit tunnel, and I creep along the descending path until it opens up to reveal a massive tomb. Three hooded figures stand before a large gravestone with three skulls, surrounded by rows of graves.

I freeze just outside the tomb's entrance, unable to move as I observe what's happening before me. Nadine is completely out of my mind as I see the guys getting initiated, one by one. The air is heavy with the acrid smell of burning flesh, making it difficult to breathe. I feel an overwhelming urge to rush over and offer comfort, but I'm frozen in place. This is a special moment for them, and I can't ruin it.

Hazen is the final one to undergo the ritual, and once he's done, the older man I spotted earlier in the car glances in my direction, so I step out of the shadows.

Nadine spins around and glares at me with intense hatred, almost making my knees buckle. It all comes rushing back to me—the drugs she gave me, the cause of my mother's addiction, and the resulting consequences.

I clench my fists and sprint over the gravestones until I'm face to face with her. I push her and she loses her balance, her eyes growing wider.

"You bitch!" I scream, and hands wrap around my waist, pulling me backward into a warm body.

"What are you doing?" Lucas snaps, holding me against his chest.

"She tried to feed me drugs and did the same thing to my mother all those years ago. She's the reason Mom's an addict and our whole life got turned upside down."

Lucas releases his grip on me and moves closer, fixing his gaze on his mother. She vigorously shakes her head while putting on a fake smile.

"She's lying. I'd never do that. You've now completed the initiation—you are a leader, and it's time to celebrate. Don't let this little rat ruin it for you," Nadine says, glaring at me, then softening her eyes as she shifts her focus to Lucas.

"Don't call her that," Lucas says in a low growl.

Nadine laughs. "Oh, don't tell me you've fallen for her?"

The only sound during a long pause is my pounding heart in my ears.

"Yes, she's one of us now," Lucas admits, pulling me under his arm.

"Stupid, stupid boy. Have I taught you nothing?" Nadine throws her head back, her laughter echoing through the room. Suppressing the urge to lash out, I grit my teeth and keep my fists clenched tightly by my sides.

From behind us, a voice bellows, "Enough!" and I spin around to see the older gentleman from the car holding a walking stick. His gray hair is slicked back above his pale, drawn face, and he coughs a few times. "This has gone on too long, Nadine. Lucas deserves to know," he says.

"Know what?" Lucas asks, glancing between his mother and father.

My heart beats faster. What does he know?

Lucas's father moves until he's within arm's reach of me.

His jawline resembles my brother's, and he has the same nose. He looks so much like Alec it's scary. "Alec LeClair is my son, and she killed—" He pauses and tears well in my eyes, spilling down my cheeks. "I'm so sorry," he whispers, reaching out, and his hand lands on my shoulder. My battered heart is squeezed by an invisible vise as I try to process what he's just said.

A loud scream echoes through the tomb, and Lucas's father's eyes go wide before there's a sickening crack, and then he's falling forward. I catch him, but his weight is too much, and we both collapse to the ground, his body on top of mine. Blood oozes from a wound on his skull and his eyes start to close. My hands are covered in red. More yelling and screaming pierces my ears, but I can't hear what's being said.

It all happens too fast. I catch sight of Nadine from below her husband's body as she drops something to the ground. I move his body off me, and he falls to my side. From her boot, Nadine retrieves a gun and pulls the trigger, hitting Lucas's father right in the chest. He groans with finality as blood blooms across his shirt from the bullet wound. With a scream, Lucas rushes toward him, falling to his knees at the dying man's side.

"What the fuck have you done?" Lucas yells, clutching his father's shirt. Nadine's hands quiver, yet she maintains her grip on the gun.

"You killed my brother," I whisper mainly to myself, but Nadine turns my way, the gun pointed at me, and she nods with a sly grin.

My ears ring and I can't think. I can't breathe. All I see is her—everything else blurs into the background. I rush at her, and she cocks the gun, but I snatch it out of her grip. Turning it around, I aim at her heart and pull the trigger.

The deafening bang pierces my ears and Nadine falls to the ground. Lucas leaves his father's side and staggers over, his gaze shifting between his lifeless mother and me. He drops to his knees, his whole body shaking as he desperately clutches his mother's hand and checks for a pulse.

As his blood-curdling scream fills the building, my ears ring. "No, no, no! Please come back." He drops her hand and starts doing compressions. I want to help, but I'm frozen in place, unable to move.

After he pauses his futile CPR to check for any signs of a pulse. "Come back. You can't leave me. Please!" he screams, falling back onto his ass and my heart splinters into a million shards of glass.

Helplessly, I watch the cascading tears and I long to ease his anguish. I want to make it better. Leaning over, I desperately grasp onto the rough ground, my trembling hands barely able to support me as I sink down onto my knees in front of Lucas.

"I'm so sorry."

I extend my hand toward him, and his attention shifts from his mother to my reaching fingers. I hesitate, then attempt to retract them, but he grips my hand. His father's blood stains my palms, leaving a lingering metallic scent in the air.

"What have you done?"

The venom in his voice sends a chill down my spine, and my hands tremble uncontrollably, while Lucas tightens his grip. He holds my gaze for a heartbeat, his eyes full of pain and betrayal, then he drops my hands, pushes himself up, and walks away without a word.

What's left of my heart breaks in two.

I turn around to seek out Hazen and Gage, but they follow Lucas out of the tomb without looking back. They are leaving me again, like before, and no one is here to help pick up the broken pieces, not even my brother.

The End

To be continued in Deadly Little Hearts

About the Author

Jenna Daring is a dark romance author living in Melbourne, Australia with her high school crush and their golden retriever Coop. When she's not writing strong female characters or alpha males, she's dreaming up the next thing, coaching or reading.

Join her readers group on Facebook here.

Be part of her VIP email list and find out more about the Daring Brotherhood here.

Also by Jenna Daring

Tens series

The Invitation – www.books2read.com/tens1

Mafia Princess of Roxbury Prep

Reclaim – www.books2read.com/roxburyprep1

Sign up for newsletter updates at https://jennalee.biz